Her Perfect Smile

BILLIONAIRE'S JEOPARDY BOOK 1

Chrissy Garwood

Her Perfect Smile

BILLIONAIRE'S JEOPARDY BOOK 1

Chrissy Garwood

Chrisolite Books,
Sorell, Tasmania
Australia

Printed in Australia

For more information contact :
Chrissy Garwood/Chrisolite Books
29 Weston Hill Road,
Sorell, Tasmania, Australia, 7172
www.chrissygarwood.com

Scripture quotations marked CG are taken from memory and not directly attributed to a particular translation. All other Scripture quotations are taken from the World English Bible British Edition and are available in the Public Domain.

Book Design: Chrissy Garwood
Cover Design: Belinda Pollard
Her Perfect Smile/ Chrissy Garwood —1st Ed.

ISBN - 978-1-922867-02-5 paperback
ISBN - 978-1-922867-03-2 eBook

I dedicate this book to my beautiful
and hardworking niece, Caitlyn Garwood.

CONTENTS

Poem

A precious child is born
destined for riches and power.
But when the storm clouds
of grief and tragedy sweep in,
she finds herself alone and unprotected.

Sorrow almost overwhelms her,
but "big girls don't cry".
She builds strong walls,
to hide her fragile heart,
invisible walls to conceal her pain.

There are daily reminders:
hide your sorrow!
Her refuge behind the walls
brings a false security –
even she believes the lie.

Time passes swiftly.
Too soon, they realise
the error of their ways.
But it is too late.
Her walls are strong.

There is no way to reach
the frightened child
safely hidden deep within
the self-imposed prison
of her troubled mind.

1

Restlessness

Isaiah 41:10b
I will uphold you with
the right hand of My righteousness.

Fat raindrops splattered against the tinted windows of the golden, late-model Mercedes. Natasha suppressed a sigh, glancing sideways at her father, Luke Jacobson. The Spendor Corporation Chief Executive Officer always sat behind Oleander, their uniformed chauffeur. Both men were tall, yet there was ample room for Luke to stretch his legs.

Her father activated the digital screen on the back of the driver's seat and tapped his portable keyboard. Columns of print replaced the Corporation palace-and-crown logo.

Luke had a ruthless reputation, ruling his business empire like a medieval king. A monarch who didn't tolerate distractions. The side of the phone conversation she could hear suggested he was negotiating an international deal.

Idle hands twitched in Natasha's lap. Her attention switched to the gold embossed logo on the lid of her father's open briefcase on the seat between them. When Luke had retrieved a file at the start of their journey, she felt relieved. Yesterday's drama was not distracting him from his usual activities. As the "crown princess", she should be copying his example.

If only she hadn't lost her briefcase.

Not lost, an inner voice mocked. *Lost is too gentle a word to describe your carelessness. You know where the briefcase is. What kept you from retrieving it?*

Father has already made the arrangements, Natasha reminded herself. Repeating that assurance didn't silence the accusations.

Is Daddy's Perfect Princess too important to deal with a mess of her making? When are you going to admit that selfishness is your greatest handicap? Your father recognises your weaknesses.

That's why he keeps asking when you're going to choose your Prince Charming.

Keeping her face clear of emotion, Natasha analysed her predicament. No one held her responsible for yesterday's attack, yet that accusing voice would grant her no mercy.

What had created a mindset where she assumed responsibility for everything? There was a familiar pattern to the internal dialogue, echoing taunts from childhood. Constant torment from boarding-school bullies about her privileged upbringing...

The only remedy was to focus on the facts. Logic always defeated irrational emotion. In less than an hour, Natasha would be in her glass tower, seated at her desk with access to the files she required.

The missing pink briefcase had been a graduation present from her stepmother, Edith. It was locked inside the brand-new car the police had towed to their city compound. No amount of anxiety would change that.

Natasha glanced at her father. Had he forgotten she was there? She could detect no evidence he had any lingering concerns about recent events.

Luke had always been strong, immovable, unstoppable and resilient. In a crisis, her father led the business empire towards victory.

On any other day, she could emulate his ability to shut out distractions. An inability to recall the details for her morning appointments was enough evidence that Natasha's mind was a scrambled mess.

Last week she had attended a seminar that included a mindfulness exercise. "Let your mind drift. If you feel the tension returning, bring your thoughts back to your breathing…"

A water droplet raced across the window. Natasha tracked its movement until the wind snatched it away. Beneath her fingertips, the cold glass was smooth and impervious. An illusion. How easily it could shatter—

Breathe in, breathe out…

Beyond the car, the countryside flashed past. The scenery was familiar, but the storm transformed it into a misty blur. A perfect canvas onto which memories from yesterday superimposed themselves against her will. Natasha could hear—

No!

Her queasiness intensified. The air inside the car was too warm. Natasha's fingers hovered above the button on the armrest, and she jerked her hand back to her lap. Opening the window might relieve her nausea, but a blast of cold air would distract her father. Asking Oleander to switch off the heater wasn't a viable option either.

The breathing exercises hadn't worked. How was Natasha to endure this torment? They were not even fifteen minutes into their journey!

As the outside storm intensified, the rain became louder than the pounding of her heart. If this were a fairytale, those darkening clouds would foreshadow a malevolent threat...

Natasha traced patterns on the glass. This long-forgotten childhood activity had once occupied her for hours. The glistening droplets would become dancers, and she was their choreographer. Perhaps it would work now? She narrowed her focus to a smaller section of glass. What piece of music would she choose? Tunes familiar after years of dancing lessons presented themselves for consideration. Debussy's *Gardens in the Rain?* Or maybe the fourth movement from Beethoven's *6th Symphony?* What about Judith Weir's *The Welcome Arrival of Rain?*

A gust of wind threw water against the glass, drowning out the inner music. The tiny dancers dissolved into oblivion. She would have to factor that into the performance. The unpredictability of her stage required something special.

Something contemporary? Ah! That new music track she had downloaded: Lindsey Stirling's *Crystallize*.

Natasha was already reaching for her phone when she remembered. Frozen for a moment, she pushed back the rising panic. Today, she had no phone. No tablet or laptop either.

Pressing against the seat, she catalogued the final obstacle. Her father liked to travel in silence. He didn't know Natasha preferred – no, needed – her music at maximum volume. Without headphones, accessing her playlist through the onboard computer was not an option.

A persistent buzzing signalled another incoming call, the third that morning. Natasha studied her father, drawn by the intensity of his voice. Luke leaned forward, his face red and his blue eyes flashing.

"I don't *care* what it *costs*. I want that story taken down from the internet BEFORE I get to the office. Buy the company if you have to! Make. It. Happen!"

Luke dropped the phone into his open briefcase. He muttered to himself before glaring at whatever was on the screen in front of him. Natasha frowned. At work, her father had a reputation as a man to be feared. But she could count on one hand the number of times she had heard him raise his voice in undisguised anger. The memories swamped her before she could stop them.

That terrifying day when Natasha was four and almost drowned in the pool...

When she was twelve and had fallen on the stairs, running away from her stepbrother...

And last night, his shout had carried across the hospital emergency department. "Where is my daughter?"

Helpless to stop the replay, Natasha dropped her head and squeezed her eyes tight.

When her father had appeared beside her bed, she had thrown herself at him. "Daddy, Daddy!"

Luke had caught her, silenced by her tears. It must have been half an hour before she came to her senses.

"I-I'm sorry, Father." The first coherent words she had said to him rang in her ears.

"Natasha?"

His voice thrust her back to the present.

Oh no! The colour drained from her face. She had spoken those words again, loud enough for her father to hear. Her racing heart became like a captured bird, trying to burst from her chest. Natasha checked to see if the chauffeur had also heard? Oleander was watching her in the mirror...

"Natasha." Luke placed his hand on her arm. "Princess, look at me."

Obeying her father was an automatic reflex. Not because she feared him, but because she loved him.

Natasha's heart cried out at the concern on his face, and she would do anything to bring back his smile.

"You don't have to do this," Luke said. "Oleander can drop me off in the city and take you back to the estate."

A wave of remorse crashed over Natasha. "I have meetings—"

"Cancelled or rescheduled," Luke said. "I know you wanted to keep busy, but I'm beginning to agree with Edith. You're more upset than you're willing to admit."

"I'm fine," Natasha said, faking a smile.

Luke shook his head. "You've just apologised for the third time. What happened was not your fault. If anyone is to blame, it's me for allowing you to drive alone."

"I'd have been right behind you if I hadn't wasted time trying to connect my phone to the car's computer."

"I should have ordered Oleander to turn around when he said you weren't following us."

"But you phoned to check where I was," Natasha said, careful to keep her voice steady. "I told you not to worry, and I promised to leave the parking garage as soon as I ended the call. Neither of us knew how heavy the traffic would be or that I'd get stuck in the wrong lane. I should have found somewhere to pull over after I missed the off-ramp."

"You make it sound like a series of random events," Luke said. "The police are convinced the kidnappers targeted you."

An instinctive denial died on Natasha's lips at the expression on her father's face.

"You're my only daughter, and I should have protected you. I won't make that mistake again. From today, you won't go anywhere without a bodyguard—"

"I don't need— Oh." Natasha covered her mouth with her hand and blinked. She couldn't remember the last time she had tried to change her father's mind. A traitorous tear trickled down her cheek.

"I'm sorry, Father."

Taking her hand, Luke held it as he studied her face. "Last night, you called me 'Daddy', and I realised how close I'd come to losing my little girl. Let me do what's necessary to keep you safe."

"If I promise not to travel alone, will you change your mind about the bodyguard?"

"It's too late, Princess."

Luke activated the screen in front of her.

Natasha focused on the coloured image before recognising the banner across the page.

Now Natasha knew why her father's favourite newspaper had been absent from breakfast this morning. Reaching forward, she scrolled past the photographic portrait, taken at her graduation ceremony.

The headline read:

HEIRESS RESCUED BY POLICE.

2

Necessary

Titus 3:14b
Learn to maintain good works
to meet necessary needs.

Skipping the rescue details, Natasha read the paragraphs portraying her as a thoughtless young woman, living a privileged life of luxury. A ditsy blonde who lacked common sense.

The journalist ignored Natasha's academic achievements, citing her father's position as CEO to explain her "meteoric rise" in the Spendor Corporation hierarchy. There was a quote from a "close friend" who described her as "reckless, haughty and selfish".

Her father would need to "rein in Princess Tash's behaviour" before she brought the Jacobson name into disrepute. Natasha blinked, thankful there was no mention of her mother's family. That secret was safe.

The story concluded with an extravagant estimation of her financial worth. There were too many zeros, elevating her from millionaire to billionaire status.

"Now you understand why a bodyguard is necessary," her father said as his phone buzzed again. "We'll continue our discussion when I finish this call."

Natasha shut out her father's presence to reread the article, paying particular attention to the literary structure. Suppressing a shudder, she acknowledged the initial paragraphs were well written, and accurate down to the finer details. That precision made the inconsistencies of the remaining sections more puzzling. Natasha searched for the journalist's name.

Tapping the digital link, Natasha read the writer's biography.

Freda Collins had twenty years of experience as a freelance investigative journalist. The listed publications included every major media outlet in the country. With a bias toward pursuing big corporations, the award-winning journalist's headlines were full of fraud and embezzlement, insider trading, hostile takeovers, and allegations about links with organised crime.

Shaking her head, Natasha deactivated the screen. A dozen responses passed through her mind. Convincing Luke there was no need to send her home remained her top priority. It was essential to prove her analytical mind was unaffected by last night's misadventure or the sensational media attention.

Natasha checked her signature smile was in place before swivelling her upper body towards her father. As she predicted, he watched her as if searching for any sign of weakness. As a child, she had believed Luke could read her like an open book, but that fear had left her long ago. She folded her hands in her lap and willed her shoulders to relax as she formed her first question.

"Where did Collins get her information? Nobody here calls me 'Tash'."

"Journalists are always reluctant to name their sources," Luke said with a small smile. "I've already commissioned an investigation."

Natasha nodded, inviting him to continue.

"Until we find out who benefits from tarnishing your reputation, you need to be careful. I've tried to shield you from the darker side of the corporate world. That's why your holiday internships were with ancillary companies. I didn't want the Spendor-Jacobson connection to open doors before you were ready."

Luke paused as if there was something else he wanted to say. Natasha considered asking what he was keeping from her but set aside the idea for a more favourable time.

"But you won't be able to hide from the spotlight now," Luke said. "Investment opportunities and requests for money will come at you from every direction. Be careful who you trust."

Natasha strengthened her smile. "You've trained me well, Father. This 'ditsy blonde' won't be easily parted from her money."

"Don't take the insults personally, Princess. Anyone who knows you will ignore the lies."

"What do you know about Freda Collins? Could she be chasing a bigger story? Is this a test to see how you react?"

"If I was the target, there'd be some mention of your mother," Luke said. "I've tried to protect you from speculation about her identity."

"Perhaps that's why Collins said I was a billionaire, a subtle hint to entice opportunistic fortune hunters. But that's not my major concern. There were eyewitness details in that article I've only shared with the police."

"My legal team are pursuing that. Either there's a leak, or somebody knows more than they should. Who knew you took delivery of your new car yesterday?"

"It would be easier to tell you who didn't know," Natasha said, dispensing with the smile. "As we agreed, I kept the information to myself. Yet by the time I had the keys in my hand, there wasn't anyone in my department who didn't know."

"Ian has already apologised for his mistake," Luke said. "He didn't expect anyone to find the online image and share it everywhere."

He frowned. "Why did you give the dealership permission to publish a picture of the handover? It would have caused similar problems if it had been your own photo. Any of your friends could have tagged you."

Except you don't have any friends.

Natasha reactivated the digital screen, careful to keep her voice calm. "I have an anonymous profile, so there was never any risk anyone could tag me. The only public online presence I have is on the official Spendor Corporation website, which is where they sourced that front page photo."

Bringing up Ian Norris's social media page, she located the photo of him standing beside her car. Natasha pointed to the hundreds of comments and reactions the post had attracted.

"Ian mentioned me by name," Natasha said. "But it isn't *his* mistake I'm unable to forgive. I should have rescheduled the handover instead of allowing you to send someone in my place. It's time I stopped allowing other people to make decisions for me."

Luke opened his mouth, and Natasha held up her hand. The words threatened to explode from her mouth, but she kept them under control.

"Please listen. What's done is done. Nothing can change what happened yesterday. But I've learned an important lesson. This is my life, and I need to be in control. If I must hire a bodyguard, I want to choose the person myself. And I don't want this bodyguard to be a Spendor Corporation employee. He, or she, will answer to me, and their salary must come from my private funds."

Holding her breath, Natasha waited for her father's response. He briefly closed his eyes, and then he smiled as he gazed at her.

"For a moment, it was as if I was listening to your mother," Luke said. "She was a determined woman who valued her independence. I've often wondered what she'd say about how I've raised you. I'm certain she wouldn't have been as patient or as gentle in telling me to stop meddling in your life. But I know she'd be proud of the beautiful young woman you've become."

Natasha was speechless.

Luke rarely talked about her mother, his first wife, who had died when Natasha was four. The silence between them stretched. Somewhere outside the car, a horn sounded, and the intense connection was broken.

Retrieving his keyboard, her father said, "I'll email Sentinel City Security." A few minutes later, Luke spoke again. "Expect a package containing the relevant information within the hour. There were three candidates who matched my selection criteria."

"Are you going to share the selection criteria with me?" Natasha asked.

Luke began to count off the criteria on his fingers. "Previous experience as a security officer; firearms and martial arts training; passed a stringent fitness assessment in the past six months, with minimum height and bodyweight requirements; available to commence immediately and a work history that includes flexible hours; good credit rating and impeccable references; must look intimidating in a suit; no dependants or significant attachments—"

"No dependants?"

"No external commitments that would distract him from his duty to protect you."

"Him?" Natasha asked. "Tell me you didn't include gender in the selection criteria."

"Of course not," her father replied, "but from the names on the list, I'm assuming all three candidates are men: Jack Smith, Eric Walker and Greg Freeman. You will have to wait for the information portfolio to find out for sure."

3

Wariness

Habakkuk 2:14 CG
For the earth will be filled with an awareness of
the glory of God, as the waters cover the sea.

The towering Spendor Corporation Headquarters loomed ahead of them. They were a block away from the entrance to the underground parking garage. The traffic was heavier than usual, and Natasha glanced at the digital clock on the screen. It was nine-twenty-six. A typical business day for her father started at eight. Today he was an hour and a half late.

Oleander eased the car through the next intersection and navigated into the required lane. The chauffeur drove past the security checkpoint without delay, heading for the elevators.

Two uniformed security guards stepped forward. Oleander leapt out to open Luke's door while the elder of the two guards, tall, broad-shouldered and sixty-something, appeared at Natasha's side of the car. The other guard scanned the gloomy car park, his hand near the holstered pistol at his waist.

"Good morning, Ms Jacobson," the guard said as he opened her door. "It's a relief to see you looking so well. I'm Caden Gosling, but everyone calls me Goose." His smile widened, and the twinkle in his eye convinced Natasha he was genuine. "And that's my partner, William Reynolds. We've been assigned to your security detail today. Will's going to keep watch near the elevators, and I'll be stationed outside your office. Nobody's going to get past us to bother you."

"Thank you, Goose."

"Everyone's upset about what happened, and if there's anything we can do to make you feel safe, don't hesitate to ask. Your father's authorised extra guards at every entrance."

With both security men at her heels, Natasha hastened to the elevators. Her father's office was on the twentieth floor, and he waited beside the elevator reserved for the senior executives. Natasha went towards the second set of doors.

"Natasha, join me in the express elevator today," Luke said. "I won't relax until I know you've arrived at your floor."

When the elevator stopped at the tenth floor, Natasha and her guards stepped out.

"Let me know when you've made your decision," Luke called after her, but the doors swished shut before she could respond.

Natasha scanned the foyer. Her eyes lingered on the updated Human Resources Department directory. It was a month since her name had been added as an Assistant Manager. She reflected on the three years of hard work that went into earning the promotion. Why was she allowing a newspaper comment about her "meteoric rise" to dampen her sense of accomplishment?

Mentally shaking herself, Natasha straightened her shoulders. No matter what had preceded this moment, she was now in familiar territory. She took a step towards the reception counter, preparing a reply for the greeting she expected to receive. But the familiar receptionist was not at her post.

Instead, one of the younger administrative assistants was behind the counter. Natasha's smile remained, yet this small change had unsettled her more than it should.

The girl hadn't registered the elevator's arrival. Natasha stared past her into the office beyond. The receptionist was nowhere in sight, but the dozens of administrative assistants in their distinctive HR uniform were busy at their desks.

After glancing left and right, Natasha made a snap decision. Why announce she was here? She might make it to her office without meeting anyone. With Goose beside her, Natasha set off. She had only taken a few steps when a voice called from behind.

"Ms Jacobson, you're here!"

Natasha turned. The girl had abandoned the reception counter and was hurrying towards her in the company of two other women. When the trio reached Natasha, they began talking over the top of each other.

"Ms Jacobson. What are you doing here?"

"We saw your photo in the paper."

"We didn't think you'd come in today."

"I'd be a mess if that had happened to me."

"Weren't you terrified?"

"Thank you for your concern," Natasha said. "Please don't let me keep you from your duties."

"How far to your office?" Goose muttered, taking Natasha's elbow and steering her in the right direction.

"The second last one, on the right," Natasha said, increasing her pace. The chunky heels on her sensible black shoes beat a steady rhythm on the polished floor. If she hadn't been wearing a slimline knee-length skirt, the temptation to run might have won.

The women were not easily dissuaded. Their voices increased in volume as they pursued Natasha along the corridor. Doors opened, and heads popped out to see what was happening. Goose signalled to the other guard. Will came to usher the three unwanted followers away.

Nodding to those who called out as she passed their offices, Natasha didn't tarry to talk to anyone. It was a relief when her own door drew near.

"Do you work alone?" Goose asked, holding her back. Natasha was uncomfortable with his wariness.

"I have a secretary. Her desk is visible when the door opens, so nobody can get to my inner office without talking to her first."

Easing the door open, Goose pushed his head into the gap. Natasha glanced along the corridor. Why was her guard keeping her out here?

Ring-ring.

The office phone was ringing. *Ring-ring, ring-ring, ring-ring, ring-ring...*

An unpleasant thought awoke at the back of Natasha's mind. Had something happened to her secretary? Her heart leapt when she heard a voice.

"Let me answer the phone."

"That's my secretary," Natasha said, pushing past Goose to enter the office.

Then a second voice called from further in, and Natasha froze.

"I'm running out of places to look. If we can't find that key in the next few minutes, I'll call Housekeeping."

The ringing had stopped, but her secretary stood with the phone receiver halfway to her ear, eyes wide and her mouth open as she stared at Natasha. Something pink dropped onto the desk and brown liquid spilled across a pile of documents. The aroma of freshly prepared coffee wafted across the room. Natasha stared at the distinctive pink cup. It was one of a pair commissioned by Natasha's stepmother. The delicate porcelain mug belonged in an unopened presentation box on her bookshelf.

"Oh! Ms Jacobson," the secretary said. "You startled me."

The secretary's eyes flew first to the inner office before noticing the spilled coffee on her desk.

"Should there be anyone in your office?" Goose asked, bringing out his gun.

The secretary screamed and collapsed onto her chair.

Natasha shook her head.

"Come out with your hands where I can see them," Goose said.

The receptionist who had been missing from the foyer stepped through the door.

"Is there anyone else in there? Stand next to your accomplice while I check." Goose kept his gun pointed at the women as he nudged the door open and surveyed the inner room.

"Do you know this woman?" Goose asked.

Natasha nodded.

The guard directed his next question to the receptionist. "What were you doing in Ms Jacobson's office?"

"Looking for her appointment book," the woman said, waving a slim pink volume.

Liar. Natasha pressed her lips together while her mind chased after a rational explanation.

Taking the journal, Goose handed it to Natasha. He dragged one of the visitor chairs behind the desk and put it next to the secretary. "Sit there," he said to the receptionist. "Both of you, put your hands on the desk. Ms Jacobson will check to see if anything is missing. No, don't turn your head to look at her. Keep your eyes fixed on me. You've caused her enough trouble already."

Slipping past him, Natasha stood in the doorway of the inner office. A few moments were all she needed to confirm the entire room had been disturbed.

Six years at boarding school had taught her to be observant. Back then, an object a few millimetres out of place in her dormitory room might be booby-trapped. Itching powder and permanent ink had been two of her tormentors' favourites.

Narrowing her eyes, Natasha dismissed the possibility of childish pranks. The women had been looking for a key. Were they trying to break into her desk, or were they interested in her filing cabinet? While that question fermented, she catalogued the evident changes in the room.

A diamond-studded pen, several crystal ornaments and a silver-framed family portrait were gathered together in the centre of her desk. One of Natasha's leather-bound books was upside down on the bookcase, and some of the other volumes were in the wrong order. The packaging that belonged to the porcelain mugs was near the coffee machine, where the second cup sat with red lipstick on the rim. On top of the locked filing cabinet, a box of imported chocolates lay open, surrounded by discarded wrappers.

Through the open doorway, Natasha heard the secretary mutter, "This is your fault. I should never have listened to you."

"Shut up," hissed the receptionist.

"I can't afford to lose my job."

"She can't fire either of us. There are rules to protect employees."

Moving to stand beside Goose, Natasha asked, "Did someone tell you to search my office?"

"I've already told you we were looking for your appointment book," the receptionist said. "Tell the guard to put away the gun. I know my rights, and I'll be making a formal complaint—"

Natasha gestured for Goose to holster his gun without taking her eyes off the defiant woman. "Go back to reception. If not for your exemplary record, your employment would be terminated immediately. Expect a written warning—"

"On what grounds?" demanded the red-faced receptionist.

"You left your assigned post without adequately covering your duties, and then you lied to a superior. Add to that, inciting another employee to breach the terms of their employment. Would you like me to continue? No?"

The receptionist headed for the door.

"One more thing," Natasha said. "I don't want to hear even a whisper about what has happened between us today."

Without another word, the woman stormed from the room.

"Go and talk to Will," Natasha said to Goose. "Ask him to keep an eye on her."

When Goose left the room, Natasha turned back to the secretary.

"Take what belongs to you and leave my office. I'm giving you one week's wages in lieu of notice."

"You can't fire me. I worked hard for this promotion."

"My predecessor hired you, and I cannot work with someone untrustworthy. Take the rest of the day off to consider what you've done. When you return tomorrow, report to the general secretarial pool on the ground floor."

"You can't do that. The salary's half what I'm making now. I have expenses—"

Natasha ignored the protest. "Be grateful you still have a job."

"My cousin was right," the secretary said, sweeping her possessions off the desk into her handbag. She threw open the outer door, sending it crashing into the adjacent cupboard. "She said I'd regret working for Ice Queen Nessie."

4

Sneakiness

Galatians 5:22-23 CG
But the fruit of the Spirit is
love, joy, peace, patience, kindness, goodness,
faithfulness, gentleness, and self-control.
Against such things there is no law.

The angry woman's departing words dealt Natasha a heavy blow. She stared at the open doorway as the secretary's voice moved further away. The woman was now complaining to Goose about her "unjust treatment". Before Natasha recovered her composure, a hand appeared, tapping on the open door.

"Is it safe to come in?" An attractive man wearing a business suit poked his head through the doorway. Ian Norris, the young executive her father had recruited to collect her car yesterday. One of her father's favoured candidates for Prince Charming, Ian didn't wait for an answer, closing the door after entering.

Natasha stifled a sigh. "Ian, what are you doing here?"

"I came as soon as I learned you were in the building," he said, leaning against the door with his hands in his pockets. The thirty-something executive smiled as he watched her face. "You're all anyone wants to talk about today."

"A phone call would have sufficed. As you can see, I'm fine."

"I had to check for myself. There was always a chance you might need a friendly shoulder to cry on. But you're serenely beautiful as always, with your signature smile in place. I should have known the legendary Queen of Calmness would never crumple under pressure."

"What did you call me?" Natasha asked, startled by the sharp pain in her chest. She was already wrestling with the old ghosts awoken by the departing secretary's bitterness. Now Ian Norris was using another title invented by Natasha's childhood enemies.

"'The Queen of Calmness'." Ian's grin widened. "That's what everyone called you at Summerlands University."

Natasha chose her words with care to maintain the illusion of calmness. "I thought you graduated before I arrived."

"Your first semester was my last, so there wasn't time for me to impress you." Ian walked towards her. "I'm still waiting for the right opportunity."

With each step Ian took, Natasha retreated an equal distance. He stopped advancing and put his hands up in surrender. "Your father said I must be patient. After what you've been through, it's going to take time for me to regain your trust."

Ian returned to the door, and as he opened it, he faced Natasha again. "Was that your secretary I saw cursing you as I arrived? I can't believe you'd fire someone without notice. What did she do?"

"I didn't fire her," Natasha said. "She's been transferred to another department. Why are you asking?"

"Yesterday, you accepted my apology, and we're still friends, so I know you're not vindictive. I'm trying to understand why your secretary didn't get another chance?"

"You didn't search my office while I wasn't here."

Ian laughed. "If I caught someone snooping in my office, I wouldn't be able to hide my anger. Everyone would know about it. I'm adding sneakiness to the list of things that don't make you lose your cool."

Ian paused on the threshold. "What did that secretary call you? 'Ice Queen Nessie'? I don't know where 'Nessie' comes from, but you're the perfect Ice Queen."

By the time Natasha thought of an acceptable response, Ian was gone. She went into her office to return her possessions to their proper place.

The used coffee mugs went on a tray, ready for someone from Housekeeping to remove them to the kitchenette down the corridor to be washed at the end of the day. Next, she went to the secretary's desk to clean up the coffee spill.

Goose burst in from the corridor. "A man came out of your office. Where did he come from?"

"Ian?" Natasha asked. "I presumed he spoke to you on his way here."

"He didn't come past reception. I should have been here, but your secretary wouldn't go quietly. He must have been lurking in one of the other offices. Are you alright?"

"Of course, I'm alright," Natasha said. "Don't be concerned about Ian. Everyone likes him."

Goose didn't seem convinced.

"Ian's popular and well respected," Natasha said. "I've not heard anyone say anything disparaging against him. His father is one of the corporation's directors. I know my father trusts him."

"I'm not sure I'd trust him, not after he snuck in here without anyone seeing him. But it's not my place to tell you who you can talk to." Goose slapped a large yellow envelope on the desk. "Were you expecting a package? The courier arrived while we were dealing with your secretary, and I signed for it."

It had the Sentinel City Security logo on it. "My father asked them to send me some information."

"Do you mind if I open it? I'm sure it's perfectly innocent – I've already had it checked for explosives residue. But I don't want any more surprises. Go into your office and shut the door. I'll bring the contents in when I'm sure they're safe."

Sitting at her desk, Natasha folded her hands together to stop herself from fidgeting. The guard's concern about Ian had her re-evaluating everything the young executive said. Didn't she have enough things to worry about without adding Ian to the mix?

"Here are the documents," Goose said, placing the envelope and its contents on the desk. He removed the disposable gloves from his large hands and dropped them into her wastepaper basket.

"You're hiring a private bodyguard?" Goose asked. "Now that I've seen how tricky it is keeping people away from you, I'll be praying for whoever you choose. He's going to need all the help he can get. I'm sure I've aged twenty years since this morning."

"Today is an exception," Natasha said, staring at the bin. "On a regular day, the most challenging things I have to deal with are paper cuts, urgent emails, and trying to juggle my meetings schedule."

"Then don't choose this man," Goose said, sifting through the documents and passing one to her. "Jack Smith. I couldn't help looking while I was checking for nasty surprises. Ex-military, travelled the world. Check out his recent employment record. He hasn't been in one place for more than a few months. He'd be bored in an office environment. You need someone prepared to commit for the long haul."

"That makes sense," Natasha said. "I know Oleander has been with my father since before I was born. What do you think about the other two candidates?"

"I always thought there was more to Ollie. None of the other drivers spends as much time in the onsite gym. You're asking for my opinion about the other two? Well, that's where things get interesting. I don't expect a young high-flyer like you to understand, Ms Jacobson. But I believe God puts people where He wants them, to fulfil His plans."

"Are you telling me God sent you here?" Natasha asked. She leaned back in her chair. "Okay, I'm listening."

Goose nodded. He picked up both files and considered them before pushing one across the desk. "I can't say anything for, or against, this man, Eric Walker. On paper, he's the better choice. But I don't think he's right for you."

After glancing through Walker's file, Natasha extended her hand for the final document. Goose seemed reluctant to hand it over.

"And now," Natasha said, "you're going to tell me what's wrong with the last one before you try to convince me to give you the job."

"Have you read the selection criteria?" Goose asked with a grin. "My wife would kill me if I accepted a live-in position. I'm about to become a grandfather. She wants me to cut back my hours, not take on more."

"Then why are you withholding that file?"

"You're looking for a knight in shining armour, and I'm trying to decide how much to tell you. You're familiar with the proverb: Don't judge a book by its cover? One glance at this man's photo and you'll want the other one. Greg Freeman's application doesn't do him justice. He comes across as a villain, but he has a good heart. I've only known him for a few weeks, but I can see God's hand upon him."

"That's the second time you've mentioned God," Natasha said.

"Hear me out," Goose replied, "and then I won't say anything else. Greg made some big mistakes when he was younger. But in the last seven years, he's turned his life around. He's debt-free and sober, and he doesn't make excuses for either his addictions or his criminal record."

"You want me to hire an addict with a criminal record?" Natasha asked. "I'm surprised he's even on Sentinel Security's books."

"I'm one of Greg's character referees," Goose said, "so I'm staking my reputation on his reliability. He's on Sentinel's books because I know the owner, Matthew Wallace. Matt is a member of my church. I asked him to imagine how he'd feel if he had a brother in a similar predicament. A man who's trying to turn his life around, but nobody's interested in giving him a second chance. I'm asking you to do the same."

"Does Freeman go to your church too?" Natasha asked. "Is that why you're championing his cause?"

"Yes, Greg attends the same church, but that's not why I'm 'championing' him. Greg's my eldest son's GA sponsor. If Greg can rebuild his life, there's hope for my boy. That's why I invited Greg to stay in my house when he moved back here. For the three weeks he lived with us, I couldn't find fault with him, and everyone says I'm a good judge of character."

To deflect her thoughts from the possibility that Goose was referring to Ian again, Natasha asked a question. "GA? That's a Twelve-Step program like Alcoholics Anonymous, for gamblers?"

Goose nodded, but before he could say anything else, his partner's voice crackled through the radio clipped to his belt.

"Hey, Goose. I hope Ms Jacobson likes flowers? Two big bunches just arrived, and downstairs said to expect more."

"I'm on my way, Will," Goose said and went to the door.

Natasha stared at the silent phone on her desk. "Why didn't someone phone me to ask?"

"I told them to hold your incoming calls until you get a new secretary. That receptionist offered to send a replacement, but you wouldn't want anyone she recommended."

Another problem Natasha needed to solve. An uncomfortable sensation crawled up her spine. Her eyes went to the used coffee mugs, the only remaining evidence of the secretary's betrayal.

Natasha sprang from her seat and hurried into the outer office. Goose hesitated with his hand on the door that led into the corridor.

"Is there something you need?" the guard asked.

"My new secretary," Natasha said before she changed her mind. "I don't suppose God has any recommendations?"

Goose laughed and tapped the nameplate on the door. "You're an HR Assistant Manager. I'm only a security guard, but I'm guessing you have access to a lot of employee files. If you can't think of a suitable replacement, you know someone who does."

When Natasha closed the door after Goose left, her hand was trembling. She reflected on his parting words for several minutes before she seized the phone on the secretary's desk and punched in a number. After the briefest preamble, she explained the purpose of her call. "At the last department meeting, you recommended an employee for a secretarial position based on her impeccable references, but you were overruled. Somebody's niece got the job."

"That would be Amanda Donavon. Would you like me to organise an interview?"

"That won't be necessary. Send me the paperwork, and she can start immediately."

5

Ugliness

Isaiah 5:20
Woe to those who call evil good and good evil;
who put darkness for light, and light for darkness; who
put bitter for sweet, and sweet for bitter!

Returning to her own office, Natasha sat at her desk and picked up the Freeman file. She began with the A5 photo attached to the outside of the folder. It was a headshot of an unsmiling brown-haired man with a misshapen nose, heavy eyebrows, and dark, angry eyes. He had a square jaw, heavy stubble on his chin, and a thick neck suggesting the rest of him was built for brawling, like a modern-day gladiator. She shuddered.

Goose's warning about not judging a book by its cover popped into her mind.

Setting aside the photo, Natasha took up her pink pen to write some notes. She clicked to activate the ballpoint, and a distracting thought carried her away. What was it about this pen that had interested the office invaders?

Natasha studied the inscription: *Happy 16th Birthday, Natasha. Love from Edith.*

A wave of nostalgia took her back in time. During the six years Natasha was enrolled at St Catherine's Academy, Edith accepted every visitation opportunity, even attending the open days. Her stepmother's steadfast devotion brought Natasha comfort during those difficult years. Natasha had never said anything about what was happening at school, but she sensed Edith understood. Perhaps that explained why her stepmother always brought a keepsake when she visited? Engraved trinkets were reserved for Natasha's merit award assemblies and dance performances.

The other students had said awful things about Edith being a "wicked stepmother", pretending to care while stealing her father's love. That was harder to bear because Luke never put in an appearance…

Dragging her mind from the ugliness of the old accusations, Natasha considered the other items that had been collected with the pen. The crystal ornaments were also engraved with names and dates. Were the intruders seeking personal information to sell to the newspapers, or was there another purpose?

Natasha frowned at the family portrait. It was taken when Natasha was four, a few weeks before her mother died. Her father never spoke about Stephanie. Nor did he explain why his marriage to the Spendor heiress must remain a secret. What had happened to transform the glamorous socialite, Stephanie Spendor, into the fragile invalid in the photo? She bore no likeness to the portrait that hung on the executive floor.

Natasha clicked the pink pen again. Pink was her signature colour. Cassie, Natasha's only friend at boarding school, had insisted Natasha needed a dramatic accent as her trademark. After Cassie provided that information to Edith, her stepmother had embraced the challenge of finding treasures in the right shade.

This pen was the first pink item Edith had bought for Natasha, but there had been many more. Today, Natasha wore pink earrings and a lapel pin matching the designer lipstick Edith had purchased...

It was also the colour of the new car, her father's gift to celebrate Natasha's recent promotion. The police said the bright pink paintwork had made it easier to track Natasha's movements...

Click. Natasha stared at the white knuckles holding the pen, and loosened her grip. She opened the folder, but her eyes would not focus on the text. Rubbing her forehead, Natasha retrieved her desk key from a secret compartment in the base of the pink desk lamp. The hiding place had been another of Cassie's innovations. Natasha steeled herself against another wave of forbidden memories, and the pain at her temples spiked.

Unlocking the desk drawer, Natasha found an unopened packet of headache tablets and pressed two into her palm. She chased the pills with half the contents of a bottle of spring water from her office mini-refrigerator. While waiting for the medication to ease the pain, she stared at the folder in her hand.

What was the challenge Goose had left her? She should deal with this application as if Freeman were her brother, in need of a second chance. Was it a coincidence Freeman shared the same first name as Edith's son from her first marriage? Edith had been a recently-bereaved widow when she and her child came to live at the estate. Natasha had been five and the boy who didn't play with girls was eight...

Click. When was the last time Natasha had thought about the boy who became her stepbrother when Luke and Edith married? She frowned.

Click. Click. A few days before she was sent to boarding school he'd said he wanted to be her friend. Yet when she came home for the holidays, he was sullen and withdrawn. It was easier to avoid him. She must have been fourteen the last time she saw him.

Three months later, she came home from boarding school to find the dining table set for three instead of four. Natasha remembered asking her stepmother where he was. After Edith burst into tears and Luke escorted his wife from the room, Natasha ate her dinner alone.

By eavesdropping on whispered conversations among the household staff, Natasha built up a picture of what had occurred. Her stepbrother had stormed out after arguing with her father, promising never to return. Natasha had not wanted to ruin the brief respite from her horrible boarding school existence by upsetting either of her parents. She pretended to be indifferent to his absence. The next time she came home she listened for news, but his name was never mentioned. It seemed as if the entire household had forgotten he existed.

Natasha shook her head in disbelief. Life had taught her about the pain of grief, yet she had allowed ten years to pass without giving any thought to Edith's suffering. How many times had she chanced upon her stepmother in an unguarded moment and turned away at the sight of her tears?

The recent conversation with Goose took on a particular significance. Perhaps God had sent Natasha to comfort Edith, and instead she had left her stepmother to deal with her grief alone. Natasha had always considered herself a good person, but there was no kindness or compassion in the way she had ignored Edith's situation.

There was no excusing Natasha's selfishness. That must be why one bad thing after another had happened recently. *You're a cold-hearted monster, and now God's going to tear your privileged life apart until there's no hiding your ugliness.*

The inner accusations awakened a dark feeling more powerful than anything Natasha had ever experienced. Her heart pounded as her spiralling thoughts descended into bitterness, self-loathing and despair...

Thunk. Natasha jerked upright in her chair.

The pen had dropped from her fingers and fallen onto the desk, breaking the spell. The pen's decorative diamonds sparkled in the light from a single sunbeam. Outside the window, the storm clouds had parted for a moment, and with that small shaft of light the heaviness inside her seemed to flee.

Had God sent the sunbeam? Natasha shook her head in disbelief at the awakening hope. *When have you ever given any thought to God?*

"God wants you to search for Him with all your heart," a voice said from a forgotten past. Nanny Sherman was another person who had disappeared from Natasha's life without an explanation. Natasha chased after the fragmented memory. What else had Nanny Sherman said?

"Now, promise me you'll never forget what I've taught you. God is always there; always ready to help you because He loves you."

If God loved Natasha, why had he taken Nanny Sherman – and her mother – away? Why—

Noises coming from the other room pulled her back into the present.

"That's your desk," Goose said. "Put your bag down, and I'll take you in to meet Ms Jacobson."

The guard pushed into her office, his arms filled with colourful bouquets. Extravagant floral arrangements festooned with bright pink ribbons. "Admirers," Goose said, dumping the flowers onto her desk. "I hope you have enough vases."

Following close behind him came a short, brown-skinned indigenous Australian woman wearing the uniform of a general administrative assistant. Large brown eyes smiled at Natasha from behind round black-rimmed spectacles. The woman appeared to be in her forties, considerably older than the untrained school-leavers who came to work in the ground floor offices. She also carried flowers. Goose took them from the stranger and added the bunch to the pile.

"This is your new secretary, Amanda Donavon. Amanda, Ms Jacobson. I'll leave you two together and watch the outer door."

"Thank you for giving me a chance, Ms Jacobson." Amanda smiled and her round face lit up. Her eyes swept around the room before returning to Natasha. "Goose told me about your last secretary. I'll work hard to prove you can trust me." Then her hands reached for one of the bouquets. "What would you like me to do with these flowers?"

Natasha retrieved the flowers from Amanda. "There are vases in the cupboard to the left of your desk. There are at least a dozen, so there's no need to go looking for more. My office resembled a florist shop in the days following my recent promotion."

"Where do I get water for the vases?" Amanda asked.

"There's a kitchenette along the corridor past reception," Goose said. "I'll fetch some—"

"No," Natasha said hurriedly, remembering the lecture she had received when she first entered the graduate program and someone reported her for washing a coffee cup.

"Amanda, call Housekeeping and ask them to deliver some," Natasha said. "The list of extension numbers is beside your phone. You'll need to give them a requisition number, so the order is processed correctly. There's a book on your desk for you to allocate the number and record the details.

"Or you could do what your predecessor did. She took bottles of spring water from my refrigerator." Natasha indicated the half-empty bottle on her desk. "My wastepaper bin was full of empties."

Amanda's response would determine whether hiring someone without an interview had been a good idea.

Frowning at the distinctive glass bottle, Amanda shook her head. "I'll call Housekeeping and tell them I want ordinary tap water. I can't believe anyone would waste that expensive brand on flowers."

"I had the same reaction," Natasha said, recalling how the secretary had complained about her employer's stinginess. "That was the first of many conversations I had about the office budget. I'll expect you to keep a strict accounting for everything you spend. We'll talk more when you've had time to settle in."

Amanda found the vases and installed the flowers in preparation to display them around the room. "Do you have a preference to which ones are closest to your desk?"

"No. I wouldn't even keep them in here, but I can't afford to offend anyone. Read out the names, so I can confirm my list is accurate."

"The pink roses are from Blaze McGilligan, the carnations from Daniel Pendragon. That mixed bunch is from Joah

Vandemeer. Zedekiah Upchurch sent those lilies, and the orchids are from Finn Quartermaster."

"I'm expecting follow-up phone calls," Natasha said, handing the list to Amanda. "Be polite, but tell them I'm not taking calls nor receiving visitors today."

Accepting the list, Amanda matched the names to the floral arrangements. "Quartermaster, Upchurch, Vandemeer, Pendragon, McGilligan. Norris? There are no flowers from Ian Norris. Should I get another vase?"

"Ian Norris has already been to see me," Natasha said.

"He came without flowers?"

"He came without an invitation."

Amanda's dark eyes widened, and Natasha regretted her harsh tone. The secretary glanced thoughtfully at the extravagant bouquets before nodding. "No visitors and screen all incoming calls."

"I've done nothing to encourage these men," Natasha said. "They're all Spendor Corporation executives, and my father hand-picked them to escort me to official functions. I'm certain he asks them to report back to him."

"Your father is Luke Jacobson, the CEO? Are you expecting him to visit?"

"If my father wants to see me, his secretary will summon me."

6

Timeliness

Psalm 57:10
For Your loving kindness reaches to the heavens,
and Your truth to the skies.

Natasha sat at her desk with her office door open, hands folded on the unread Freeman file. She told herself this inability to focus had nothing to do with the creepiness of a room where everything had been disturbed. No, she was assessing Amanda's phone-answering skills. For the first time, she regretted the layout of the two offices. All she could see of the outer room were two vacant visitor chairs. Goose must be seated closer to Amanda's desk.

Amanda's polite engagement with the incoming callers was faultless. But it was the easiness of her conversation with Goose in between the calls that captivated Natasha. Amanda told him she had been overseas for a decade, working for a well-known international charity.

"What made you decide to come home?" Goose asked. "It sounds as if you loved your job."

There was a pause in the conversation. Natasha leaned forward to hear Amanda's answer.

"You'll probably think I'm mad," Amanda said, "but I believe God called me home. I was going to enrol in Bible College, but He had other plans."

"Those 'other plans' brought you here?"

"In a roundabout way. To be honest, I expected God to open doors immediately, so it was shocking to find I couldn't get a job. I'd been the private secretary for the charity CEO, with excellent references, yet I couldn't even get an interview. It seemed as if every door slammed in my face.

"My bank account was almost empty, and yet God continued to ask me to trust Him. A friend got me some waitressing hours in a café, but it wasn't enough to cover my living expenses. Another week and I'd have admitted defeat and gone home to my family."

"Then I was offered the admin assistant job downstairs," Amanda said, "and I knew God hadn't forgotten me. The timeliness of God's provision always amazes me."

Out of her chair before she could stop herself, Natasha hurried to the other room.

"Did you want something, Ms Jacobson?" Amanda asked, rising to her feet.

"Timeliness," Natasha said, slowing her breathing to regain her composure. "Say that sentence again."

"Um, the timeliness of God's provision amazes me."

"Did you ever meet a girl called Cassandra Thorborgson-Smyth? She's dead now, but we were at school together. Cassie had curly red hair and freckles, and her parents were international diplomats."

"No," said Amanda. "I never met Cassie. Why are you asking?"

"Timeliness was our code word. We spent hours rehearsing how to use it in a sentence, but we never came up with a phrase that included God."

"Why did your friend need a code word?" Goose asked. "Does it have anything to do with her death?"

"The code word was for me," Natasha said. "But I don't want to talk about that. Cassie loved word games. Amanda, please provide Goose with a notepad and a pen, and the same for you. Then write down the first three words you think of that end with the letters n-e-s-s."

Watching as the pair completed the task, Natasha spoke as soon as she regained their attention. "I'll go first. My words today are weirdness, seriousness and wrongness."

"My list is righteousness, faithfulness and timeliness," Amanda said.

"I've got righteousness and faithfulness, too," said Goose. "My final word is hopefulness."

"Thank you," Natasha said. "You both believe God directed you to my office today?"

They answered without hesitation. "Yes."

Natasha smiled as a flicker of hope quietened the restlessness of her thoughts. "You believe He sent you to help me and you're both in the right place, at the right time? Everything that's happened in the past twenty-four hours suggests I'm in the wrong place."

"Have you considered looking at things from a different perspective?" Goose asked. "What if God sent us to tell you He's here, waiting to transform your situation if you let Him?"

"There's a Scripture that says all things work together for good," Amanda said, and Goose added his voice to finish the phrase, "for those who love God."

Nodding, Natasha moved towards the inner door. "I'd like to continue this discussion in my office. Amanda, switch the phones back to reception – I showed you the process before." Then Natasha raised her finger to her lips in the universal signal for silence and gestured for Goose to lock the outer door. "Come along. We'll have coffee while we talk."

Amanda and Goose exchanged glances before complying with her requests and joining Natasha in her office. She directed them to prepare the refreshments while she moved her chair to supplement the two seats at the circular table beside the window.

Natasha played the part of an idle executive, gazing out at the city from her seat. Amanda and Goose conversed as if morning tea was their only concern. When the coffee mugs and a plate of sugar cookies were on the table, Natasha sent Goose to switch on the stereo on a shelf closest to the door.

"A little more volume, please," Natasha called as classical music flooded the room.

When Goose had joined Amanda at the table, Natasha spoke.

"There's a signal jammer woven into the music. I'm feeling paranoid today, yet something tells me trustworthiness is an attribute you both share."

"Why do you keep using words ending with 'ness'?" Goose asked.

"I wondered if either of you had noticed," Natasha said. "Cassie and I weren't the only ones who played word games at boarding school. The 'mean girls' peppered their conversations with seemingly innocent phrases to remind me I couldn't escape them. It became constant, which is why everyone called me Nessie. Not one of the adults suspected it was more than a nickname."

"Nessie?" Amanda asked.

"After the Loch Ness Monster," Natasha said, studying the sugar crystals on her cookie. "I was twelve when I arrived at St Catherine's Academy but I'd already perfected the ability to hide my emotions.

"At first, Cassie agreed my best defence against the bullying was not to react. But after three months of keeping up the pretence, she realised we'd created a problem for ourselves. It became a contest among my tormentors to see who could come up with the next outrageous scheme.

"Calling me Nessie was Cassie's idea, a kind of exposure therapy. I don't know how she got them to adopt it. She played the outraged friend to perfection, so nobody suspected. While the mean girls used the same phrases to taunt me, Cassie and I neutralised the negative connotations with our word games."

"Why are you telling us this?" Goose asked.

"I don't have enough evidence, but this morning's newspaper article suggests someone with knowledge about my past *difficulties* intends to profit from my recent misfortune. I've already had two people address me by a St Catherine's Academy title."

Goose stiffened. "Who? I've been with yo—" He narrowed his eyes. "That secretary? I didn't pay any attention to what she was saying. And the man who snuck into your office while I was trying to get the secretary to leave? I knew I should have gone after him."

"Ian offered a plausible explanation," Natasha said. "Nobody outside this room can know that I suspect an old school bully has resurfaced."

"What are you going to do?" Amanda asked.

"Take advantage of the 'timeliness of God's provision'." Natasha picked up the folders from her desk and passed them to Amanda. "My father expects me to hire one of these men as my bodyguard. I'm unable to concentrate long enough to read the files. I'll leave you to read them while Goose escorts me to the restroom. You will notice Goose is a referee for one of them. Please try not to let that prejudice you against the others."

Following Natasha into the front office, Amanda placed the files side-by-side on her desk.

Goose notified Will they were about to leave the office, and then he stepped into the corridor to check the way was clear. Natasha held her head high, activating her signature smile. Focusing on her destination, she avoided eye contact with anyone.

7

Foolishness

Returning to her office, Natasha approached Amanda's desk. "Have you formed an opinion?"

"It was easier than I expected, Ms Jacobson," Amanda said. The three folders were arranged across the desk. "I eliminated Jack Smith as soon as I saw the list of overseas organisations he'd worked for. Two of them were mining companies I recognised from my time with the charity. There were rumours the security guards they employed were thugs who took bribes. He might have been one of the innocent ones, but you can't afford to take the chance. I've written a note and added it to the file for future reference."

The rejected folder went into the filing tray on the desk. Amanda looked at the remaining folders.

"That left me two candidates. One of them, Eric Walker, seemed to have everything going for him. The right qualifications and experience." Amanda picked up the photo. "And he's attractive for his age, so he'd fit in with the business executives you work with. The choice seemed obvious, so I phoned one of the referees. I got more than I bargained for, only making it as far as the referee's secretary. When I mentioned Walker's name, the secretary almost shouted at me through the phone.

"She said she dated him for six months. At first, Walker was the perfect gentleman. So perfect, she let him stay overnight on their second date. He asked her to keep quiet about their relationship, claiming Sentinel City Security had a non-fraternisation policy and he'd lose his contract. Once she agreed, they never went out in public. He always came to her apartment. Walker never offered to pay for the extra food and drink she purchased for him. Walker promised he'd marry her as soon as his divorce came through.

"She discovered he'd been telling similar lies to another woman in the company – there was no wife. After the two women compared stories, there was a messy public row.

Walker didn't deny anything and laughed about how easily he'd been able to deceive them. He said women always found him irresistible, and he'd have no trouble replacing either of them."

With a thud, the Walker file dropped into the tray with the other rejected one. Natasha stared at the remaining folder.

"I know," said Amanda. "Greg Freeman's not done himself any favours with that photo, but do you remember the old saying about not judging a book by its cover? God looks at the heart of a man to determine if he's good."

Natasha flipped open the folder and found the contact phone number.

"Goose, phone your friend. If he doesn't answer, that will be a definitive sign we've misread the situation, and God doesn't want me to hire this man."

"And if Greg answers?" Goose asked.

"Amanda, take notes, so Goose doesn't have to remember everything I want him to say. At the first negative response, Goose will bring the conversation to an end..."

Natasha spoke fast, afraid if she paused for even a second, the foolishness of this enterprise would render her silent. After giving Amanda only two questions, Natasha was satisfied this was as far as the interview would go.

Amanda and Goose took their role as advisors more seriously than expected. At their insistence, the interview questions increased. Twenty minutes elapsed as the trio discussed the interview procedure, including differing predictions about how the interviewee would respond to some of the questions.

"Ready?" Amanda asked, her fingers hovering above the keypad on the desktop phone. Goose held the receiver, waiting for the call to connect.

Nodding, Natasha rested her hands on her copy of the questions to maintain the illusion of calmness.

Goose frowned as he waited for Freeman to answer the call, and then the wrinkles vanished from his brow. "G'day, mate. This is Goose. I've got something confidential to discuss with you. Are you free to talk?" After listening for a moment, Goose smiled. "Look, mate, first I must tell you this is a job interview. I've got a long list of instructions in front of me, and I'll be in trouble if I don't get this part right. Think carefully about what you say when the questions start because a wrong answer will bring the interview to an end. Do you understand?"

A momentary silence, and then Goose spoke again. "Are you okay with taking part in a conference call?"

He paused to listen to the response.

"Four people: you, me, Amanda – she's the secretary taking notes, and your potential employer." He paused again. "I can't answer that question. That information comes at the end of the interview. Are you willing to participate in this conference call?"

"He says yes," Goose said to Amanda, and she pressed the required button to amplify the call. "Right, mate. Now everyone at this end can hear you. Say hello and introduce yourself."

"Ah, um. Hello. My name is Greg Freeman, and I'm thankful for this opportunity. I'm presuming you know I'm a recovering addict. I'm looking for a fresh start, and I'm ready to prove I'm a diligent and reliable worker."

"Nice to meet you, Greg. I'm Amanda. I have a few questions. Are you ready?"

"Ask your questions, Amanda."

"Do you agree to keep the details of this phone conversation confidential?"

"Of course."

"Are you available to commence a full-time position today?"

"Today? I have an appointment Gent, but I can cancel it. I'll do anything to convince you I'm the man for this job."

"Anything?" Amanda asked, departing from the agreed script. "Be careful what you ask for, Greg."

Natasha resisted the urge to correct Amanda, forcing herself to remain silent and allow the situation to progress to the inevitable conclusion.

"Next question," said Amanda. "Are you prepared to accept a live-in position?"

"The job comes with accommodation? That's a resounding yes. I'm paying by the night here at Kitchener's Hotel."

"Is your social calendar clear? The successful applicant would be on call twenty-four-seven."

There was an extended pause before Freeman answered. "I've got my Twelve-Step meetings and church. As long as my employer allows me to fit those in around my work obligations, I'm free."

"My turn again," said Goose. "I'm going to ask a series of questions, and I want you to give me your immediate response. First, I need a word starting with the letter Q."

"Quick."

"Three words that end with n-e-s-s? I'll give you an example: coldness."

"Right, hmm..." Freeman said. "Forgiveness, thankfulness and faithfulness."

"What do you think of when I say the word foolishness?"

"A fool is easily parted from his money."

"Cleverness?" Goose asked.

"The opposite of foolishness? No, the ability to make good decisions. Not to be confused with trickiness – trying to gain an unfair advantage over someone."

"Which best describes you?" Amanda said.

Natasha didn't need to check the list to confirm this was not one of the prepared questions. Amanda smiled in her direction, and then her lips formed a silent, "Trust me."

"I'd like to think I'm wise enough to avoid trouble," Freeman said. "And clever enough to realise you're playing a word association game with me. Goose, are you still there? If not for your part in this strange interview, I'd hang up."

Amanda covered her mouth to hide her grin, and Natasha tapped the sheet of questions, waving her hand at Goose to respond to Freeman's comment.

"Don't hang up, Greg," Goose said. "I'm asking you to trust me. Here's the next question. Which of the following would you prefer: a low-paying job with an extended contract; or a single payment of fifty-thousand dollars for a day's work?"

"Did you say fifty thousand?" Freeman's voice deepened to a harsh growl. "My integrity is not for sale. Goose, I'll give you thirty seconds to explain what this is about."

"I've heard enough," Natasha said, rising to walk over to Amanda and lean closer to the phone. "Mr Freeman, thank you for your cooperation during this unorthodox interview. Congratulations, you have progressed to the next stage."

"Who are you?" Freeman asked.

"The answer to that question will be provided when we meet. Please come to the Spendor Corporation Headquarters in the city. Are you familiar with that location?"

"I know it."

"When you arrive, call this number, and my secretary, Amanda, will come down to escort you to my office." Without waiting for a response, Natasha pressed the disconnect button.

"Why did you do that?" Goose asked. "He's not going to come."

"Then I'll know for certain," Natasha said. "Choosing Freeman was nothing more than pandering to my foolishness."

8

Surrealness

Colossians 1:13
Who delivered us
out of the power of darkness,
and translated us into
the Kingdom of the Son of his love.

Natasha jumped when Goose appeared in the doorway to her inner office.

"Will called on the radio," the security guard said. "Amanda and Greg have stepped off the elevator."

"Go and meet them."

As soon as Goose left, Natasha surveyed her desk, removing the documents she had spread out to conceal her idleness. The pressure in her head had not eased since Freeman phoned from the downstairs lobby, proving her prediction wrong. Not only had he arrived, but he made the journey in less than half an hour.

Natasha's heart pounded as she battled the urge to leap up and lock her door. Resisting the temptation to check her appearance again, she reminded herself Freeman needed to impress her, not the other way around.

The surrealness of the situation intensified her growing anxiety. If she had realised how emotionally fraught this meeting would be she might have left the choice of bodyguard to her father.

Over the classical music playing in the background, Natasha listened for sound in the next room. Her diligence was rewarded by a jumble of lowered voices followed by the closing of a door.

"Take off your wet jacket, Greg," Amanda said. "You can't meet your new boss looking like a drowned rat."

"I haven't been offered the job yet," the newcomer's voice said, "and I might not accept it."

"Of course, you will," Amanda said. "I told you on the way up: God's at work here. Couldn't you have stayed on the covered side of the street when you came from the bus stop? Your hair's a mess."

Freeman laughed. "I don't think your boss wants to hire me for my good looks."

"Stop bothering the man, Amanda," Goose said. "You're making *me* nervous."

"Remember to smile when you go in, Greg," Amanda said.

"That smile takes more than ten years from your face."

"How old do you think I am?"

"I know how old you are," Amanda said. "I've seen your file. Fifteen years younger than me, so show some respect for your elders. The twenty-seven candles on your last birthday cake don't mean anything because, without that smile, your face puts you on the wrong side of fifty."

"There's nothing wrong with fifty," Goose said.

"Fifty looks good on you, Goose," Amanda said. "But you're happily married and settled. Greg's single and unemployed. He should be worrying about his appearance. First impressions are important. Now, follow me, and I'll introduce you. Ms Jacobson, Mr Freeman to see you."

Natasha stared at the doorway as Amanda advanced towards her desk, but Freeman came no further than the threshold.

The smile faded from Freeman's face as he folded his arms across his chest. Natasha blinked at the contrast in size between the diminutive secretary and the big man.

Dressed in faded denim jeans and a black tee-shirt, his bulky frame blocked the doorway. His brown hair was untidy and damp, much longer than it had been in the photograph. And he'd forgotten to shave.

Noting the hostility in his stance, Natasha's rehearsed welcome stuck in her throat. Her courage fled, and the anger in his opening remark stole the colour from her face.

"Natasha. I should have known this was a set-up. Your father's outdone himself this time."

"What are you talking about?" Natasha asked. "What's your relationship with my father?"

Freeman strode towards her desk, and the slim executive leapt to her feet to face him. The angry man leaned forward and stared into her eyes. Natasha held herself still, retreating in her mind to the safe place where she could hide her fear.

"You really don't recognise me, Queenie?" he said, dropping onto one of the visitor chairs. The furniture groaned in protest. Freeman shook his head as a sad smile stretched across his face. "I caught a glimpse of uncertainty in your eyes, but you're still hiding behind that perfect princess smile."

"Oh," Natasha said.

The room tilted sideways.

This man was not Greg Freeman, but Gregory Leonard Cross, her stepmother Edith's missing son.

Holding her breath, she closed her eyes against the blurriness at the edge of her vision. A parade of memories assaulted her as she eased herself onto her chair. Her first encounter with the boy who eventually became her stepbrother had occurred when she was five.

An angry boy had appeared in her nursery doorway, "I don't play with *babies*." His mother was her new governess.

In the first six months, Gregory had progressed from calling her a "stuck-up little princess" to settling on the name "Queenie". It had been her fault. During a chance encounter in the playground, he'd stolen her favourite ball. "Queenie, Queenie, who's got your ball?" Natasha should have walked away instead of commanding him to give the toy back. After that, he'd pretended to bow whenever he saw her...

"Ms Jacobson," shrieked Amanda. "Goose! Goose! Get in here. Ms Jacobson's fainted."

Jerking upright in her seat, Natasha defended herself from the unnecessary ministrations. "I did *not* faint. Amanda, there's no need to fuss."

"What's happened?" Goose asked, bursting into the room.

"He's one of them!" Amanda pointed at Freeman. "Get him out of here."

"How is Natasha's fainting *my* fault?" Freeman asked. Then unexpectedly he started to laugh.

"Greg, I put in a good word for you," Goose said, "and this is how you repay me?"

"I can't believe I fell for his trickiness," Amanda said. "I've brought one of those nasty name-callers into her office."

"Be quiet and sit down, all of you," Natasha said, using the tone she reserved for male colleagues who needed reminding of her right to be there.

"I didn't faint," Natasha said, "but I definitely have an unbearable headache."

Amanda and Goose froze, and Greg leaned back, his large hand concealing the lower half of his face. His shoulders were shaking.

"Amanda," Natasha said, directing the secretary towards the chairs at the window table behind her. "Greg is not one of those 'nasty name-callers'. He only called me Queenie so I'd recognise him."

"Then why is he laughing?" Amanda asked, dragging the chair closer to Natasha.

Goose placed himself in the chair beside Greg.

"Why are you laughing?" Natasha said to Greg. "There's nothing funny about this situation."

"Always the perfect princess," Greg said. "You collapsed onto that chair with the grace of a ballerina performing to her audience."

"I did *not* collapse," Natasha said, keeping the quiver from her voice, "and you are a very poor audience if all you can do is laugh at me. You almost gave me a heart attack when I realised who you were."

"Heart attack?" Greg asked. "That's nothing to the shock you've given me. What were you thinking, Queenie, luring me into your office with the promise of a job?"

"You two know each other?" Goose asked.

"Remember, Goose, when you said I should treat Greg as if he was my brother?" Natasha asked.

"Y-yes?" Goose said, narrowing his eyes.

"I did," said Natasha.

"I am," said Greg.

After a few seconds of stunned silence, Amanda and Goose started talking.

"What?" Amanda said to Natasha. "You're the long-lost stepsister Greg told me about as we were coming up in the elevator?"

"Greg," Goose said, "why didn't you tell me you're related to the CEO's daughter?"

"I'm not related to the CEO's daughter," Greg said. "My mother married Natasha's father when I was fifteen. End of story. People presumed I received preferential treatment, but I couldn't live like that. I'd rather be an unemployed loser."

"My father would have helped you," Natasha said, "if you'd asked him."

"I'd better go," Greg said, pushing upward with his legs.

Goose shook his head as he caught hold of Greg's arm. "Now is a time to listen."

"You're quoting Scripture at me?" Greg said to Goose, returning to his seat. "Can't you see this isn't going to work?"

Facing Natasha again, Greg said, "Isn't it obvious, Queenie?" He paused, smiling at Amanda, as if confirming that word choice was intentional. "I don't want your father's help. I've seen how everyone acts around him, trying to appease him, and I can't play that game."

"I'm not my father," Natasha said. "I'm not trying to help you. I'm the one who needs help. If this is a game, then I'm the one with everything to lose. I need a bodyguard I can trust, and I chose you before I realised you were Edith's son."

"Trust goes both ways," Greg said. "After the way I treated you when we were children, why would you expect me to trust you?"

"That's an excellent question," Goose said. "Pardon me for asking, Ms Jacobson, but if he's your brother, why didn't you recognise him? He might have changed his appearance, but surely the name would have told you who he was?"

"Stepbrother," Natasha rubbed her forehead before she continued. "He was a scrawny teenager the last time I saw him, and his name was Gregory Cross. He bore no resemblance to the mean gorilla glaring out of that photograph."

"Who are you calling a 'mean gorilla'?" Greg asked, raising one of his bushy eyebrows. "It's not like you, Queenie, to be malicious with your words."

Amanda leaned forward, waving a finger towards Greg. "You've done nothing to disprove it."

9

Stubbornness

1 John 1:9
If we confess our sins, He is faithful and righteous
to forgive us the sins and to cleanse us
from all unrighteousness.

"That's enough," Natasha said, pulling open her desk drawer and extracting the headache tablets. She read the instructions on the box before glancing at her watch. Taking a deep breath, Natasha returned the pills to the drawer and reached for her water bottle.

The room fell silent.

"How bad is that headache?" Amanda asked.

"Wrong question," Greg said. "Can I see that box?"

Natasha reopened the drawer and brought the ibuprofen tablets back into view. Amanda took the packet and delivered it to Greg.

"Over-the-counter medication," Amanda said. "Nothing that warrants your frown."

Greg opened the packaging and checked the contents. "You took two this morning? Was this packet already in the drawer, or did you bring it with you?"

Natasha gestured towards the drawer.

"Why are you asking Ms Jacobson these questions?" Amanda asked.

"Stop calling me Ms Jacobson, Amanda. You know too many of my secrets," Natasha said. "I'm including you in that request, Goose. Please use my first name while we're among friends."

"So I'm your friend now?" Greg asked. "It's nice to know where I stand. Apart from Goose and Amanda, who else do you trust with your secrets? Does my mother know you have these pills?"

"Why do you think I keep them locked in my office?"

"Why the secrecy," Amanda asked, "over a packet of pills I can buy anywhere?"

"When I was four," Natasha said, "my mother died. I don't know the details, but my father doesn't permit any non-prescription medication in the house. He also worries about my health. I've learned not to show the slightest sign of illness unless I want the doctor to visit."

Natasha smiled. "I'm not a fragile flower. My father doesn't need to know I use over-the-counter medication for the occasional headache."

"Today's headache is more severe," Greg said.

"This headache is a reward for my stubbornness," Natasha said. "It was a mistake to pretend I'm unaffected by everything that's happened."

"Can we pray for your headache?" Goose asked.

"Pray for my headache?" Natasha asked, dark spots flashing before her eyes as the band of pressure around her head tightened. "Why would you want to pray—"

"What an excellent idea," Amanda said. "You stay right there, Ms, er, N-Natasha, and we'll gather around you."

"They can pray for me from there," Natasha said, sitting upright as Amanda placed a hand on her shoulder. "I didn't know praying was a hands-on exercise."

"In the New Testament," Amanda said, "there's an instruction to lay hands on the sick, and they'll be healed."

"Natasha doesn't like anyone touching her," Greg said. "Goose and I can pray from this side of the desk."

"What do I have to do?" Natasha asked.

"Nothing," Amanda said. "Sit there and relax."

Greg laughed. "Sorry, Amanda. Asking Natasha to relax looks as if it's having the opposite effect."

"Be quiet, Greg," Amanda said. "Natasha, ignore him. Close your eyes. You don't have to look at that annoying man."

Natasha obeyed. A shiver ran up her spine, and darkness pressed in. She took a deep breath and started counting backwards from one hundred inside her head.

"Goose, you'd better pray first," Amanda said. "I've got some repentance and forgiveness to work through before my heart attitude is right."

Losing count, Natasha started again.

"Heavenly Father," Goose said. "Your Word tells us to pray for each other. We're here in obedience. Thank You for hearing our prayers. We know You listen to our petitions when we ask for healing in the precious name of Jesus Christ. Lord, Natasha has been under a lot of stress, and this headache isn't helping. We ask that You release her from the pain."

When Goose finished, a heavy silence amplified the beating of Natasha's heart. Having abandoned her counting, she almost opened her eyes.

"Stubbornness." That single word from Greg was like a spear thrust into her heart, a blow that was repeated when he continued to speak. "I believe stubbornness is the key. Lord, You heard Natasha confess this headache is a reward for her stubbornness. We ask You to take her stubbornness and replace it with a willingness to listen to Your voice."

Her mind screamed for the torment to stop. Relief washed over Natasha when Greg's verbal assault ended.

"Teach Natasha how to trust Your provision," Goose said, "and how to trust those You send to help her."

"Yes, Lord," said Amanda. "Teach Natasha to trust those You sent to help her."

A rush of heat started where the secretary's hand rested on Natasha's shoulder and spread outward.

Amanda's voice continued. "Forgive each of us for adding to Natasha's stress. We don't fully understand what she's going through, but You know everything, Lord. We're here as Your servants, and we want to be a help and not a hindrance. Please deliver Natasha from this headache, and protect her from those scheming against her. We claim victory over her enemies, both those we can see and those in the spiritual realm. Please bring healing to her body, her heart and her mind, in Jesus' name. Amen."

Removing her hand from Natasha's shoulder, Amanda asked, "How do you feel?"

Natasha glanced at the hopeful expression on Amanda's face and smiled. She lacked the words to adequately answer that question without hurting her new friend.

"A little better, thank you," Natasha said. "I think I'll go home as soon as Greg and I conclude this interview."

"So there really is a job on offer?" Greg asked, leaning forward. "Does your father know you're hiring a bodyguard?"

Something Natasha couldn't define had changed in the room's atmosphere. It was easier to believe he was Edith's son. Perhaps it was the way his smile reached his eyes.

"It was my father's idea." Natasha's answer came without effort. "I found out on the way to work this morning. He'd already drafted the selection criteria, and I asked him to allow me to conduct the interviews. He agreed without hesitation."

"Why does your father think you need a bodyguard?" Greg asked. "You live in a walled estate with armed guards patrolling the grounds. I presume you travel to and from the city with your father, and here in this building, Goose and his colleagues are always on duty."

"Haven't you seen this morning's newspaper headlines?" Goose asked.

"No. Is this another tricky interview question? Have I disqualified myself from consideration?" Greg moved as if intending to leave.

"Sit down," said Amanda, pushing him back in his chair. She disappeared into the front office. When she returned, Amanda tapped Greg across the chest with a folded newspaper. "While you're reading that, I'm going to order

Natasha's lunch from the cafeteria."

"Order enough for all of us," Natasha said, her eyes locked on the newspaper. "And Goose had better check on Will. The poor man has been stuck near the elevator all morning."

"Are you sure you want to be alone in the same room with Greg?" Amanda asked as Goose prepared to follow her instructions.

"Consider this the next stage of the interview process," Natasha said. "If Greg and I can't be polite to each other while you're in the next office, then this arrangement will never work."

Goose departed, already talking to his partner on the radio as he went. Natasha couldn't bear to watch Greg glaring at the newspaper. She drained the remaining water from the bottle and was fetching a replacement when Goose called from the doorway.

"Ollie's on his way," Goose said. "He's carrying a pink briefcase, and he's told Will he's not leaving until he personally delivers the briefcase into your hands."

"Your briefcase was in your car?" Greg asked, tossing the folded newspaper onto her desk. "I'm surprised your father allows you to drive alone."

"I wasn't supposed to be alone," Natasha said. "I only took possession of the car yesterday, and it was my first opportunity to drive it. The plan was for me to follow behind my father's car, but everything went wrong."

"We'll talk about what went wrong," Greg said, "after you've gotten rid of Oleander."

"Why does Natasha need to get rid of Ollie?" Goose asked. "His loyalty to her father is beyond question."

"I'm not questioning his loyalty," Greg said. "But if I was still a betting man, I'd put everything I owned on Oleander taking one look at me and throwing me out."

"Why would Ollie throw you out?" Goose asked.

"He never liked me."

"I'm sure that's not true," Natasha said.

"He was there the day I chased you through the house and caught you on the stairs. None of the household staff would leave us alone together after that. Why do you think your father sent you away to boarding school? He couldn't get rid of his new wife's rebellious son, so he made sure his precious princess was out of reach."

"Natasha?" Goose asked. "Did Greg try—"

"Of course not," Natasha said, shaking her head. "I was twelve. It was a harmless game of chasings."

"It may have seemed harmless to you, but I was an adolescent boy who couldn't resist a cute girl in a tutu. If you'd shown me any encouragement..."

10

Uneasiness

Isaiah 43:19
Behold, I will do a new thing. It springs out now.
Don't you know it? I will even make a way
in the wilderness, and rivers in the desert.

A loud knock on the main door brought the disturbing conversation to an end. Natasha pressed the call button on her desk phone. "Unlock the door and bring Oleander in," she told Amanda before gesturing to her other companions.

"Goose, take Greg over to the table and keep him quiet. Perhaps Oleander won't recognise him."

"Mr Oleander to see you, Ms Jacobson," said Amanda, appearing in the doorway. The secretary moved aside to allow the visitor to enter.

Oleander was wearing his chauffeur's uniform. He surveyed the room as he stepped towards Natasha's desk and placed her briefcase firmly in front of her. His eyes lingered on Greg's face while his right hand disappeared into his jacket pocket. Natasha held her breath, uneasiness over this intrusion reactivating the almost-forgotten headache. When Oleander's hand reappeared, he offered her the missing mobile phone.

"The battery is flat, Miss Natasha," Oleander said. "But I thought you'd prefer to have it back in your possession."

"Thank you, Oleander," Natasha said. "I'm sorry you had to visit the police compound."

"It was nothing. I had my reasons to volunteer for the task." Oleander walked around the room, examining the cards attached to the five floral arrangements. "Pendragon, Vandemeer, Upchurch, McGilligan, Quartermaster." He turned back to Natasha with a smile. "The first reason was to satisfy my curiosity. Did you know I'm thinking of writing a novel in my retirement?"

Pausing in the process of finding her phone charger, Natasha said, "I didn't know you were retiring."

"Neither did I," Oleander said, choosing a chair in front of Natasha's desk. "Not until your father mentioned the possibility. That brings me to another reason for me wanting to examine your car. Your father has stopped listening to my advice. He still asks for my input, but then he seeks a second opinion. I must apologise, Miss Natasha, for not disobeying his orders and turning back to find you yesterday."

"Why would my father tell you not to come back for me?"

"Your father believed you were enjoying a *private moment* with the young man assisting you with your car."

"A private moment?" Natasha asked. "With Ian Norris? What gave my father the idea that I'd want…"

A chill rippled through Natasha as she recalled two of her morning conversations. First, her father had told her to forgive Ian, and then that young executive had shared advice her father had given him. Natasha resisted the urge to ask the chauffeur if Ian was her father's new advisor.

Instead, she blinked, reminded herself to smile, and reached for the briefcase. As she pulled it across the desk, the forgotten newspaper came with it and fell into her lap. Natasha thrust the paper onto the desk, careless about the crumpled pages.

"Where did that come from?" Oleander reached for the newspaper, refolding it neatly. "Your father issued orders for every copy in the building to be retrieved and destroyed."

"I found it in my desk drawer," Amanda said. "I didn't know about the order."

"Put it in a safe place," Oleander said to Amanda, handing over the newspaper without taking his eyes from Natasha's face. "It might prove to be important."

Maintaining her smile had never been more difficult. Natasha's initial uneasiness had grown into an internal tempest. "Are you implying Ian Norris had something to do with the newspaper story?"

"Did I say that?" Oleander said. "Curious you think there might be a connection. I wonder if anyone else has considered that possibility? Your security team should discuss that while making plans for your future."

"I didn't know I had a team," Natasha said. "My father only mentioned one bodyguard."

Oleander smiled, showing his teeth. "I walked in, expecting to talk my way past my old friend Goose before I could see you. But instead, I faced your formidable new secretary. Here's Goose sitting in your inner sanctum, alongside a man who looks more like a nightclub bouncer with a chip on his shoulder than the bodyguard I know he is."

"What do you want, old man?" Greg asked.

"Charming as always, Master Gregory? How far into the interview did you get before Miss Natasha realised who you were?"

"It's Freeman now," Greg said. "How did you recognise me?"

"Curiosity has always been my weakness," Oleander said. "The investigators Luke hired gave up looking for you, but my persistence was rewarded. I tracked you and your grandfather across borders, and I witnessed the rise and fall of your overseas sporting career. I know all about the scandals and the different aliases you used. When I learned you were back, I wondered how long it would be before you made contact. I must confess, I was surprised to hear your name mentioned as a potential bodyguard."

"Does my father know?" Natasha asked. "Is that why you're here?"

"My answer depends on why Master Gregory is still here," Oleander said.

"It was either this 'mean gorilla'," Amanda said, "or a philanderer who can't keep his hands to himself."

"I had my money on the philanderer," Oleander said. "I heard someone suggest that having to fight off his inappropriate advances would be an efficient way to teach Natasha the dangers of singleness in a man's world." He didn't sound happy about it.

"I don't like what you're implying," Natasha said, gripping the edge of her desk.

"Neither do I," Oleander said. "There's one thing that's been puzzling me since I arrived. I expected more flowers."

"Flowers?" Natasha asked. "What do flowers have to do with this discussion? I'm sure there'll be more deliveries tomorrow. Nobody knew I was going to be here today."

"*Some*body knew you were here."

"Ian Norris," Goose said. "He snuck in to see her."

"We're back to Norris again," Oleander said with a frown. "And he didn't send flowers. Hmm, there's a puzzle here. There must be more to him than his permanent smile and silver tongue?" He folded his hands and smoothed the wrinkles from his brow. "Perhaps he phoned his closest rivals and told them about his triumph? They had to settle for sending flowers while thinking of the missed opportunity to offer her comfort."

"He didn't offer any comfort," Natasha said.

Oleander leaned back against his chair as if he had no intention of leaving. "Interesting, isn't it? If anyone asks, I came to deliver the briefcase, and then I was invited to stay for lunch."

"Why would Ms Jacobson ask you to stay?" Amanda said. "You'll report everything to her father."

"I think we can trust him," Greg said.

Amanda spun towards Greg. "You've changed your tune."

"If Oleander intended to report me to my stepfather," Greg said, "I'd never have made it inside the building. I'm voting we trust him."

"I agree with Greg," Goose said. "Ollie's got insider information."

"You're talking as if this is a great conspiracy," Natasha said.

"It has all the important elements for a good novel," Oleander said. "A beautiful heiress survives a kidnapping attempt, and then an unflattering story appears in the newspaper. The article hints a 'close friend' has betrayed our heroine's deepest secrets. Frightened and confused, the heiress questions everyone's loyalty. Her workplace is broken into, and someone has bugged her office. A man with dubious motives sneaks past security and corners her alone. Does this man have anything to do with the aforementioned problems, or is he merely an opportunistic predator?

"The reluctant heroine turns to an unlikely band of friends, each with a different reason for helping her. There are three supporting characters: a security guard who believes in miracles, a silver-haired charmer who fancies himself as an amateur detective, and a feisty woman recently returned from overseas looking for a righteous cause."

Oleander smiled. "The hero is an ugly man with an unsavoury past who is secretly in love with the heiress.

"Add a shadowy cast of villains, a group of ambitious men her father has encouraged to pursue the heiress. Is one of these suitors behind her recent troubles, fighting a dirty campaign to gain an advantage over his rivals? Or is there an unknown enemy yet to reveal him- – or her- – self?"

As soon as Oleander finished his lengthy monologue, the other three responded without restraint.

Amanda said, "You're not helping…"

Goose began with, "How do you know these things?"

"I never said I was in love with her," said Greg.

Natasha withdrew into her mind, registering what they were saying without showing any reaction. She took another sip of water before she spoke. "There's one more plot complication to add to Oleander's fanciful story."

"What is it?" Amanda asked.

"Is the heiress the target? Or is there a more sinister plot to bring down the family empire?"

11

Wrongness

Lunch was a noisy, chaotic experience, and Natasha spent her time observing the others. The group crowded around the table near the window. After Goose prayed a blessing, the others devoted themselves to eating.

Amanda had ordered two regular and two large Italian luncheon specials, and there was plenty of pasta and pizza to share between them. Nobody seemed to notice Natasha had the same piece of cheesy crust in her hand throughout.

After the food disappeared, Amanda prepared coffee while Goose removed the packaging to a bin in the other room. Greg was discussing Oleander's visit to the police compound.

"I'll forward photos of the damaged car to your mobile, Greg," Oleander said. "The kidnappers broke the driver's side window without damaging the door panels, and reached in to open the door. From everything we know, I don't think this was an opportunistic event."

"The photos only show the aftermath," Greg said. "I'd like to hear Natasha's version of events."

"The newspaper gives a realistic account," Natasha said. "When I read it this morning, it was as if I was standing outside the car witnessing everything as it happened."

"The newspaper doesn't tell us what you saw from inside the car," Greg said.

Amanda placed the final mugs on the table. "There's a theory people need to retell their story twenty or thirty times before they've processed the trauma enough to make a healthy recovery."

Goose returned and added his opinion. "If you try to keep this to yourself, Natasha, it will bring you a bitter harvest in the future."

"I do not want to retell my story twenty times," Natasha said.

"We're not asking you to," Greg said. "If you put in enough detail, then once will be enough."

"Where in the story do you want me to start?" Natasha asked, folding her hands in her lap to immobilise them.

"Start at the beginning," Oleander said. "Tell us about the first part of the journey before you realised anything was wrong."

"Wrongness can be attributed to everything yesterday," Natasha said. "It began when I arrived at the office and had to reschedule my meetings. This meant I wasn't able to pick up my car. Someone went in my place."

"That someone being Ian Norris," Oleander said. "I was in the guard room when he drove the car into the parking garage. By the time he found you to hand over the keys, I don't think there was anyone in the building who didn't know you'd asked him to do it."

"I didn't ask him. My father made the arrangements, and nothing went right afterwards. But I don't want to talk about Ian. For numerous reasons, I was late leaving the office."

Natasha pushed aside the negative emotions that awoke at the reminder.

"Instead of starting the car and following Oleander home," Natasha said, "I was distracted by a flashing message on the dashboard's digital screen. The computer wanted to synchronise with my phone and demanded a code. Ian assured me—"

"What was Ian doing there?" Greg asked.

"My father sent him to apologise for an earlier problem."

"What kind of problem?" Greg asked.

"If you keep interrupting me," Natasha said, "I'll never finish this story."

"It was a social media post," Oleander said. "Suggesting Ian and Natasha were a couple. I'll show you later. Sorry, Natasha. Please continue."

"Synchronisation was supposed to take a few minutes, but there was a problem with the code. The one I was given had seventeen characters, and the computer wanted eighteen."

"Ian again," Oleander said. "He wrote down the code and insisted on staying with her until she got it right. Her father should never have left her alone with him."

"Stop blaming Ian for my mistakes," Natasha said. "I panicked when my father phoned to ask me where I was, and I rushed off without resolving the problem."

"I haven't met him yet," Greg muttered, "but Ian Norris is on my watch list."

Ignoring the interruptions, Natasha resumed her story. "I didn't pay enough attention to where I was in the traffic. My annoyance over another driver's behaviour led me to miss the off-ramp."

"What was the other driver doing?" Greg asked.

"The other driver?" Natasha asked.

Torn from her self-reproach, she was thrust into a recollection so clear she could smell the new car's leather interior, feel the steering wheel beneath her fingers, the pressure of her feet on the pedals, and hear the traffic sounds.

Alone and unobserved, all the colourful details were overlaid with her unfiltered emotional reactions.

Raw.

Intense.

Real.

Natasha considered her audience, wrestling with a choice. She could give them the bland summary she'd given the police officers who interviewed her. There would be more interruptions and further questions to extend the process... But if she offered them a more animated glimpse of her experience, there was a chance they might allow her to continue to the end.

"The other driver was weaving in and out of the lanes behind me. I saw him in the rear vision mirror, and then he was beside me in the outer lane."

"Before I realised what was happening," Natasha said, "he had crossed into my lane, and I had to stomp on the brakes to avoid a collision. I promised myself I'd never take the freeway during rush hour again.

"My knuckles were white from gripping the wheel, and I had to prise them loose as I slowed."

"I found a gap and switched to the next lane," Natasha said and the scene was right before her eyes. "But the car I wanted to avoid also changed lanes. I was too focused on getting away from him and not paying attention to the road signs."

"You weren't using the dashboard navigation system?" Amanda asked.

"The digital screen was still asking for the code," Natasha said. "I couldn't make a phone call, I had no GPS, and no music to help calm my nerves."

"You missed the off-ramp?" Greg said. "Why didn't you take the next one?"

"I waited until the last minute to signal my intention to take the exit, in case that crazy car tried to stop me. I was halfway into the slip lane when a different car overtook me on the inside. I was forced back into the onward lane."

"Did you think you were being targeted?" Greg asked.

"Not then," Natasha said. "I was concerned about how late it was. The sun had set, and it was harder to recognise the landmarks. Once I got off the freeway, I knew there had to be a turning up ahead that would take me back to where I needed to go.

"The crazy driver was still ahead of me, although he seemed to have given up trying to make my journey more difficult. I paid attention to the road signs, slowing at each intersection and searching for the one I needed.

"Another car appeared behind me with its headlights on high beam, almost blinding me. It came close enough that I expected to feel a bump. I sped up, and the car chased me.

"I watched my mirrors and almost missed a road sign that flashed past. The intersection appeared, and I threw my car around the corner.

"I wouldn't have attempted the turn if Oleander hadn't been my driving instructor. His driving lessons finally made sense, but I'd rather not know he'd been preparing me for high-speed pursuit. The other car missed the turn.

"Speeding along the tree-lined country lane, I didn't register my mistake until it was too late. Around the final corner, a closed gate blocked the road. There wasn't time for me to turn around before my pursuers came to a screeching halt behind me.

"While I watched the mirrors, I undid my seatbelt," Natasha said. "I searched for my phone with one hand while I locked the doors. My phone was not on the seat where I'd left it, and I leaned down to search for it on the floor while keeping my eyes on the side mirror. A shadowy figure stepped from the other car."

12

Resourcefulness

Matthew 5:6
Blessed are those who hunger and thirst for
righteousness, for they shall be filled.

Losing herself to the retelling, Natasha closed her eyes. Her heart was racing as if she had been exercising, and she felt breathless. Her survival had depended on her resourcefulness.

Bang! Natasha hit the table with her hand, and she jumped at the loudness of the sound. "Bang. The side window is gone. There's glass everywhere." Her hands raised and her fingers shimmied down like rain in a storm, her ears hearing the tinkling noise again.

"Black leather gloves." She held up her hands and spread her fingers, examining them. "Like Oleander's driving gloves. Is it Oleander? Is this a test?" Natasha frowned. "No – this man is too short, and Oleander would never wear a hat and sunglasses at night. The man is unlocking the door. Go away." Natasha pushed with her hands. "I'm in the passenger seat, escaping. Black gloves grab my legs. I kick and kick. The man steals my shoe, calling me names I won't repeat."

Natasha glanced over the opposite shoulder. "The passenger door moves behind me. I didn't open it – I'm falling. Someone grabs me. I can't move my arms. There's a second man! 'I've got her.' He's squeezing me, lifting me up. I scream and kick and lose another shoe. He throws me against a car, my car. His arm is under my chin, and he shoves something into my mouth. Fabric, scrunched up like a ball. Bleah – tastes horrible, smells like rags from the garage. I try to push the rag out with my tongue. Nausea burns the back of my throat, but I force myself to swallow.

"There's another voice. Who is it? Oh, black glove man. 'You can't escape, Ms Jacobson.' I stop struggling. He's laughing at me. There's a cloth in his hand, and he's pressing it over my face. My eyes are watering, and a chemical smell stings my nostrils. Everything starts to fade."

Opening her eyes, Natasha took a deep breath. She glanced down at the coffee Amanda had given her before she began her story. The beverage was still warm, and she savoured several mouthfuls. The memory lost its power. "Please don't ask me to remember that again."

"The newspaper article doesn't have anything else until the police found you," Oleander said. "But that's not all you remember."

Natasha looked at him over the brim of her coffee mug. "Have you seen the police report?"

"No," said Oleander. "But I've known you since birth. I have the added advantage of having accompanied your stepmother to more than one of your school drama performances. A girl who can pretend to be dead, despite being tossed around the stage like a rag doll for half an hour, would have no trouble persuading anyone she was unconscious."

"You're right," Natasha said. "I don't think the police believed me when I said I was pretending."

"You pretended to be unconscious?" Greg asked.

"As soon as they mentioned my name, I knew I was more valuable to them alive. So I gave them the helpless victim they wanted, and they removed the drugged cloth too soon. The drowsiness didn't dissipate immediately. That made it easier not to resist while my hands were bound behind my back. They also tied my feet together and put tape over my mouth. The second man, the one not wearing black gloves, carried me over his shoulder.

"The men who attacked me were not the two arrested

when I was rescued. My eyes were closed, but I heard enough to be certain there were at least five men there, and they'd come in three cars. After discussing their pursuit, they boasted about what they'd spend their payment on." Natasha took a breath. "One of them speculated about how much ransom my father would pay to get me back. He was told 'the Big Boss' had 'inside information' and my kidnapping was only the beginning."

"What did he mean?" Oleander asked.

"I didn't find out. One of the others silenced him, and then I was thrown into the getaway car. My face was shoved against the rear seat, and after a heavy blanket dropped on top of me, the door closed. I heard both front doors open and shut before the engine started.

"The driver said, 'Axel, where are we going?' Axel swore at him for using his name – my head was closer to the driver's side of the car. Axel insisted it was safer if a 'blabbermouth' didn't know anything. 'Blabbermouth' stopped talking, and the car accelerated. I was almost thrown onto the floor when we careened onto the main road. Axel said the driver would be in trouble if the 'package' was damaged before delivery. He then told a few horror stories about other 'employees' who upset the Big Boss. I'll spare you the gory details. I wasn't sure I believed him, but the police became more animated when I told them.

"By then, we were back on the freeway, and there were other cars nearby. I could see lights flashing past. Axel said to take the next off-ramp, and about five minutes later Blabbermouth started screeching, 'Police! There's a roadblock!' Axel told him not to panic. It was 'just random breath testing'.

"Every instinct told me to sit up, but I maintained my pretence. Just as well, because Axel reached back to shake me to see if I was awake. 'She's still out cold. Play it cool. There are a few cars pulled up already, so they'll probably wave us through.'

"Blabbermouth told Axel what he could do with his advice and swerved into a side street.

"Axel shouted at him. 'Now they'll think we've got something to hide.'

"The driver thought 'an unconscious girl tied up on the backseat' was sufficient justification."

Natasha fell silent and stared at her cup of coffee.

"Did the police give chase?" Amanda asked. "Is that how you were rescued? The newspaper was light on the details."

"Blabbermouth kept checking his mirror," Natasha said, "and there was no sign of any pursuit. He thought he'd gotten away, but when he turned the next corner, there was a patrol car waiting for him. A second patrol car pulled out of a side street and came up behind us. I could see the flashing red and blue lights. I waited until the first police officer tapped at the driver's window. That's when I sat up."

"Keep going," Oleander said. "You've almost reached the end of the story."

"Things got a bit crazy after that," Natasha said. "Someone shone a bright light in my face, and I couldn't shield my eyes. Everyone was shouting. No, not everyone. Blabbermouth was crying, pleading for police protection from the Big Boss. I think Axel attacked him before trying to escape. The rear door of the car opened, and I was dragged out. Several police officers hovered around me, assuring me I was safe and there was no need for me to be anxious or afraid. I had tape over my mouth, so I couldn't ask them if I looked anxious and afraid.

"The police untied my hands and feet, and I peeled off the tape. I told them my name and address and asked them to call my father. They asked if I knew who these men were, and how I came to be tied up in the back of their car. I gave them answers. Then different police officers came and asked the same questions. I was careful to give them identical answers. I asked how long it would be before my father arrived. I heard someone phoning for an ambulance. It was only when the ambulance arrived I realised it was there for me."

13

Childishness

Romans 8:26
In the same way, the Spirit also helps our weaknesses,
for we don't know how to pray as we ought.
But the Spirit Himself makes intercession for us
with groanings which can't be uttered.

"I told them I was fine," Natasha said, "but nobody would listen."

"Who did you tell?" Oleander asked.

"The police. The officers talked about me as if I wasn't there. And the paramedics when the ambulance arrived. Everyone thought I was suffering from shock because I wasn't crying or hysterical. The consensus was my behaviour wasn't normal. I almost told them I'd never been normal. Instead, I said, 'big girls don't cry'."

"Did that help?" Oleander asked.

"No," said Natasha. "When I arrived at the hospital, the doctors wouldn't listen to me either. They insisted on giving me a sedative. I woke up screaming." She stared out the window. "I think that's what affected me the most. My father was there to witness my lapse of control."

"Luke Jacobson has a lot to answer for," Greg muttered.

Oleander shook his head. "You're directing your anger in the wrong direction, Gregory. If anyone's to blame, it's me."

"Why are you saying you're to blame, Oleander?" Natasha said. "I've always been thankful for your advice."

"What advice?" Amanda asked.

"I'm the one who told Natasha big girls don't cry. Countless times I've had cause to regret those words."

"But you shouldn't have any regrets," Natasha said. "Those words have carried me through many difficulties. That's why what happened at the hospital is so troubling. I can't believe I lost control of my emotions."

"I was there at the hospital," Oleander said. "After the ordeal you'd been through, a few tears are nothing to be ashamed of."

"A few tears? I blubbered for at least half an hour."

"More like twenty minutes, and then you took a deep breath, apologised to your father for your childishness, and put your emotions back into whatever vault they've been locked in for two decades."

"Two decades?" Amanda asked. "How old was Natasha when you told her she wasn't allowed to cry?"

"Do you want to tell them, or shall I?" Oleander asked Natasha.

"I'll tell them," Greg said.

"You weren't there," Natasha said.

"I arrived six months later," Greg said. "You were five by then, but only four when it happened. Your mother had recently died, and your father forbade anyone to tell you. You overheard your Nanny talking about the restriction and ran weeping and wailing right into the swimming pool.

"Oleander dived in, uniform and all, to save you. Everyone was still whispering about the averted tragedy years later. But that was not all they were whispering about. That was the last time anyone ever saw you cry, look sad, or even lose your temper.

"You walked around with that perfect smile stuck on your face. Calm and quiet and in control, refusing to react to anything or anyone. Why do you think I gave you such a hard time?"

"It's in the past," Natasha said, rising to her feet. "I'll find the contract Sentinel City Security emailed me, and Greg can sign it."

Oleander leaned forward. "I don't want you to think I'm telling you how to do your job, Natasha. But check the small print."

"Check for what?" Natasha said, pausing halfway to her desk.

"You'll know when you see it."

Natasha sat before her computer and opened the file. She scrutinised the document line by line while the others continued their conversation behind her.

"Why don't you tell Natasha what she's looking for?" Greg asked.

"There might be nothing to find," Oleander said.

"Then why add to her stress by suggesting there would be?" asked Amanda.

"Wouldn't it be a standard contract?" Goose asked Oleander. "Like the one I sign every year?"

Natasha looked away from the computer. "Amanda, take Goose into your office and get him to access his personnel file. Print out his contract, and I'll check to see if there's anything else I've missed."

Amanda and Goose hurried from the room.

"You found something?" Greg asked, moving to the chair on the other side of her desk. Oleander came with him to occupy the second chair.

Tapping the screen with her fingertip, Natasha spoke. "A little clause that requires my bodyguard to accept instructions from 'designated others' in my absence. It also gives the 'designated others' authorisation to terminate employment without notice."

"Designated others?" Greg asked. "How are these *others* designated?"

"Of course, there's my father," Natasha said, "and anyone he verbally issues authority to in your presence."

Greg shook his head. "I'm not taking orders from your father, and I'm certainly not listening to anyone he nominates."

"You won't have to," Natasha said. "I'll create a new version that makes this a mutually exclusive agreement between us. In my absence, you will be free to decide on the appropriate action within the terms of the agreement."

"Here's Goose's contract," Amanda said, coming to stand behind Natasha's desk. While the young executive compared the document with the new one on her screen, Goose remained in the doorway.

"Natasha, are you qualified to change contracts?" Goose asked.

"More than qualified," Oleander said. "She has a Masters Degree in Commercial Law she keeps under wraps."

"Ollie, you have an answer for everything," Goose said. "Tell me this. Is someone at Sentinel City involved in this conspiracy? I'd hate to think my friend Matt is trying to exploit Natasha's vulnerability."

"I can't answer your question definitively, Goose," Oleander said, "but probably not. The additional clauses would have come from Natasha's father. Luke agreed without hesitation when Natasha asked to supervise the employment process, which suggests her father had already made adequate provisions to control the outcome."

"I object to being called vulnerable," Natasha said, sending the document to her printer. She also dispatched the payroll authorisation and other employment forms. There was no need to verify these as she'd generated new versions for Amanda a few hours earlier.

"If my father authorised those changes, it would only be to protect me. But I'm not dismissing your advice, Oleander. From now on, I'll double-check everything before I add my signature."

Amanda retrieved the newly printed documents and passed them to Greg.

"Can I see Goose's contract?" Greg asked.

Goose nodded. Amanda took the single page document from the desk and gave it to him.

"I'm not going to be a Spendor Corporation employee?" Greg asked Natasha.

"No," Natasha said. "NASSJA Enterprises is my private company. Until today, I've only had part-timers on my payroll. You and Amanda are my first full-time employees."

"How long have you had your own company?" Amanda asked.

"Eleven years. Starting the company was my friend Cassie's idea. We were both fourteen. She thought I should do something creative with my money instead of letting it build up in the bank. My father helped me with the paperwork. He was the first director, but that role came to me when I turned eighteen."

"What does your company do?" Greg asked.

"I invest in small start-up companies, mostly information technology. I also offer research and development grants for student projects."

"You inherited money from your mother?" Amanda asked.

"No," Natasha said, making a conscious decision to unlock another secret.

"My mother's estate went to my father, except for her shares. They returned to her father, Stephen Spendor. My grandfather outlived my mother by a decade."

"Stephen Spendor?" Amanda's eyes grew wide. "*The* Stephen Spendor who started the Spendor Corporation? Your grandfather owned all this?" The secretary's arms stretched towards the walls and the ceiling.

"Outside this room, nobody knows he was my grandfather," Natasha said. "My grandfather was particular about who had shares in his business empire. My mother didn't have any shares until she earned her seat on the Board of Directors when she was forty. She was his only child, and I'm his only grandchild, but Stephen didn't believe anyone should have a free ride.

"If I become a Director one day, it will be because I've met the conditions stipulated in his will. I've asked my father not to tell me what those conditions are."

"So, who controls your grandfather's empire now?" Amanda asked.

"The Directors are minority shareholders, working with the CEO. The bulk of the Spendor fortune is held in a trust fund."

"Where did your money come from?" Greg asked. "Does your father control your finances?"

"I've been financially independent since I was twelve," Natasha said.

"My grandfather opened an account for me when I was born and put money in each year on my birthday. There was an annual meeting with my grandfather to discuss how the money had been spent.

"My father answered on my behalf until I was old enough to understand the accounting processes. The costs associated with employing my nanny, and later my governess – Greg's mother, Edith – came from that account.

"Anything leftover was available for me to spend, and we called it my allowance. When I went to St Catherine's Academy, there was more than enough to cover the school fees and extra tuition.

"That's when Cassie suggested I divert some of my allowance into small investments. Every idea we developed seemed to generate more money.

"I think my grandfather approved because, after he died, the trust fund continued the annual payments. When Cassie and I went to Summerlands University, I paid her first-year tuition and purchased us an apartment."

"Your grandfather more than approved," Oleander said. "He told your father the Corporation's future would be safe in your hands."

"That future's a long way off," Natasha said. "Recent events have taught me I have a lot more to learn. Now, if Greg can sign that contract, it's time to go upstairs and tell my father about my decision."

14

Carefulness

Proverbs 21:21
He who follows after righteousness and kindness
finds life, righteousness, and honour.

After the necessary documents were signed, Natasha handed them to Amanda to process. "I'll take my briefcase with me. I'm planning to go home after I've seen my father. Message me if anything comes up I haven't already talked to you about."

"I'll be praying for you to have a good rest," Amanda said.

Outside the office, Natasha turned to Goose. "Stay here, please. I'll feel better if I know Amanda's not left unprotected. I'll talk to my father about having a permanent security presence monitoring my office."

Natasha walked towards the elevators with Oleander at her side and Greg a pace behind them.

"We'll take the express elevator," Oleander said, producing his access card.

When the doors closed behind them, Oleander turned to Greg, straightening the collar on the younger man's damp jacket. "Don't smile. You're here to protect Natasha. Everyone you meet could be a potential threat. Stand close enough that nobody can touch her without you dealing with them first. Cross your arms. That emphasises your size, and don't hide your tattooed knuckles. What did Amanda call you? A mean gorilla? That's better."

"Is that really necessary?" Natasha asked.

Oleander ignored her and retrieved Natasha's briefcase from her hand. "I'll look after that. Try to maintain the illusion you're weakened by your trials. Walk slowly, and dim that smile. If anyone approaches you, don't look them in the eye. Instead, glance at Freeman as if you need reassurance he's there. We don't know what your father has heard about this morning's events, so be careful."

"I'm the Queen of Carefulness."

"Today, you need to take that to the next level, Natasha. Remember not to be too casual with your bodyguard. He's Freeman when he's on duty."

The elevator doors swished open at the twentieth floor. Natasha took a deep breath and stepped out behind Oleander, aware Greg was at her shoulder.

Oleander led them past the uniformed guards. Across the foyer, the receptionist glanced up.

"There you are, Oleander. Mr Jacobson has been asking for you. Please take Ms Jacobson straight in."

Oleander went to the door bearing the nameplate: Luke Jacobson – Chief Executive Officer. He knocked, opened the door and ushered Natasha in. Greg followed, and Oleander closed the door behind them. The CEO's suite made Natasha's spacious office seem small.

Natasha stopped a few steps from the chairs in front of her father's desk, waiting for permission to approach. Her father sat behind his desk, sorting through some printed documents. Oleander waved for her to advance as he took his position beside the large desk. Natasha shook her head. Why was Oleander asking her to break the formal protocol?

Oleander gestured to Greg. The newly appointed bodyguard placed a hand on her upper back and applied light pressure. Natasha leapt forward, her heart racing and the colour bleaching from her face. She fell into the padded armchair. Frowning at Greg, she watched the hint of a smile disappear from his face.

"You're back, Oleander," Luke said, not looking up.

"Yes, sir. I've brought Miss Natasha to see you. With your permission, I'll drive her home when this interview is over."

Her father's head jerked upward, first looking towards where she usually waited and then finding her closer. Surprise registered on his face. Luke was quickly upright, coming around the desk towards her. "Princess, you're pale. Oleander, has Doctor Hamilton been called?"

"No, sir. Miss Natasha would not allow it."

Natasha jumped to her feet. "I-I'm sorry, Father." Why was there a tremor in her voice?

Greg's hand returned her to the chair, and then his back appeared in front of her. She tugged on the hem of his jacket. "Freeman, what are you doing? You know this is my father. We came here to see him."

"Freeman?" Luke asked.

Greg stepped sideways, and Natasha smiled despite her father's stormy expression. She waved Greg back, relieved he no longer crowded her view. Her father dropped onto the chair beside her and reached for her hand. It took her a few moments to realise he was checking her pulse. She withdrew her hand.

"There's no need, Father. I'm fine. A little tired, but fine."

Luke studied her face before glancing at the big man standing behind her chair.

Refusing to look at Greg, Natasha waved a hand in his direction. "Father, this is Freeman, my bodyguard. Oleander gave him a lecture about potential threats, and it seems Freeman has overreacted."

After glancing at Oleander, who hadn't moved from his station, Luke scowled at Greg.

"Is there a problem?" Natasha asked her father.

"Of course not, Princess," Luke assured her. "But I am surprised you chose this man." Her father stood and offered his hand to Greg. "Welcome, Freeman. I'm Luke Jacobson. If your presence keeps my daughter safe, you will earn my heartfelt gratitude."

"I don't want your gratitude," Greg said, dismissing the offered handshake. He kept his arms crossed over his chest. "I've agreed to protect your 'princess', but I don't want anything from you."

"Freeman!" Natasha cried. "Where are your manners? You mustn't speak to my father like that!"

"It's okay, Queenie," Greg said. "It's not the first time your father and I have disagreed over his generosity."

Luke took a step back and stared at Greg. "Who are you? Oleander, I asked you to oversee the decision making."

Natasha's eyes flew to Oleander.

He shook his head. "I'm sorry, sir, but you underestimated your daughter's resourcefulness."

"By the time I arrived," Oleander said, "Miss Natasha had already made her decision. Persuading *him* to accept the position was the real challenge. Consider it a miracle she chose the best candidate without realising who he was."

"Stop speaking in riddles, Oleander," Luke said. "Natasha, who is this man?"

"Freeman is Edith's son," Natasha said.

"He's what?"

"Edith's son, sir," Oleander said. "I verified his identity. He's returned to reconcile with his mother. Might I suggest, sir, you keep his relationship with your wife confidential? At least until the media speculation has died down."

"Oh." Luke frowned at Greg. "You're right, Oleander. I don't want Edith drawn into this publicity nightmare." Then the executive shrugged, and a smile appeared on his face. "Gregory, your mother will be delighted to see you. I'll phone the estate, so Edith knows you're on the way."

"Make sure you tell her I'm called Freeman," Greg said, "and I'm coming as Natasha's bodyguard. I don't expect any special treatment."

"While you're on duty, you won't get any," Luke said, already halfway towards his desk. "But Edith won't forgive me if I put you in the servant's quarters. You can have your old room. Of course, you'll eat with the family." Luke directed his attention to Natasha. "Is there anything else, Princess?"

"I've emailed a copy of the contract to you, Father." Natasha stood. "I made a few changes. I've also asked the security guards to remain near my office. I don't want any more unpleasant surprises. Could you authorise the additional security arrangements? Of course, I'll expect an invoice for the expenses."

She took a few steps towards the door. Greg went ahead of her and opened it. Natasha hesitated for precisely five seconds, dropping her eyes to the floor, before she turned back to her father. "I thought I'd feel safe in my office, but I was wrong. I had to hire a new secretary."

"A new secretary, Princess?" Luke asked.

Was it her imagination, or was her father's reaction milder than she'd anticipated? "I can't talk about it, Father." To her consternation, a genuine sigh escaped.

"Please excuse me; I want to go home."

That statement reawakened her father's concerned frown. "Don't worry about anything, Princess. I'll make the necessary arrangements." He addressed his chauffeur as she left the room. She lingered at the threshold listening to his instructions.

"Oleander, after you deliver Natasha home, take Freeman to collect his luggage and ensure he has a *better* grasp of his responsibilities. There's no need to hurry back. Collect me at the end of the day."

"Certainly, sir," Oleander said, following Natasha and Greg from Luke's office. As soon as they were in the foyer, Oleander hustled them towards the elevator.

"That went better than I expected," Oleander said after the doors closed and they were descending. "Now, to get you home without any further drama."

"Where are we going?" Natasha asked when the elevator stopped at the third floor, and Oleander ushered them forward. Her headache was back, and she was finding it harder to command her feet.

"Turn right at the end of this corridor and take the sky bridge to the shopping centre across the road. Make your way to the rear underground car park. I'll collect you from there."

"I'm not in the mood for games," Natasha said.

"Come on, Queen of Carefulness," Greg said, taking her arm and leading her away. He called back over his shoulder. "Don't be too long, old man. Your princess is almost asleep on her feet."

"I am not," Natasha said, pulling herself free.

"Then walk faster," Greg said. "I don't remember you being so slow when you were younger."

Natasha increased her speed, her mind wrestling with a logical response. What was it he had said that bothered her the most?

Finally, as they stepped from the sky bridge into the bustling shopping centre, she came up with an appropriate reply. "I'm surprised you remember me at all. I wrote to you, and you never answered."

"You wrote to me?" Greg said, leading her towards a store directory. After studying the maps of the different levels, he spoke. "We need to go that way."

Natasha took off in the desired direction, slipping through small gaps in the crowd. It must have been more difficult for Greg because he didn't appear beside her for another five minutes.

"I'll take back what I said about you being too slow," Greg said. "Give me some warning before you try that again."

"You're supposed to anticipate what I'm going to do and take the appropriate action."

Greg laughed. "I've never trusted any of my predictions about you. Your face doesn't give any clues, but I'm guessing you're annoyed about something. You said you wrote? I didn't get any letters from you. But I know I wrote to you, and I was hurt when you never replied. You wrote to my mother asking questions about everyone except me."

"That's because I put all my questions in the letters I sent you."

"I never got them," Greg said, steering Natasha down an escalator and then guiding her through the shoppers towards the lower level.

"I wrote every week for a term. I even slipped a letter under your door when I came home for the holidays. Then I sat opposite you at dinner, and you ignored me."

"I never got any letter," Greg said, pointing towards the car park exit. "But I did see the 'Keep Out' sign you put on your dance studio door. The door was always locked, even when I was sure you were in there. It was obvious the sign was put there for me."

"Of course it was written for you. I was angry and upset. The locked door was for you, too. My dance studio had been my safe place, and you ruined that. I had nightmares for weeks after you appeared from nowhere, making fun of me."

"I didn't make fun of you," Greg said as they entered the darkened underground space. He led Natasha across the pedestrian crossing, peering through the gloom. "I was genuine when I said you were a beautiful dancer."

"Then you shouldn't have chased me."

"Is it too late to say I'm sorry?" Greg asked.

A car appeared beside them. Greg opened the rear passenger door of her father's gold Mercedes, bowing before her. "Your chariot awaits, Queenie."

15

Sleepiness

Natasha climbed into the car. "Thank you, Oleander. Greg thought it was a race. Now I'm exhausted. I might fall asleep on the way home."

"Gregory, get in the back with Natasha," Oleander said. "Her father will terminate both of us if she wakes from a flashback and jumps from the car."

"Move over," Greg said, shoving Natasha across the seat. "If you're sleepy, you can lean your head against my shoulder."

Scrambling across to sit behind the driver, Natasha fastened her seatbelt. "I don't need your shoulder." She turned towards the window and closed her eyes.

The car moved out into traffic. Natasha pressed her burning face against the cool glass. Sleep was elusive, but she could always pretend...

"Master Gregory, you still haven't acquired any manners," Oleander said when the car was on the freeway.

"Stop calling me that," Greg said. "Freeman will do. Is she asleep or pretending again?"

"Does it matter?" Oleander asked.

"I suppose not. I've got nothing to say to you I wouldn't say in front of her."

"You haven't made it easy for her to like you."

Greg laughed, a sharp sound, lacking warmth. "I don't want her to get too attached to me. Her father wouldn't want me to become a permanent fixture. I'm here until this emergency is over, unless she finds a more suitable bodyguard. Someone like Goose would be perfect."

"What makes Goose more suitable?"

"He's mature and reliable."

"And happily married?" Oleander suggested.

"There's that," Greg said. "Her perfect smile wouldn't be a problem for Goose. I thought I'd gotten over my schoolboy crush, but she's exquisite now she's grown up. I'd like to kiss all her problems away."

Natasha almost stopped breathing. She sensed Greg leaning closer. What would she do if he tried to kiss her? Could she keep up the pretence?

"If you act on that desire," Oleander said, "I'll stop the car and break both your legs. Kissing a princess without her permission is a criminal offence."

"I only said that to see if I got a reaction," Greg said. "I'm still unconvinced your princess is asleep. If you'd break my legs over a stolen kiss, old man, what would you do if I was a real threat?"

"You wouldn't be here if I thought you were a threat."

Silence filled the compartment. Natasha's focus began to drift. Perhaps sleepiness would carry her away before she heard anything more – Greg spoke again, but his voice was becoming muffled as if thick glass separated them.

"What game are you playing, old man."

Oleander's answer was also distorted. "One that began before you were born."

"You're talking in riddles again," Greg said.

"I've served the Spendor Corporation my entire life. I shouldn't need to explain about that kind of commitment to a Christian."

"I've signed a contract. What more do you want?"

"Haven't you pledged to wholeheartedly serve God?"

"You can't compare a commitment to God with service to a corporation…"

Something hard and smooth pressed against Natasha's face. Her eyelids fluttered. She was inside a car, leaning against a side window. She could see across three lanes of stationary traffic. The car must be on the main road, stopped at a set of traffic lights. The fog of sleepiness clung to her, and her eyes closed again.

A man spoke from beside her as the car eased forward before gathering speed. "Don't dismiss God too easily…"

Natasha's chest tightened. Who had spoken, and why were they talking about God? Before the panic took over, her inner voice of reason reminded her where she was. By then, she had missed all but the conclusion of Greg's statement.

"Not even a conniving old man like you can deflect God from his purpose."

Why was Greg calling Oleander a "conniving old man"? And what was this purpose? She fought against the mental confusion, catching fragments of the chauffeur's response.

"…realise I've been wrong… I still have the letters."

Natasha didn't want to hear any more, but she couldn't move. Her eyes refused to open, and her tongue seemed stuck to the roof of her mouth.

"How did you get my letters?" Greg asked.

"I had someone at St Catherine's Academy intercept them," Oleander said. "Her grandfather believed she was too young to receive love letters."

"You read them?" Greg asked. "I knew you didn't like me, old man, but I never thought you'd stoop so low. Did you show them to my mother? Did Luke see them?"

"I'm the only one who read the letters. I kept Stephen Spendor informed, but Luke and Edith knew nothing about them. Natasha's grandfather was confident you'd lose interest when she didn't reply."

"What about the letters she wrote to me?"

"Who told you about them?" Oleander asked. "Did Natasha? I'm surprised, but perhaps that's an encouraging sign. She was a more dedicated writer than you, although her daily letters dropped off to once a week.

"As the months went by without an answer, the letters grew shorter. I found it harder to read the last few. And then there was the final note she slipped under your door. A maid found it and delivered it to me. Natasha offered you one last chance to prove you were her friend."

Greg said something Natasha didn't hear.

Oleander continued without pause. "I carried out my orders. My actions destroyed every chance she might build any form of relationship with you. Her grandfather was confident more appropriate friendships would become available as she adapted to boarding school."

No! Natasha screamed, but no sound escaped her lips.

Her heartbeat skipped and danced. She was stuck in a living nightmare.

Greg was silent for a long time before he replied. "God says I have to forgive you."

"Don't be premature with your forgiveness," Oleander said. "Natasha was not the only schoolgirl who wrote."

"What? Who else wrote to me?"

"Cassie."

"Cassie? Natasha's friend? Why did *she* write to me?"

"Cassie thought you had 'behaved despicably'. To repay you, she sent you an ancient Gaelic curse—"

"Cassie cursed me?" Greg said. "Do you know how I can contact her?"

"Why do you want to contact her?" Oleander asked.

"You know I'm committed to the Twelve Steps. I'm supposed to contact everyone I've injured so I can try to make things right."

"It's too late for Cassie. She died six years ago."

"Six y— How did she die?" Greg asked.

"Why do you want to know?"

"People who dabble in curses invite evil into their lives."

"Is that what you think happened to Cassie?" Oleander asked. "Her letter was nothing but a childish..."

The swirling grey mist surrounding Natasha spun and expanded like a cosmic galaxy, drawing her into the darker centre. She fell, twisting and tumbling, uncertain which way was up. The darkness gave way to colourful shards of light and then she crashed into a solid surface.

Natasha's eyes flew open. The part of her brain that always had to be in control whispered this was a dream. She was back in a dormitory room at St Catherine's Academy. This version of the familiar nightmare had delivered her to the room she shared with Cassie when they first met. Natasha was not surprised when her dream-self turned, and the girl with the untameable red curls was pacing the room. Cassie was rehearsing a poem she had found in an old book in the library.

"Be cursed, thou enemy of my friend. Abandoned by your family, and betrayed by your allies, may disaster befall you in a foreign land..."

"Stop!" Natasha cried.

The girl morphed into a beautiful young woman. The dormitory disappeared, replaced by the university apartment. Nineteen-year-old Cassie was dressed for a party. "Come with me, Natasha. All you do is study. One night isn't going to make a difference to your grades..."

"Wake. Up!" Natasha struck herself, not wanting this final vignette to play out. She didn't want to see what lay at the foot of the stairs. Her feet refused to obey, taking her out the door. She was running, not pausing as the final landing came into view. "No! No! No—"

A dark figure appeared in front of her. Natasha screamed and lashed out at the man who shouldn't be there. The phantom was one of her attackers from the foiled kidnapping. His arms wrapped around her...

"Wake up, Natasha. Wake up."

Blinking, Natasha stared into Greg's face. His arms pinned her to the seat. Oleander was staring at her over Greg's shoulder from the front of the stationary car.

"I'm awake," Natasha said, pushing against Greg's chest. "Let me go."

"Not until you tell me why you were screaming and slapping your face," Greg said as he loosened his grip.

"It was only a nightmare. Nothing to concern you."

"How much of our conversation did you hear?"

"What conversation?" Natasha said. "You woke me, so you know I've been asleep."

"You were shouting at Cassie," Greg said.

"Shouting at Cassie is how that dream always ends."

16

Cursedness

How could Natasha find out more without confessing she'd lied about listening? When Oleander pulled back onto the road and the journey continued, both men were silent. She couldn't get Greg's comment about curses out of her mind. Cursedness was an appropriate description for the way her life was unravelling. Oleander seemed unconcerned, but a glance in Greg's direction suggested there was more her bodyguard wanted to say. He was back on his side of the car, staring out the window.

Oleander decelerated to negotiate the next intersection, and for a moment, she caught the chauffeur watching her in his side mirror.

"I thought the nightmares had stopped," Oleander said. "The Summerlands University counsellor said you no longer needed your appointments."

"I stopped seeing the counsellor because her suggestions helped," Natasha said, seizing the opportunity. "Oleander, how do you know I saw a counsellor? Those appointments were supposed to be confidential."

"The university pastoral care team kept me informed," Oleander said. "Luke and Edith were on a business trip when Cassie died. I was the next emergency contact, after your grandfather's death."

Natasha thought about that for a moment. "You've never accompanied my father when he's gone interstate or overseas. I've always wondered about that when you're so indispensable when he's at home. It was also peculiar you accompanied Edith when she visited me at St Catherine's Academy. All that time, you were spying on me and reporting to my grandfather. Did my father know?"

"I've always reported to your grandfather. I was your mother's driver before she married Luke."

"You became my father's driver after she died?"

"I was assigned to your father seven months before you were born," Oleander said. "Your mother's withdrawal from public life coincided with Luke's appointment as CEO. People presumed my assignment to your father was a matter of convenience."

"Didn't my mother continue working for the Corporation until she died?"

"Once your mother was appointed as a Director, motherhood was her next goal. She pursued that with the same single-minded determination. Falling pregnant was easy, but carrying a child to full-term proved more difficult. The doctors thought the stress associated with being the sole Spendor heir was responsible for her miscarriages. Your grandfather never forgave himself for not realising she postponed motherhood because she was waiting for that promotion."

"I didn't know any of this."

"You weren't supposed to," Oleander said.

"Why are you telling her now?" Greg asked, intruding into the conversation.

"Stephen Spendor was determined Natasha would not face the same demons that tormented her mother. That's one of the few things he and her father ever agreed on. I've come to believe they were both wrong to keep the truth from her."

"'Demons' is an interesting choice of word," Greg said, "for someone who discounts curses and has no time for God."

Natasha's heart felt as if it had been torn in two. Curses, and her mother, in the same breath. She wanted the conversation redirected to a safer topic – any topic – yet the desperate words were out in the open before she could catch them. "Who said anything about curses? We were talking about my mother."

"Your mother believed she was cursed," Oleander said. "She thought God was punishing her for trying to have a child without first committing to a husband."

"But – but my father..."

"Your grandfather respected her request for secrecy about her hasty marriage to Luke. That pregnancy failed like the earlier ones, and everyone feared for her sanity. Against the doctors' orders, she immediately tried again. The day Stephanie discovered she was pregnant with you, she resigned from the Corporation and effectively disappeared."

"Didn't anyone ask where she was?" Natasha asked.

"She sent messages to her friends about going to an exclusive health spa. Rumours spread that she'd suffered a breakdown. Nobody knew the truth. Stephanie spent the next seven months in seclusion within the walls of the newly constructed Jacobson Estate. Doctor Hamilton visited so often your mother became his only patient. You came early, and despite everyone's assurances, she refused to accept you would survive. You only had to cry, and Hamilton was summoned.

"But that was not Stephanie's only obsession. She feared someone would steal you if they learned you were the new Spendor heir. For your first years, only the doctor and the household staff knew of your existence. Your birth and Stephanie's marriage to Luke remained closely guarded secrets until your grandfather died. Even now, only the original Directors and the Trustees of Stephen Spendor's estate know who you are."

"How did Luke explain Natasha's sudden appearance, later?" Greg asked. "I remember being dragged away from my school friends to accompany the little princess on public outings."

"My father told the truth," Natasha said. "He told them my mother had died, but refused to name her or reveal anything more."

"But what about you?" Greg asked. "The girls at school would have asked—"

"It was easy to pretend I didn't know anything." Natasha closed her eyes, memories of boarding school crowding her mind. She frowned, voicing a secret she had never shared. "Cassie thought my ability to maintain my composure regardless of the circumstances was extraordinary. That's how I convinced everyone I was the 'perfect princess with the perfect life', and persuaded them nothing anyone could say or do had any impact. Cassie was sure it was a blessing. But she was wrong. I've been cursed since before I was born."

"You mustn't say that, Natasha," Oleander said. "Too many people made sacrifices for you."

"For once, I agree with the old man," Greg said. "People care about you, Queenie. God cares about you. Even if you're right about being cursed, you don't have to let that determine your future."

"How can you say that?" Natasha asked. "Cassie cursed you because of me, and that ruined your life."

"Cassie's curse didn't ruin my life," Greg said. "I did that without help from anyone else. Since the Garden of Eden, everyone's been born under a curse, but that's not God's ultimate plan for humanity. Once I came to my senses, I let God pick me up and put me on the right path. I've never looked back. And I'm not the only one. If you ask Goose and Amanda, they'll tell you all Christians share a similar story. Without God, everyone's life is under a curse, but Jesus paid the price to transform it into a blessing. You only have to ask. It's a free gift."

Natasha shook her head. "I'd like to believe you, but now my mind has identified this new label I can't let 'cursedness' go. I had six years of attending daily chapel at St Catherine's, but I never made the connection. I need time to think. I don't want to hear any more about breaking curses, Greg. Either keep quiet or discuss something else with Oleander that has nothing to do with me."

The heavy silence following her outburst continued for ten minutes. Tormented by thoughts she couldn't control, Natasha's regret intensified with each kilometre. She gazed at the passing landscape. Oleander was not helping. She was sure he was deliberately driving slowly.

"Greg, why did you leave?" Natasha asked.

"What were you told?"

"I wasn't told anything."

"You could have asked," Greg said, shifting in his seat.

"I tried, but after your mother burst into tears..."

"I never meant to hurt my mother, but I couldn't stay. Not after your father— Sorry. I have to stop blaming other people."

"I'm the one who raised the subject," Natasha said. "If my father was responsible, I'd like to know."

"Sport was the only thing I had any talent for," Greg said. "My college coach thought I could make it as a professional, and I worked hard to prove him right. A few months before I turned eighteen, a national football club offered me a place in their junior development squad. Big money, independence, but more importantly, I could get away from your father's disapproval. Luke thought I was too immature for the big league. Said I'd ruin my life. And by association, bring the family name into disrepute."

"It takes courage to stand up to my father," Natasha said. "You accepted the offer?"

"No. The offer was withdrawn. Luke told me he phoned some influential friends, and then he suggested an alternative. If I enrolled in a university degree, he'd buy me a place on a local team. I was hurt. I said things I now regret, packed a bag and left. When I walked out the gates, I promised myself I wouldn't return until I'd proven him wrong."

"Oleander said my father tried to find you. Where did you go?"

"Nobody knew my father's family kept in touch with me. When Dad died, they blamed my mother, and they weren't happy when she moved away. I had an open invitation to stay with Grandpa, so that's where I went."

"I'm glad you had someone to take care of you."

"Grandpa was a wily fox, but he was also a realist. He knew your father would come after me, so he changed our identities and we went overseas. When I asked if the passports were legal, Grandpa told me not to worry. That should have been a red flag. Looking back, I realise Grandpa was already connected to the wrong people."

Natasha shuddered. "Wrong people?"

Images from the previous evening's foiled kidnapping were back to torment her.

"The kind who opened doors to unbelievable opportunities," Greg said. "I didn't stop to consider what Grandpa's friends might want in return for their investment. I took their advice, trained harder, used the right supplements, and bulked up to the size I am now. They persuaded me to swap football codes, and I signed for an important team.

"For three years, Grandpa and his friends kept me on a tight rein. They called it 'protecting their retirement plan'. Dating was prohibited – that would distract me from my game.

"Apart from the occasional alcoholic drink, recreational drugs were forbidden. That set me apart from my peers, who made headlines with sex and drug scandals. The media began calling me the Choirboy. I was a rising star with a spotless reputation. The money came pouring in.

"But when I turned twenty-one, my minders changed strategy. Grandpa boasted I was his 'personal banker', and visits to his favourite casinos became a daily occurrence. Of course, I'd have a few drinks to celebrate winning my football games. Once I'd had enough to drink I would bet on anything, anywhere, anytime."

Greg took a deep breath. "I thought I had everything under control, but I was a disaster waiting to happen. Everything unravelled when there were match-fixing allegations, and the money trail ended with me. I couldn't even remember betting on my game..."

17

Sickness

The gates to the Jacobson Estate opened automatically as the golden Mercedes approached. Natasha glanced at Greg to assess his homecoming response, but his expression was neutral. Oleander continued past the guard station without stopping. The long driveway passed through landscaped gardens that were not at their best after weathering the morning storms. At least the rain had stopped.

Expecting to see Forest and his team of gardeners repairing damage, Natasha scanned the grounds. The workers were nowhere to be seen. As the Mercedes drew closer to the white mansion, their absence was explained. The front steps were crowded with rows of people. Every employee must be there, both the permanent staff and the casual day workers.

They were arranged as if this was a formal homecoming scene from one of the historical dramas her stepmother enjoyed and the butler and housekeeper were obsessed with. Natasha grimaced. When her father had brought her home from the hospital in the early morning hours a similar welcome had played out, with everyone assembled in their sleepwear, but apparently they were going to do it all over again.

Movement on the steps heralded Edith's appearance. For a fleeting moment, Natasha thought everyone was there to welcome Greg until Doctor Hamilton joined her stepmother on the lowest step. He placed his medical bag at his feet.

"I was hoping I could slip into the house without a fuss," Natasha said.

The car crawled closer to the covered forecourt.

"You're supposed to be creating an illusion," Oleander said. "How will you convince anyone you're weakened from your ordeal if you don't let them see you?"

"I'll create a distraction," Greg said.

Kincade hovered beside one of the forecourt's supporting columns. Wearing his formal butler's uniform, he stood ready to open Natasha's door. Greg didn't wait for Oleander to stop the car. He exited the car and stood between Kincade and her door before Natasha could react. For a big man, her bodyguard was quick on his feet. Natasha released her seatbelt and stared out the window.

"Kincade, you haven't changed a bit," Greg said, taking the butler's hand and pumping it up and down. He waved to the other staff. "Thanks for the welcome, but please excuse me. We'll catch-up later. I've got work to do."

"Master Gregory?" Kincade asked, taking a step back as he stared up at Greg.

"It's Freeman now, Kincade. I'd be grateful if you'd pass that information on to the other staff. I'd like to put my time as Master Gregory behind me. I'm sorry, but I'm going to do you out of a job today. I remember how you enjoyed carrying your little mistress into the house after an exhausting excursion, but she's my responsibility now."

Greg wrenched open the car door, and Natasha swung her feet out. Before she could stand, Greg gathered her into his arms and stormed the steps past the open-mouthed onlookers.

"Someone get the door," Greg said. "I don't want to drop her on my first day."

One of the maids opened the door, and Greg carried Natasha into the foyer.

"Put me down," Natasha said quietly. "I can walk without your help."

"This is much more fun, and it gets both of us away from that awkward scene on the front steps."

"Gregory," Edith said, running to catch them at the foot of the staircase. "What are you doing?"

"You'd better come with us, Mum. Does Natasha have the same room?" He didn't wait for an answer, taking the stairs two at a time.

"You're not coming into my room," Natasha said. "Put me down."

Greg tossed her a few centimetres into the air and caught her again. "If you want me to put you down, you'll have to play to your audience. Kick and scream, make an unseemly row."

Turning to her stepmother, Natasha made an appeal. "Edith, please tell him to put me down."

"Gregory," Edith said. "Your behaviour is unacceptable. Put your sister down immediately."

"Sorry, Mum. I refuse to acknowledge her as my sister. Natasha has employed me for protection, and that's what I'm doing. Please tell her I'm temporarily immune to her princess commands."

He moved as if to toss her again. Natasha threw her arms around his neck.

"That's better," he laughed. "Mum, your princess has had a very tiring day, and I have orders to ensure she rests. Did I see Doc Hamilton hovering at the door? Tell him not to come into her room until I've conducted a thorough check for danger."

"The only danger is you," Natasha said. "Why are you doing this?"

"I need to remind everyone that if they treat me like Edith's long-lost son, I'll pick up teasing you where I left off when I was fifteen. But if they address me as Freeman, I'll behave like a professional bodyguard. A good servant always knows his place."

Natasha stared at Greg. "Freeman, put me down."

"Certainly, Queenie." Greg lowered her feet to the landing at the top of the stairs. "Your wish is my command."

Striding toward her suite of rooms, Natasha tried to calm her racing heart. "I'm sorry, Edith," she said when her stepmother caught hold of her hand. "He wasn't like this before I employed him. I should have chosen one of the other candidates when I realised who he was."

"Stay here with Mum," Greg said to Natasha, pushing past to stand in front of the door to her suite. "While I check your room, you need to make up your mind. Either you trust the decisions I make as your bodyguard, or you dismiss me today."

Without waiting for a reply, he opened her door and closed it behind him.

Natasha groaned, pressed her hand to her forehead, and turned to the railing that overlooked the ground floor.

Doctor Hamilton appeared beside her.

"Please don't fuss," Natasha told the doctor. "I didn't come home because I was sick. A nap and some time alone are the only remedies I need."

The doctor walked away, whispering to her stepmother. The pair kept their eyes on Natasha, and she bowed her head as she waited for Greg to re-emerge from her room. With the estate surrounded by high walls and security guards patrolling the grounds, why did he think there might be any danger within the mansion? She shuddered, remembering the shock of finding intruders in her office. The Spendor Corporation headquarters also prided itself on excellent security.

Natasha hugged her waist as she faced her door.

Finally, Greg emerged. "All clear, Natasha," he said. "There's no one hiding anywhere, and I've turned on the stereo." He flashed a cheeky grin. "But you should have warned me to wear protective glasses. There's pink everywhere!"

"Freeman, wait downstairs. When Doctor Hamilton leaves, your mother will want to talk to you. Then find Oleander. I don't want to see you again until you sit opposite me at dinner."

Greg bowed and left.

"This way," Doctor Hamilton said, guiding Natasha through the door into her sitting room. "I'm here, and I'm not going until I've conducted a thorough examination."

"Nobody is listening to me today, Doctor," Natasha said as she perched on a pink sofa.

While the doctor checked her blood pressure and heart rate, she surveyed the immediate room. There were subtle changes to suggest where Greg had searched. He'd even looked behind the other sofa. Through the open connecting door, she could see her canopied bed. The frilly quilt and pillows had been disturbed. Had he suspected someone might be hiding under the bed, or was this another strategy to unsettle her?

Natasha allowed that question to distract her as she endured the doctor's customary prodding and probing. She studied the expression on the man's careworn face, the furrowed brow, and the nervous habit of glancing toward her stepmother. Finally, he sat back and returned his equipment to his bag.

"I told you I was fine," Natasha said.

Doctor Hamilton peered at her over the top of his glasses. "Hmm. Fine is not the word I would have chosen. Your heart is racing, and your blood pressure is higher than usual. You said you wanted to take a nap. Perhaps I should give you a sedative?" The doctor turned and addressed Edith. "A single tablet, something mild."

"No," said Natasha. "I don't want a sedative. What I want is for everyone to stop treating me like a child."

The doctor opened his bag, removed a small bottle and unscrewed the cap. He reached for her hand and pressed a small white tablet into her palm.

Natasha stared at the tablet. "Is it any wonder my blood pressure is up and my heart is racing? I've got a name for my sickness." She leapt to her feet, threw the pill onto the floor, and raised her voice. "Nobody. Is. Listening."

"Of course we're listening," Edith said, hurrying to Natasha's side. "Tell us what has upset you, and we will make it right."

Groaning, Natasha folded her arms and sank back onto the sofa. "What if you can't make it right?"

Edith sat beside Natasha. The doctor retrieved the tablet and remained standing.

"Can either of you erase the memory of last night's kidnapping?" Natasha asked. "Or undo any of the troubling revelations since then? Can you rewind time? Can you restore my lost friendships, or erase the horrors of boarding school?" She took a deep breath. "Can anyone bring back my mother?"

The doctor staggered backwards, and Edith flinched, her eyes filling with tears. The visible signs of Natasha's frustrated anger retreated instantly before their obvious pain. She uncrossed her arms and reinstated her smile. She hesitated for a moment before reaching across to pat Edith's arm.

"I didn't mean to hurt you, Edith. Please don't think I'm asking anyone to try and make any of those things happen. I know caring for me hasn't been easy. Someone told me today God has a purpose for everything. You're upset now, but because of my troubles, your son is home. You should go to him."

"You asked about your mother?" Doctor Hamilton said, shaking his head. "Stephanie's death is my greatest regret. I've always wished I could have done more to ease her suffering."

Edith stiffened, and Natasha sat straighter, studying the elderly man's face.

"How did my mother die?"

The doctor sat down on the other side of Natasha, opened his mouth and closed it again. He glanced towards Edith and then back to Natasha. "Y-you want to know h-how she died?"

"Yes. I'm almost twenty-five, and I want to know how my mother died."

"Y-your f-father s-said..." The doctor appealed to Edith with upturned hands. "Mrs Jacobson, please!"

Reaching for Natasha's hand, Edith began. "Your mother was being treated for postnatal depression..."

"Thank you, Edith," Natasha said. "I don't need to hear anymore. I've always suspected I was responsible, but it's good to have it confirmed."

"You were not responsible," Doctor Hamilton said. "Your mother had been unwell for a long time. It was not your birth but the inability to provide you with a brother or sister that weighed upon her mind. She was exhausted, both emotionally and physically, following yet another miscarriage." He paused. "The week your mother died, tests confirmed a diagnosis of early-onset menopause... If I had known how she would react to that news..."

He rose from the sofa and picked up his bag. "If I have been overzealous with your care, I apologise, Miss Natasha. You were always a quiet, uncomplaining girl. I hope you understand why I've spent more time listening to the concerns of your parents than considering your feelings. I'll endeavour to do better next time. I will leave you to rest."

"Goodbye, Doctor. I'll try to be more like that uncomplaining girl next time."

"Don't do that," he said. "It's an honour to see what a thoughtful young woman you've become."

18

Forthrightness

Psalm 85:7
Show us Your loving kindness, Lord.
Grant us Your salvation.

When Natasha awoke from her afternoon nap, her bedroom was darker than she expected. She threw off a blanket that hadn't been there when she lay down.

Scanning the shadowy room, she noted someone had closed the bedroom curtains. The only illumination came through the open door leading to her sitting room. The soft yellow light suggested it came from one of the smaller reading lamps.

Snatching her phone, Natasha cried out when she saw the time and leapt from the bed. Dinner was at seven and she had less than fifteen minutes to make herself presentable.

Her father would be wearing his business suit, but Edith usually wore something casual. Natasha looked down at her crumpled business shirt and fumbled with the buttons as she hurried to her dressing room. At least she'd had the good sense to remove her tailored uniform skirt before she lay down.

Natasha was reaching for another crisp white shirt when she remembered a fourth person would be at dinner. Would Greg be wearing his jacket, or could she expect him to show up in a tee-shirt and jeans?

Her hand dropped to her side, and she moved from the row of shirts towards the casual dresses. Many of these had never been worn.

Everything in Natasha's wardrobe had been selected by her stepmother. Shopping was something the young executive avoided. But it was one of Edith's favourite pastimes, and her stepmother always carried one of Natasha's debit cards.

Natasha trusted Edith completely and never questioned any purchase. Edith continued to add garments without ever exceeding Natasha's strict budget.

In the centre of the dressing room, a bright pink ballgown was displayed on a dressmaker's model. Natasha smiled. The gown would not be out of place in a fairytale movie. It was Edith's most extravagant purchase.

When Natasha first tried it on, the young executive had spent a delightful afternoon swirling around her dance studio. She imagined the expression that would appear on Greg's face if she entered the dining room wearing this dress.

Shaking her head, Natasha dismissed the idea. The dress had tiny buttons at the back and was impossible to put on without assistance. A more serious consideration dimmed her smile.

The dress was not one of Edith's spontaneous purchases but a special commission for an upcoming gala event. Her father was hosting a fancy dress ball to celebrate Natasha's twenty-fifth birthday. Luke had not consulted Natasha before he'd sent out the invitations to two hundred and fifty guests, including the most senior Spendor Corporation executives.

Tap tap tap.

"Miss Natasha, are you there?" The voice belonged to Delores, the newest member of the household staff. The housemaid was the teenage niece of one of the security guards and had been with them for three weeks. "Kincade sent me to find you. Dinner is ready."

Natasha pulled the closest dress from the hanger and wriggled into it. "I'm almost ready," she said, spinning to check her appearance in the mirror. The blue skirt twirled as she moved, displaying pink flowers hidden within the loose folds.

"You should dress up more often," Delores said, appearing behind her in the mirror. The girl's forthrightness was unsettling. The maid shooed Natasha towards the ensuite bathroom. "Go and fix your hair, and I'll find the right accessories. Do you want heels or flats?"

"Flats. I'll have to hurry. I can't believe I overslept."

Natasha removed her smudged makeup. There was no time to replace the foundation or eye colour. She flicked mascara across her lashes before swiping pink colour across her lips.

"You were sound asleep when I came in and closed the curtains," Delores said, appearing in the bathroom with full hands. "I've found blue ballet flats to match your dress and a pair of retro, pink flower earrings.

"I've also brought a choice of bracelets and this cool watch. I haven't been in your dressing room before. You have some amazing things, but half the shelves are empty, so there's scope to add more. I'd love to go shopping with you."

"My stepmother does my shopping for me," Natasha said, brushing the tangles from her long blonde hair. "Usually, she's the one standing where you are, making suggestions. You said you closed my curtains. Did Edith ask you to check on me?"

"Here, let me help," Delores said, snatching the brush from Natasha's hand. "Pass me that big clip. You're not doing yourself any favours pulling your hair back so tight. It suits you better like this." A cascade of curls dropped from a high ponytail.

"Mrs Jacobson was busy talking with your bodyguard," Delores said. "Freeman's been given the bedroom on the other side of your dance studio, next to the old nursery. Your stepmother was roasting him for manhandling you, and when she realised I was listening, she sent me to check on you. From the way everyone's whispering, I'm guessing Freeman has been here before. Is he a relative?"

"I'd better get downstairs," Natasha said, making a quick selection from the jewellery. She fastened the flower earrings and rushed to the door as she slipped on two bracelets. "Thanks for your help, Delores."

"Call me Dee Dee," Delores said. "All my friends do. I'll stay here and tidy up. Enjoy your dinner."

Natasha fumbled with her watchband. "Please don't tidy up. I'm very particular about who touches my things."

"I'm sorry," Delores said. "I was trying to be helpful. Everyone else in this house is old, and I thought you might appreciate a friend closer to your age."

"Let's go downstairs," Natasha said, uncomfortable with this conversation.

They were a third of the way down the stairs when Delores spoke again. "Why won't anyone tell me about Freeman? When he carried you into the house, he caused such a stir. Anyone would think he'd hooked up with you."

"I'm only going to say this once," Natasha said, hesitating on the step. "My father does not tolerate inappropriate behaviour." She frowned at the maid before continuing down. "If there's even the hint of a rumour that Freeman has 'hooked up' with anyone in this house – and I'm including myself in that statement – there'll be trouble. I can assure you it won't be Freeman packing his bags."

"But your father—"

"Delores, six years at boarding school taught me the importance of respecting house rules. Please apply yourself to your work and avoid speculation about Freeman or anyone else."

Continuing her rapid descent, Natasha neared the bottom of the stairs. Delores kept pace with her, but asked no further questions.

"Do you enjoy working here?" Natasha asked the teenager.

"It's better than flipping burgers, and the pay's better," Delores said. "I'm grateful for the free meals and the great accommodation, but I'm not planning to be a housemaid forever. Most of what I earn goes towards my uni degree."

"I didn't know you were a student. What are you studying?"

"Fashion Design, first semester. That's why I was keen to check out your wardrobe."

"Being this far from the city doesn't inconvenience you?" Natasha asked.

"No. Most of the assignments are online, and if I have to go in for a lecture, I swap my day shifts with the other maids."

They reached the bottom of the stairs.

"Look, Kincade's glaring at me," Delores said. "I'd better go. Thanks for being cool about me barging in. I meant what I said about being friends. If you want to talk about clothes, or anything – like men and stuff – you know where to find me."

The teenager hurried away, leaving Natasha to approach Kincade alone.

"Good evening, Miss Natasha," the butler said, opening the door. "Your father is already seated."

Natasha thanked him and hurried to the square table. The seating arrangement was the same as when Natasha and Greg were children. Luke and Edith faced each other, with Greg between them on Edith's right. Edith smiled and waved Natasha forward.

Luke was lecturing Greg and failed to notice her arrival. "As soon as Oleander drove through the gates, you should have considered yourself off-duty."

"I'm never off-duty," Greg said, standing to acknowledge Natasha's presence. He had swapped his black tee-shirt for a blue one and was still wearing faded jeans.

Her father glanced at her.

"Father, I apologise for being late," Natasha said. "My afternoon nap lasted longer than I expected."

Her father nodded, and she lowered herself onto her chair. After Greg resumed his seat, the servers came forward with the first course. Greg bowed his head before dipping his spoon in the thick vegetable soup. Natasha checked if either Edith or her father had noticed Greg silently praying over the meal. They were already eating.

The atmosphere was tense.

After taking a few mouthfuls, Natasha set aside her spoon. Greg ate with enthusiasm and was offered a second bread roll which he used to wipe the bowl clean.

"Tell Mrs C the soup was delicious," Greg said to Kincade when the servers returned to clear away the bowls.

Natasha stared at the mountain of roast beef and vegetables placed before Greg, and then relaxed when a much smaller portion appeared before her.

"Mmm, this is good," Greg said between mouthfuls. "I've eaten in some fancy restaurants, but I've never found anyone who can out-cook Mrs C."

"I asked Mrs Conneally to prepare your favourite dishes," Edith said. "There's butterscotch pudding for dessert, but I'm wondering whether you will have any room. I don't understand why there's so much food on your plate."

"I'm more concerned about how little is on Natasha's plate," Greg said, pointing his fork at his employer. "I didn't realise one of my responsibilities would be to keep her from starving herself."

Natasha focused her attention on her plate and loaded her fork. She dipped the food in her gravy, convinced three pairs of eyes watched her. After chewing carefully and swallowing, she repeated the process, praying she wouldn't choke.

"I'm not starving myself," Natasha said. "I'm just not very hungry this evening."

"You weren't hungry at lunchtime, either," Greg said. "And I checked with Mrs C. Breakfast was half an apricot, eaten as you walked to the car. I learned a lot about nutrition while I played football.

"You've not eaten enough today to nourish your traumatised brain. That's one of the reasons you slept so long this afternoon. I'm sure your father agrees with me: you're not returning to the office unless your appetite returns."

19

Suspiciousness

After dessert, Natasha's father stood to make an announcement. "Kincade, bring coffee to my downstairs study. The ladies will retire to watch television and have their coffee there. Edith, I apologise for taking Gregory away on his first evening home, but I have matters to discuss with him."

"There's no need to send Natasha and Edith away," Greg said, "but I agree we need to go somewhere more private." He also stood, looking at Natasha. "Queenie, are you happy with the downstairs study, or would you prefer to adjourn this discussion to your sitting room? Oleander and I swept the rest of the house this afternoon, and he's been clearing your rooms while we're eating dinner."

"Father's study," Natasha said, pushing back her chair. Her legs were shaking. Edith appeared beside her.

"Why are you bothering Natasha?" Luke demanded, suspiciousness written in his stance.

"I don't take orders from you," Greg said, silencing her father with a gesture. "I've included you in the briefing because it's your house. If you don't agree to my terms, I'm taking Natasha to live somewhere else."

Natasha almost lost her dinner as her father's face turned red. Edith reached out and held Natasha's hand.

Greg continued to address Luke. "The last thing I want is to take your precious princess away from you. Oleander agrees with me; your estate is the most secure location. But until we know who targeted Natasha, we require your complete cooperation."

"How dare you recruit Oleander for your subversion!" Luke said.

Greg laughed. "Oleander has always been a law unto himself. My subversion is a minor thing when compared to his suspiciousness."

He turned to Kincade. "Coffee in the study, thank you. Please tell Oleander we're ready for his report."

Kincade glanced to Luke for confirmation.

"Do as he says, Kincade. It's the only way I'm going to get any answers." Then Natasha's father switched on his smile and offered his arm to his wife. "Come along, Edith." He extended his other arm to Natasha, and together they progressed across the foyer with Greg following behind.

The downstairs study windows faced the driveway, and bookcases lined the other three walls. A polished Tasmanian blackwood desk to the side accommodated a desktop computer. Half a dozen leather armchairs occupied the central space, arranged around a matching blackwood coffee table.

A big man already occupied one of the armchairs. Natasha frowned, trying to recall his identity. The man looked up from a handheld electronic device and stood to acknowledge her father.

"Wallace, what are you doing here?" Luke asked.

"Oleander called me to update your security protocols," Wallace said. "The technicians will be here in the morning to install the new cameras."

"What new cameras?"

Wallace glanced at Edith and Natasha. "Good evening, Mrs Jacobson. I apologise for intruding on your evening." He extended his hand, and Edith shook it. Next, he turned to Natasha. "Miss Jacobson, I haven't had the pleasure of meeting you in person. I'm Matthew Wallace from Sentinel City Security. My team will do everything within our power to guarantee your safety."

Murmuring a reply, Natasha accepted the firm handshake. Her father signalled for everyone to be seated. He chose the chair opposite Wallace. Edith sat beside her husband with the windows at her back. She invited Natasha to sit near her. Greg remained standing behind Natasha's chair as he watched the door.

"You were talking about new security cameras," Luke said.

"We'll be installing cameras covering access points to the upper floor."

"Why?" Luke asked.

Reaching into his pocket, Wallace placed a small black object on the table. "Oleander asked me to bring the listening device he found in Miss Jacobson's car. He wanted to compare it with the ones he found during the latest sweep of the house."

"What listening device?" Edith asked.

Greg pressed his hand on Natasha's shoulder as Luke leapt to his feet. Her father seized a heavy leather-bound book from the nearest shelf and slammed it down on the fragile object. Natasha flinched.

"There was no need," Wallace said, removing the book and sweeping the fragments into his palm. "I'd already deactivated that one." He slipped the broken pieces into a tiny plastic bag and returned them to his pocket.

"Luke, why are there listening dev— Oh," Edith said. "Is that how the kidnappers knew where to find Natasha?"

"An excellent question," Oleander said, appearing in the open doorway. He entered the room with Kincade at his heels. They each carried a tray. "When everyone has coffee, I will be happy to provide some answers."

The trays were left on the table while Kincade distributed the coffee mugs. Oleander closed the door before sitting beside Wallace. Kincade placed a mug in front of Oleander, collected both trays, and then moved towards the door.

"If that is all, sir," Kincade said to Luke, "I will brief the other staff about the new security measures."

Without waiting for a response, Kincade backed towards the door and left.

"Oleander, you have some explaining to do," Luke growled.

"Thank you, sir," Oleander said before turning to Wallace. "Is this room secure?"

Wallace nodded. "I've stationed one of my men in the garden outside the window. Another guard is watching the kitchen where the servants are gathered. Nobody can get close enough to eavesdrop, and the devices you found aren't sophisticated enough to be used remotely."

"How many devices are we talking about?" Luke asked.

"Four." Wallace patted his pocket. "The first one was found in Miss Jacobson's car. Anyone could have put it there. Freeman located one in her bedroom. Since then, we've swept the house and located one more, hidden in Miss Jacobson's dance studio. I also retrieved one from her city office. All four were identical in design and manufacture, suggesting a common source. Finding two in the house implies a security breach."

"Have you questioned the household staff?" Luke asked Oleander.

"I left that for Freeman to oversee," Oleander said. "We're assuming whoever targeted Miss Natasha will want information about her new bodyguard. This afternoon, Freeman and Kincade spoke with individual staff members. Each interview included a unique false detail which should identify the source of the leak."

"What if the offender is Kincade?" Luke asked. "He knows everything. What's to stop him from framing someone else?"

"I shared specific information with Kincade nobody else heard," Greg said. "And I've done the same with you and my mother. I'm sorry, Mum, but not even you are above suspicion."

Natasha opened her mouth to protest, and Greg pressed on her shoulder. "Queenie, anyone could be leaking information without realising they are helping your enemies. It's better if nobody shares anything about you or your security arrangements with anyone else."

"Oleander, how do we know Freeman didn't plant the bugs?" Luke asked.

"If he did," Oleander said, "he would have needed advanced information about her car."

"He could be working with an accomplice," Luke muttered.

"For Freeman to be part of this conspiracy," Oleander replied, "his recruitment would have happened *before* the kidnapping attempt. When did you contact Wallace to request a bodyguard?"

"You were there when I made the call from the hospital," Luke said, "so don't try and point the finger of suspicion at me. I didn't call Wallace until after the police spoke to me. "

Luke continued his defence. "You were also present when Wallace sent the list of potential bodyguards. You know Freeman wasn't my first or second choice."

"A divided house is a defeated house," Wallace said.

"What?" Luke asked.

"That's a Christian proverb," Oleander said. "Wallace is warning that disunity among us is counterproductive. It increases the probability the next attack against Miss Natasha will succeed."

20

Highness

The two weeks preceding Natasha's twenty-fifth birthday were uneventful, and the daily security sweeps uncovered no more listening devices. Her father declared the increased security measures effective and refused her request to cancel the extravagant celebrations.

Today's preparations were testing her smile. Finally, her appearance met the exacting standards of the hair and makeup team Edith had recruited for the occasion.

The professional photographer's camera flashed a final time, and Natasha must leave the privacy of her suite.

Staring at her reflection, Natasha almost didn't recognise herself. Her blonde hair was piled high and held in place with a sparkling tiara that matched the pink diamond earrings and necklace. The ballgown had a tight strapless bodice to emphasise her curves and the full skirt ballooned out from her tiny waist. She swished the layered skirt, catching a glimpse of the pink high-heeled shoes.

"The guests are waiting, Princess," Luke called from the sitting room. "It's time for your grand entrance."

Natasha's father wore a black and gold costume with a purple cape, topped with a regal crown. Beaming, he offered Natasha his arm. "You are even more beautiful this evening."

Edith's crown was smaller. "I'll see you at the bottom of the stairs." Her flowing blue dress swished as she kissed Natasha on the cheek and rushed from the room.

A single trumpet blast sounded below.

"Ladies and gentlemen, Her Royal Highness, Queen Edith, your hostess for the evening."

A small group of classical musicians played a lively tune, and then there was a triple blast from the trumpet. "Ladies and gentlemen, His Royal Highness, King Luke and Her Royal Highness, Princess Natasha."

To accompanying music and multiple camera flashes, Natasha and her father descended slowly. Guests wearing elaborate costumes filled the foyer.

Halfway down, Natasha spotted a line of men stationed at the foot of the stairs, wearing identical gold crowns. Her father's favoured junior executives: Daniel Pendragon, Joah Vandemeer, Zedekiah Upchurch, Blaze McGilligan and Finnegan Quartermaster. Their matching red jackets had black capes attached at the shoulders.

Natasha searched the crowd for her faithful bodyguard. Since Greg's appointment, his intimidating presence had effectively dissuaded these would-be suitors from pursuing her.

"Perhaps the one you seek is standing over there?" her father said.

Glancing in that direction, Natasha saw a familiar man wearing a crown. After saluting her, Ian Norris pushed through the crowd to join the other 'princes'. Two questions troubled her. Why did her father think she was looking for *him*; and why was his costume blue?

"Where's Freeman?" Natasha asked.

"He's in the security hub," Luke said, guiding her down the final steps.

"With two dozen of Wallace's best officers among the guests," Luke continued, "Oleander agreed Freeman's presence in the ballroom was unnecessary."

A hot sensation awoke in her chest. Natasha thought she'd kept this reaction hidden from her father, but the pressure on her hand increased. Edith appeared beside her, and the camera flashed again.

Luke raised his voice. "Honoured guests, thank you for attending my royal ball. Tonight there will be dancing and feasting as we celebrate my daughter's twenty-fifth birthday."

He lifted his arm, and a trumpet sounded.

"It would not be a proper ball without a royal proclamation. I have invited six worthy princes to seek the princess's favour." A ripple of laughter ran through the crowd and Luke's eyes twinkled as he shot a smile at his daughter. "After that trumpet announces the midnight hour, my daughter will name her Prince Charming."

Natasha's perfect smile remained firmly in place, even though, inside, she was drowning. The five "red princes" pressed forward, talking over each other in their eagerness to impress her. Natasha kept smiling while her father gave light-hearted assurances they would have equal opportunities. Ian waited until the red princes had withdrawn before he approached and offered a brief greeting.

Over the next half an hour, Natasha welcomed other guests with her father by her side. She nodded politely, thanking everyone for their compliments while tapping her toes to the music flowing into the foyer from the ballroom. The guests seemed satisfied with her token response before moving on to bask in Luke's presence.

"Has His Royal Highness forgotten this is not a business meeting?" Edith asked, interrupting the proceedings. "You're keeping the guest of honour from her dancing."

Luke frowned for a moment, and the man before him withdrew. Her father bowed to Natasha. "Princess, may I have the honour of your first dance?"

Natasha curtsied before entering the ballroom's double doors on her father's arm. Fairy lights twinkled across the three window alcoves along the opposite wall and around every doorway. Pink floral arrangements decorated all three rooms, and hundreds of pink balloons with trailing ribbons shimmied to the music from the vaulted ceiling. She paused to thank Edith for overseeing the decorations.

The spacious ballroom could accommodate double the number in attendance this evening. Natasha scanned the room. Only a quarter of the guests were on the dance floor. Everyone seemed to be staring at her. They gathered in clusters, seated or standing around the circumference of the dance floor, or assembled near circular tables in the open rooms on either side.

The current dance ended, and the dancers moved aside as her father directed Natasha onto the parquetry floor. The forty-piece orchestra occupied the central alcove with the darkened garden behind them. The conductor bowed to Natasha before signalling the musicians to play a fast waltz.

Her father began the dance with precision. When Natasha had synchronised her movements to follow his lead, Luke gazed over her head around the room. At first, Natasha wondered what he was thinking, but then she lost herself to the music. Her movements became more graceful as her heart sang in appreciation. The quality of the orchestra's performance soothed her lingering concerns about the extravagance. Having personally selected their playlist for the evening was worth every cent.

Even if it exceeded everything else on your party budget?

At first, Natasha's father had declined her offer to contribute to the expenses, only relenting after she revealed her current bank balance. Having seen the food and alcohol invoices, she was thankful to have assumed control of everything else.

Reminded of her responsibilities, Natasha scanned the room for the additional wait staff hired for the event. Men and women in black uniforms circulated among the guests, distributing refreshments from long tables in the alcoves on either side of the orchestra. Others were coming and going through the paired kitchen doors.

The familiar music was nearing its end when Natasha's father steered her towards the outer edge of the dancers. One of the 'red princes' loomed into view. Her father guided her around the perimeter, where the other four waited at intervals like vultures encircling their intended prey.

Where would she be when the music stopped? Natasha swivelled her neck, looking at the four exits as the dance continued. There was one in each corner of the ballroom. Both the kitchen and foyer doors were too far away, but the doors on either side of the windows seemed promising. One led through a side room into the garden and the other into the restroom corridor.

Lost in her inner turmoil, Natasha mistimed a step, drawing her father's attention.

"The contest is about to begin, Princess." Luke smiled warmly. "Ian's willing to wait until you've danced with the others. There's no need to let anyone know you've already made your choice. Let the music determine the first dance."

There were so many inaccuracies in her father's statement, Natasha didn't know which to address first. Her confusion would prove costly.

The waltz ended, and Luke released Natasha into the eager arms of Joah Vandemeer. In quick succession, she was passed to Blaze McGilligan for the third dance, and then Zedekiah Upchurch claimed her for the fourth.

All three men held her too close, but she was reluctant to protest, having witnessed their passionate outbursts during workplace discussions. Natasha could not risk an embarrassing confrontation in front of her father's guests.

The one-sided conversations with her dance partners followed a pattern. Each man acclaimed her beauty, declared their admiration for her father, and then boasted about their personal attributes. Next, they denigrated the other suitors before assuring her they would be devoted lovers. Natasha hid her growing agitation behind her professional smile.

As the fourth dance concluded, Natasha searched for a safe face. She spotted Oleander near the refreshment table, dressed in a long black gown and a professor's hat.

Zedekiah asked, "Who are you looking at?"

"I'm thirsty," Natasha said, pulling herself free.

"Hey, Pendragon," Zedekiah said to the next 'red prince'. "Bad luck. Natasha needs a drink."

Daniel Pendragon rushed to the table, selecting a glass. "Champagne?"

"Fruit punch," Natasha said, ignoring the offered glass.

While she sipped her non-alcoholic drink, she approached an empty chair. Daniel swallowed the champagne in a single gulp before selecting a second one and dragging another chair beside her.

"Thank you for allowing me time to rest," Natasha said. "I'd forgotten partner dancing is exhausting."

"Your father said dancing was your favourite pastime."

Natasha nodded. "But not ballroom, though I love classical music. The formal dancing was my father's idea."

"He organised lessons for us, so you wouldn't be without a partner."

"My father thought of everything."

"You're smiling," Daniel said, "but you don't sound pleased."

"I'm sorry," Natasha said. "From the earlier conversations, it seems my father has suggested I'm looking for a husband. I'm not. If I'd known about his plan, I'd have hired a dance partner to save me from this awkwardness."

"I'll go," Daniel said. "Finn's on his way. He'll be happy to sit with you."

The fifth prince appeared in the vacant seat a few seconds later. Finnegan Quartermaster was a tall, thin man who wore round spectacles and had his dark hair combed sideways to hide a receding hairline.

"You're looking lovely this evening." Finn said, blinking in quick succession. "Not that you don't look lovely all the time, but in the office, it's easier to forget you're not one of us. You have a good head for business, which you must have inherited from your father. I've always admired Luke…"

21

Quickness

"You should have warned me," Natasha hissed at Oleander as she passed him on her return to the refreshment table.

"And spoil the evening's entertainment?" Oleander said. "You still have one prince expecting a dance. Here he comes now."

After placing her empty glass on a tray, Natasha turned to face Ian Norris.

He bowed before her. "Princess Natasha, may I have the honour of this dance?"

Accepting his hand, Natasha accompanied Ian onto the dance floor. He seemed content to follow the music without any attempt at conversation, and Natasha relaxed. The tune ended, and the dancers around them dispersed to look for new partners. Ian released Natasha and bowed again. "Thank you for the dance. May I escort you back to the waiting princes? I'm certain they're eager for another opportunity to win your favour."

"Don't," Natasha said, startling herself with the quickness of her answer.

"Then would you honour me with a second dance?"

Ian was already guiding Natasha into position for the next dance, and when the music resumed, she followed his lead. As they twirled around the room, she sought Oleander, but he had left the refreshment table.

"Your bodyguard isn't here?" Ian said.

She smiled. "There are more than enough security officers among the guests."

He raised his eyebrows. "Then I'd better be on my best behaviour. Tell me, did you give the other princes the same warning?" He gave her a roguish smile.

"None of you should need a warning," Natasha said. "My father's presence should be deterrent enough. Earning his disfavour would be a career-ending mistake."

"Not everyone is as obsessed with their career as you are."

Natasha glanced at Ian's face as the pressure on her lower back intensified where his hand rested.

"You work too hard," Ian said, lowering his voice. He

looked above the heads of the dancers to where her father was standing, before leaning closer. "Your father agrees with me."

For a few rotations, Natasha maintained her silence before she asked, "Why have you been talking about me with my father?"

"Your father approached me," Ian said, "the week after you entered the graduate program. You surprised Luke when you refused the deputy director's position he had reserved for you. He didn't understand why you didn't want any special consideration."

"It wouldn't be fair," Natasha said.

"Your obsession with fairness was another of Luke's concerns."

The music slowed, signalling the end of the dance. "Thank you for granting me a second dance." Ian spun Natasha so she could see her earlier dance partners hurrying towards them. He released her hand, but his other arm remained around her waist. "After all, it's only *fair* the others have the same opportunity."

"I'm going to the restroom," Natasha said, pulling free and raising the front of her skirt to facilitate a quicker escape.

"I told Luke not to worry." Ian matched her pace as Natasha wove among the guests. "Once you realised none of your peers shared your ideals, you'd stand up for yourself."

"With your father's approval, I started a rumour that you didn't deserve to be in the program. Your first weeks with the Corporation were tough, but you exceeded my predictions." Ian grinned. "Not only did you prove you weren't an empty-headed bimbo, but you refused to sit quietly in the corner. It was satisfying when you accepted tasks the other graduates thought beneath them. They scoffed at your long hours and attention to detail. Too late, they realised you'd outmanoeuvred them for the more prestigious assignments. Well done!"

"Why are you coming with me?" Natasha asked as she dashed along the corridor. "Even an 'empty-headed bimbo' could find her way to the ladies' room."

"But would she make it back to the ballroom?" Ian said, reaching for her elbow as she dodged left to cater for two women walking in the opposite direction. "What if she emerges from the restroom to be ambushed by one of her many admirers? There's a doorway leading out to the garden at the other end of this corridor."

Natasha shook herself free from his arm and stared at him. "Is that a threat?"

Ian laughed. "I'll keep the others distracted for you. But don't be too long. You don't want them thinking the next challenge is a game of hide and seek."

Watching Ian walk away, Natasha shook her head before

stepping into the restroom. Sighing, she entered one of the cubicles and locked the door. She sat down on the closed lid and dropped her head forward into her hands. Ten minutes passed as she listened to women coming and going in the room. Finally, the whir of the hand dryer stilled, the outer door closed, and the room fell silent. Natasha was alone with her thoughts.

Soft footsteps crossed the polished floor and stopped outside her door. Someone knocked softly, and then Edith's voice asked, "Natasha? Are you okay? Ian Norris asked me to come and check on you."

Holding her breath, Natasha listened to the pounding in her ears as her heart beat rapidly.

"Natasha," Edith said again. "I know you're in there. Why are you hiding when you have two hundred and fifty guests here to celebrate your birthday?"

"Why am I hiding?" Natasha unlocked the door and rushed out. Edith took a few steps back, and words flew from Natasha's mouth without restraint. "I told my father I didn't want a celebration. There might be two hundred and fifty guests, but they're here for my father, not me. Not one of the people I wanted to invite made his guest list."

"I'm sorry. I should have insisted your father invite your new friends, but his intentions were good. As you rise within the Corporation, you will socialise with these people. And they're not *all* here for your father. Your princes adore you—"

"They're here because my father offered them financial incentives," Natasha said, turning on the tap and swishing water around the basin. She raised her eyes to look at Edith's reflection in the mirror. "The CEO's daughter is a desirable commodity."

Edith's smile disappeared, and her eyes widened. "Natasha! How can you say such an ugly thing about your father?"

The heat of Natasha's anger drained away with the same quickness as the spiralling water. In a calmer voice, she turned to Edith. "It's true. Ask any of them. They have each confirmed there is an agreement with my father. The lucky man who can persuade me to marry him gets Spendor shares and a position on the Board."

Edith frowned before forcing a smile. She moved towards the exit. "I'll talk to your father. When he finds out how unhappy you are…"

Natasha hurried over and pushed the door closed. "Please don't tell him I'm unhappy." She straightened her shoulders and reinstated her smile. "Thank you for coming to check on me. Please go back to the party. I'll be back in the ballroom in a few minutes. Having witnessed your response, I realise how foolish I've been."

22

Farsightedness

Psalm 23:6
Surely goodness and mercy shall follow me
all my days of my life, and I will dwell in
the LORD's house forever.

After Edith left, Natasha practised her smile in the mirror. The door swung open and two grey-haired women entered the restroom. Watching them in the mirror, the birthday girl pretended to tuck a strand of hair back into place. She had not been introduced to either of these women.

"There you are, Natasha," said the younger of the pair before hurrying to a cubicle. That small woman was wearing a Jane Austen-inspired regency dress.

Her stockier companion had chosen a fairy godmother costume. She came towards the basins, waiting for Natasha to turn around. "Jessica thought you'd gone outside to the gardens with one of your beaus."

"It's a perfect night for a romantic stroll, Bertha," Jessica said from behind the closed door.

"You're forgetting Natasha is a sensible girl," Bertha replied loudly. Her fairy wings quivered.

"Stephanie didn't care what people thought of her scandalous behaviour," Jessica retaliated. "No man was safe from her schemes. Don't deny you're relieved Natasha hasn't taken after her mother in that regard."

What!? Natasha was torn between a desire to escape this uncomfortable situation and her growing curiosity. How did these women know her mother's name? Oleander said it was a secret.

"Stephanie was not known for her farsightedness," Bertha said, "but moderated her behaviour before the end."

"Stephen had to compensate for her lack of 'farsightedness'," Jessica said. "We wouldn't be celebrating his granddaughter's birthday if he hadn't future-proofed his legacy."

Bertha shrugged her shoulders, lowering her voice to address Natasha. "Sorry for the shouting, dear, but since Jessica turned sixty-nine, she's had trouble with her hearing. She's too proud to admit she needs hearing aids."

"There's nothing wrong with my hearing, Bertha," Jessica said. "Stop maligning my reputation before I've had a chance to introduce myself. It was *you* who wanted a private word with Natasha this evening. *I* was prepared to wait until after tomorrow's Board meeting."

The reference to the Board was a vital clue. As the identities of her visitors dawned on her, Natasha wondered why they had not been introduced at the start of the evening. These women were members of an exclusive club. Apart from her mother, there had only ever been two female Spendor Corporation Directors. One had been on the Board since the beginning. The other had been promoted from among the career executives thirty years ago, six months ahead of Stephanie.

"Fiddlesticks, Jessica," Bertha said. "You've done nothing but complain about those persistent young men."

Jessica emerged from the cubicle to wash her hands. "Nominating six Prince Charming candidates was not one of Luke's better ideas. Nobody can get anywhere near the guest of honour."

"Well, she's here now," Bertha said, "and there's not a Prince Charming in sight. But hurry up. Natasha needs to get back to her party."

"It's a pleasure to finally meet you, Natasha. I'm Jessica Becker-Tompkins, and my outspoken friend is Bertha Doncaster."

"That's the formalities dealt with," Bertha said. "You look lovely tonight, Natasha."

"Yes," Jessica said. "You're the perfect princess. Your grandfather would have been proud."

"Thank you," Natasha said. "It's an honour to meet you both. Apart from my father and some of the household staff, I've never met anyone who claimed to know my mother."

The two women exchanged glances.

"I was Stephanie's godmother," Bertha said. "That poor girl showed so much early promise..."

"That's a conversation for another occasion," Jessica said. "Bertha and I wanted to be part of your life when you were growing up, especially after your mother's tragic demise, but Stephen asked us to keep our distance."

"But he kept us informed about your progress," Bertha said.

"We've followed your career with interest," Jessica added. "It's commendable you started your first company at fourteen. And you haven't let all that education go to your head. You've remained humble and teachable, despite earning three degrees in the time it takes most young people to get one. Your mother took six years to complete her degree, and then she barely scraped through with a pass."

"If only your poor mother hadn't wasted her opportunities..." Bertha wiped away a tear. Both women fell silent.

"Please don't say something like that," Natasha said, "and then not explain what you mean. I want to know more about my mother."

"Be careful what you wish for, princess." Bertha raised her wand and waved it in the air. "If I were a real fairy godmother, I'd make you forget everything we said. A little knowledge can be a dangerous thing."

"My father never talks about her," Natasha said. "All I have are a few photos. Please, there must be something you can tell me?"

Bertha sighed. "Your mother was a confident, beautiful and intelligent woman. Everyone loved her."

Jessica snorted, reaching for the wand. "So we're playing good fairy, bad fairy, are we, Bertha?" She waved the wand. "Learn from your mother's mistakes, Natasha. Stephanie had a wild reputation. She broke hearts everywhere she went. You wouldn't find her hiding in the restroom at a party. Your mother would have led your six princes on a merry dance while flirting with the other guests."

"All that ceased," Bertha said, snatching back her wand. "Stephanie gave up partying when she became a Director."

"Only because Stephen told her she needed to change her behaviour," Jessica said. "When she learned of my appointment as Director, she threw a terrible tantrum.

Stephen told Stephanie she'd squandered too many opportunities. If she wanted a position on the Board, she had to prove she was ready. No more turning up late and leaving early, expecting other people to cover for her."

"I think we've said more than enough," Bertha said, catching hold of Natasha's arm. "There's a room full of people expecting your return."

"I'll check if the way is clear," Jessica said, opening the door and stepping into the corridor. "James and Landon are at the other end, having another of their clandestine meetings, but there's no sign of those pesky princes."

Before Natasha could protest, she was out of the restroom. She glanced toward the two men Jessica had mentioned. Facing away as they whispered together, they were wearing dark, hooded cloaks.

"Come along, princess," Bertha said.

The men glanced in her direction and pulled back their hoods. One of them was Oleander. She'd never heard anyone refer to the chauffeur by anything other than his surname. How could she persuade these women to reveal more information?

"Bertha! Jessica!" the unknown man said, hurrying along the corridor towards them. "Please wait."

Oleander loitered until the other man reached them, then disappeared around the corner.

"Not now," Bertha said, pulling Natasha closer. "We're on an important mission."

"We have to get *our* princess back to the ballroom," Jessica added, claiming Natasha's other arm.

"Don't let me delay you on your mission, ladies," the smiling grey-haired man said. "But first, I beg you to allow me to introduce myself to *our* princess. Miss Jacobson, Landon Greenville, at your service." He executed a stiff bow. "I'm delighted to finally make your acquaintance. I was one of your grandfather's closest advisors."

Natasha recognised the name of another original Director. She frowned. He wore a professor's costume that seemed identical to Oleander's. She didn't remember seeing any other professors. The closeness of her companions constrained her from offering him the customary curtsey. Nodding her head, she reinstated her smile. "Thank you, Mr Greenville. Please call me Natasha."

"And you must call me Landon. With your permission, Natasha, I would like to accompany you and your delightful companions."

"We have the situation under control," Bertha said, pulling Natasha in the direction of the ballroom.

Landon chuckled as he fell into step behind them. "Of course you do, Bertie. But James is expecting trouble, and it won't hurt to have me as your rear guard."

"What kind of trouble?" Jessica asked, glancing over her shoulder at Landon.

"He didn't say," Landon said. "You know how secretive he's been. He asked me to deliver a message."

"What now?" Bertha muttered.

"Protect tomorrow's secrets."

"We don't need reminding," Jessica said, but her grip tightened on Natasha's arm. "Neither of us would betray Stephen's vision by speaking out of turn."

"We understand what's at stake," Bertha added. "Right now, the objective is to get Natasha safely back to the ball."

Without further discussion, Natasha's companions drew her forward. The heavy silence compelled the young woman to speak. "Everyone is talking in riddles tonight."

"It's for your own good, dear," Jessica said, patting Natasha's hand.

"I'm not sure I believe you," Natasha said. "But I'm guessing you're involved in one of my grandfather's schemes. I'd rather trust his 'farsightedness' than whatever my father and those princes have in mind. Find me some excuse to avoid spending the whole evening dancing with them, and I'll be forever grateful."

23

Boldness

1 Chronicles 16:8 CG
Give thanks to the Lord. Proclaim His greatness.
Tell everyone what He has done.

It was almost ten o'clock, and as the music of another dance faded, Natasha smiled, preparing to make her escape before anyone else claimed her for the next dance. She thanked Finn for the dance and checked her surroundings. Since her return to the ballroom, Ian was the only prince she hadn't danced with, and he was nowhere in sight.

Finn caught her hand and dragged Natasha from the dance floor. "Ian's over there, talking to your father. I want to know what Ian's up to."

"Perhaps he's given up the challenge?" Natasha said.

"Don't let him con you," Finn said. "There's no way he'd give up after working so hard to win."

Finn lowered his voice. "Ask yourself why we're wearing this shade of red that clashes with your dress, while he's wearing blue. Guess who organised our costumes?"

Glancing at his red jacket, Natasha replayed her recent conversations with the other princes. Only Finn had avoided criticising the others, which added to the impact of his comments. Natasha frowned. Joah had warned her not *everyone* was playing fairly. Was he talking about Ian? Blaze had told her to ignore what *anyone* else said about him. Ian again? Zed had asked her to ignore baseless rumours, assuring her of his wholehearted devotion and fidelity. Daniel had insisted he was the only one who valued her career.

Recalling Oleander's negative comments about Ian following the kidnapping attempt, Natasha studied the prince in the blue coat. The *boldness* in Ian's posture, the confident tilt of his head, and the way his hand rested on her father's arm rang alarm bells.

"It's your turn to dance with Natasha," Finn told Ian.

Luke smiled at Natasha, but there was something in his eyes that set her nerves jangling. "Ian has offered to forfeit his dance to help you open your birthday cards."

"I don't need any help," Natasha said to her father.

Shaking his head with a rueful smile, Luke said, "Accepting Ian's help is non-negotiable. It will provide valuable insight into how well you work together as a team."

"That's an excellent idea," Finn said. "I'll signal the others. It's only fair everyone plays a part in this opportunity."

Ian shrugged. It was her father's turn to frown.

Flanked by Ian and Finn, Natasha headed for the ballroom exit. She stopped halfway across the empty foyer, shaking her head. "What happened to the pink castle where everyone deposited their cards?"

The repurposed dollhouse should be near the front door with a guard watching over it. The ball was a charity fundraiser and donations were included with the cards. Both the guard and the shoulder-height, heavy wooden cube were missing.

The remaining suitors arrived while Natasha spun slowly, inspecting the room.

"We should call the police and report a robbery," Zed said. "There'd be a fortune in charity donations in those cards."

"Don't act prematurely," Ian said. "There's no point calling the police until we've conducted a thorough search. I'll stay here with Natasha, while the rest of you spread out and look."

"Who appointed you the leader, Ian?" Finn snapped.

The other princes added their voices to his protest.

"I'll find it myself," Natasha muttered as she turned away.

Her actions ended the argument as everyone scattered to search the foyer.

"Over here," said Blaze, his voice coming from near her father's downstairs study.

Everyone converged on his location.

"Someone left the pink monstrosity outside this room," Blaze said, patting the wooden box that was decorated to look like a medieval castle, complete with tubular towers at each corner of the flat roof.

Finn snorted. "Labelling Natasha's castle a monstrosity won't win you any points."

"This is where I'm counting the donations," Natasha said, opening the study door. She leaned inside and checked the room.

Everything in the study seemed to be as she'd left it. Her laptop was on her father's desk beside a tall stack of shallow baskets. Returning her attention to the hallway, she scanned the area for security cameras and found none. "There's supposed to be a guard."

Blaze checked the child-sized arched doorway on the front. The heavy bottom-hinged drawbridge sealing it shut was secure.

After Zed attempted to push his arm through the narrow slit near the top, everyone agreed nothing could be retrieved using that method. Meanwhile, Joah circled the castle, tugging on the rear-facing padlocks that kept the dollhouse from unfolding to reveal the inner rooms.

"Please take it to my father's study," Natasha said, leading the way.

"Step back," Blaze said, "and I'll wheel the 'pink monstrosity' into the room."

"Put it in front of the window," Natasha said. "I'll check the computer hasn't been tampered with."

A few clicks confirmed the database forms worked, and the printer was ready. When Natasha glanced up, five princes were standing to attention on the opposite side of the desk.

Behind them, Ian was inspecting the tables set beside the longest wall. He turned with a decorated gift bag in his hand, examining the label on the bottle of wine he'd found within.

"I can see why you thought you didn't need any help," Ian said. "You've already organised the thank you gifts."

"Put it back," said Joah. "You're supposed to be helping, not swanning around as if you own the place."

With a shrug, Ian returned the bag to the table before approaching the pink castle. "Do I have permission to lower the drawbridge, Natasha?"

"I'll get you a letter opener," Natasha said.

Searching the desk drawers, she found a silver one. She dropped it into the top basket beside the pink dinosaur-shaped letter opener her friend Cassie had given her years ago. She emerged from behind the desk, carrying the baskets. "I wasn't expecting any helpers. I'm unconvinced your presence improves my efficiency. Your contempt for my strict procedures is no secret. If I catch anyone ignoring my instructions, or taking a shortcut, I'll banish the lot of you. Is that understood?"

A chorus of agreement followed her remark. Natasha placed the baskets on the flat castle roof before offering Ian the letter openers. He stared at them for a few seconds before grinning and choosing the pink dinosaur. Stabbing the tape sealing the side edges of the drawbridge, Ian ripped the blade through the joins to unseal the hatch before unfastening the clips.

The heavy castle drawbridge dropped to the floor with a loud crash. An avalanche of envelopes in various colours and sizes tumbled from the opening. Natasha leapt back as the men scrambled to stem the flood of envelopes.

Ian battled the shifting mass of paper, shoving cards back inside the castle. The other helpers retrieved envelopes from the floor and tossed them onto the castle roof.

Shaking her head, Natasha sifted through the untidy pile of envelopes to reach the stack of baskets. "One card to a basket."

Selecting an envelope, she employed her father's letter opener. Explaining her detailed process step by step, she matched her actions to her words as she carried the basket from the castle to the desk. Her original plan had required her to process the cards in batches of thirty.

These extra helpers complicated everything, but if they could work together, that would save her valuable time.

Crossing to the desk, Natasha spun the laptop towards her. She resisted the urge to push her audience away when they pressed forward to look over her shoulder. "The database is sorted by guest name..." A few keystrokes brought up the correct record, and she focused on the accompanying cheque. "Complete every box..."

Tap tap tap...

The printer on the desk clicked and whirred. "The cheque goes into the cashbox, and the receipt joins the card in the basket."

Finn snatched the paper from the printer and handed it to her.

"Now we come to the task only I can do – the thank you notes. I was planning to sit here..."

Natasha scooped up a pile of notepads from beside the printer and a couple of pink pens, adding them to her basket. "But I'll move to the coffee table. There's a lap desk in that corner."

Zed rushed to obtain the portable desk and delivered it to Natasha. The armchair she'd selected was closest to the door, providing her with a good view of the room.

"Thank you, Zed. I'll address the notes and place the processed birthday cards here." She tapped the table. "They have to be pinned on display boards." She pointed to folding stands near the door. "We'll move the display into the foyer when we're finished. The receipt and note go into a labelled gift bag with the bottle of wine, and the basket returns to the castle for another card. Any questions?"

The men shook their heads.

"I'll leave you to decide how to proceed while I write this note. Please don't leave me sitting idle."

"Here, take these baskets," Ian said. "I've been opening envelopes while Natasha gave her instructions."

"So have I," said Blaze.

"I'll enter the data," Finn said, claiming the chair behind the desk. "Zed, come and confirm..."

24

Chilliness

John 8:12
Again, therefore, Jesus spoke to them, saying,
"I am the light of the world.
He who follows Me will not walk in the darkness,
but will have the light of life.

Lowering her eyes to the card in her hand, Natasha shut out the conversations in the room. She concentrated on the music drifting through the open study door.

After taking several calming breaths, she studied the card. The cover image was pretty, and the printed greeting inside rhymed nicely, but the sentiment sounded hollow. Natasha couldn't remember meeting the people who had signed the card.

Natasha sighed as an air of chilliness entered the room. Sorting through her notepads, Natasha selected the briefest handwritten message. She was thankful that she made the effort to write these ahead of time.

By the time she had written the guests' names at the top, Joah was beside her with another basket. She swapped it for the one in her hand and considered Joah's progress as he hurried to the gift bag table.

He shuffled along, loitering over the labels before he pounced on a decorated bag. After inserting the thank you note and receipt, Joah flashed a confident smile in her direction. She shouldn't have let him catch her watching him.

Natasha pretended to focus on the next card as he disappeared behind her on his way back to the castle. When Joah reappeared, he thrust the empty basket towards Daniel. The pair spoke before Joah strode past Natasha on his return to the desk.

Ian and Blaze were opening envelopes. Daniel carried a stack of baskets towards the desk. Finn typed at the computer while Zed dictated numbers from a cheque. Reminding herself she could not afford to sit idle, Natasha opened the next card. Another impersonal greeting from people she didn't know.

When Joah returned, she swapped her basket for the two he'd delivered. He studied her handwriting. "You wrote the labels on the gift bags, too. Did you also pack them?"

Impatient to escape his scrutiny, Natasha nodded.

"It must have cost your father a fortune," Joah said. "You didn't need to include a pair of goblets with the wine."

"I paid for the gifts," Natasha said. "I'm a tough negotiator, and the total cost was below my projected budget. My father agreed I could add any savings to this evening's charitable donations." She selected a notepad and clicked her pen in dismissal.

A few minutes later, a shout erupted from the desk. "Hey, Ian!" Zed waved a slip of paper. "We came to a consensus about our donations. Why are there two extra zeros on your cheque?"

The chilliness in the room intensified, and Natasha shuddered.

"The rest of you came to a consensus," Ian said, brandishing the pink dinosaur letter opener like a laser pointer. "My accountant agreed a more generous donation would assure Natasha I wasn't after her money."

"Don't believe anything he says," whispered Daniel, appearing beside her to take the cards she'd already processed.

Leaning closer, Daniel continued to speak as he sorted the cards according to size. "Ian never spends a cent unless it's guaranteed to return with interest."

In a louder voice, he continued, "I'm taking these to the display boards. You guys had better work faster, or we'll still be here at midnight."

"I certainly hope not," said a woman's voice.

Natasha almost dropped her pen as she spun towards the door. Why were Jessica, Bertha and Landon here?

Jessica continued, "Perhaps the presence of three Directors will inspire you to new heights of efficiency?"

Her words had the opposite effect, halting every activity.

Bertha and Jessica commandeered chairs on Natasha's right while Landon sat closer to the desk.

"Chop chop," said Bertha, clapping her hands. "Back to work."

The young men resumed their tasks, and Natasha opened another card.

Jessica leaned toward Natasha. "How are you enjoying our teamwork exercise?"

"Are you claiming responsibility?" Natasha asked.

"You said you'd be forever grateful if you didn't have to dance with them all evening," Bertha said. "I told you to be careful what you wished for."

"Why are you here, Bertie?" Ian asked, and the others stopped working again.

"Ian, have you gone mad," Daniel hissed. "You can't talk to a Director like that!"

"It wouldn't be the first time," Bertha said with a grin. "I've had to endure his insolence since he was in nappies. You asked why I'm here, Ian?" Bertha waved her wand. "I'm Natasha's fairy godmother, and I'm thinking of turning *you* into a toad."

Ian laughed. "Save your threats for the others, Bertie.

"Stop calling me Bertie."

"You're even grumpier than usual," Ian said. He stopped work and took a step closer. "Is it true you fired both deputies after last week's fiasco at the General Meeting? Is that seven this year, or eight?"

"You cheeky—" Bertha began.

Jessica placed a hand on her friend's arm. "Ignore him. His appointment as one of his father's deputies has clearly gone to his head."

"You didn't tell us you were a deputy to the Board, Ian," Blaze said.

"It's not as important as it sounds," Ian replied.

The three directors stiffened, and the 'red princes' stopped work and stared.

As the silence stretched, Ian shrugged. "My father always sought my advice, and the appointment made my role official. A Spendor Corporation deputy only attends General Meetings and doesn't have voting rights."

"The significant decisions happen behind closed doors," Ian said, "at the monthly Executive Board Meetings."

"Your tongue is too free for my liking," Bertha said, shaking her head as if seeing Ian in a new light.

"You don't have to worry about us," Blaze said. "Luke made us sign a confidentiality agreement."

"That's right," said Zed, and the others added their affirmation. "Anything that's said here won't go beyond these walls. Is Ian right about vacancies on your team, Ms Doncaster? It's obvious Luke has nominated Natasha, but are you here because he's recommended one of us for the other position?"

"You couldn't be more wrong," Jessica said. "Natasha's not going to be Bertha's deputy, and our presence has nothing to do with vacancies. We're chaperones."

"Since her father's announcement this evening," Bertha said, "poor Natasha hasn't had a moment's peace."

"I don't know why you've come dressed as princes," Jessica said. "Ruthless pirates or greedy fortune hunters would be more appropriate."

"That's harsh," Ian said. "Let's redeem our reputations and prove we're worthy of any challenge our princess sets."

"I'm surprised you're making any progress," Landon said to Natasha. "You focus on your thank you notes, and I'll keep an eye on these rogues."

The Directors talked quietly among themselves, but Natasha could sense their watching eyes.

Ten minutes later, Finn appeared beside Natasha. "Have you finished with these?"

She nodded, and he picked up the baskets from the table. He looked at the note in the top basket before reaching for one of the notepads.

"Young man, stop being a sticky-beak, and get back to work," Jessica said, retrieving the notepad from Finn. "Natasha, I'm impressed. Handwritten notes are rare these days."

"My father said the guests would appreciate the personal touch," Natasha said.

"I'd have been happy with your signature on a printed note," Finn said, "but then I'm not someone who can afford to donate thousands of dollars." He glared at Ian, who appeared on the other side of Natasha's chair and reached for a pile of processed cards.

"Talking about me again?" Ian asked. "It's ten-thirty, Natasha. Don't let Finn keep you from your work. There are more notes to write, and you don't want to miss the unveiling of your cake at eleven."

Without waiting for a reply, Ian headed toward the display boards.

"Aren't you glad we volunteered to help you," Finn said.

"Get back to work," Jessica said, shooing him away.

25

Clumsiness

"That's the last of the cards," Joah announced. He waited until Natasha glanced toward him before he tossed the dinosaur letter opener into a basket and handed it to Ian.

"Have you checked the floor?" Ian asked. "Your clumsiness is legendary, and you've probably lost some under the box."

"The only clumsiness in evidence tonight," Blaze said, joining the pair beside the box, "was when you opened the hatch, Ian – cards went everywhere. You're trying to shift responsibility."

"It doesn't matter who is responsible," Ian said. "The only way to be certain is to look underneath."

The three men shoved the box aside.

"You were right," said Blaze, pouncing on an envelope. "Hey, this is addressed to someone called Nessie."

"Are you sure it came out of the box?" Daniel asked from behind the computer. "There are only four spaces left in the database and four cards waiting to be processed."

"Someone told me Natasha's pet name at school was Nessie," Ian said.

The colour had drained from Natasha's face as she stared at the unopened card Blaze waved in the air.

"Give it to me," Joah said, retrieving the pink letter opener.

"Careful," said Blaze. "Don't rip the envelope. There's something drawn on the outside. Look, it's a pink dinosaur."

"The same dinosaur as this letter opener," Joah said as he withdrew the card and flipped it open. "There's no cheque. Is there a Cassie on the guest list?"

For the first time that evening, Natasha felt as if she was alone and invisible.

The men continued inspecting the card.

"Listen to this poem," Joah said. "Goodness, Nessie! Please accept this silliness..."

"Hey, be careful, Joah," Ian said. "Something fell out of the envelope."

Joah ignored Ian. "To celebrate your birthday's timeliness! Your brightness outshines my darkness…"

"Move your feet," said Ian. "Whoever Cassie is, she gave Natasha a real present."

"There's no Cassie in the database," Zed called from the desk.

"Your kindness cancels out my cruelness…" Joah stepped sideways and continued reading. "Your rightness balances my wrongness. Your gentleness overpowers my bossiness…"

Nobody seemed to notice Natasha's reaction. As she struggled to her feet, the equipment in her lap slipped towards the floor.

"I've found it," Ian said. "This dinosaur pendant—"

"Your friendliness redeems—"

CRASH!

The lap desk hit the coffee table, throwing baskets into the air as Natasha's arms and legs refused to obey her instructions. The room spun, and the floor pushed upward to meet her.

Bertha and Jessica cried out. "Natasha!"

Finn appeared, blocking her view of the room. He shoved Natasha into the armchair, crouching beside her. "Natasha? What's wrong? You look as if you've seen a ghost."

Throwing her hands over her face, Natasha burst into tears. From the bustle around her, she realised everyone was rushing to her aid. She inhaled deeply, swiping at her tears. "Please go back to your tasks. I do not need assistance."

"The clumsiness award is yours tonight, Nessie," Ian said, stepping around the clutter on the floor. He reached for her hand, dropping the dinosaur pendant and gold chain into her palm. "Here's your prize."

Wrapping her fingers around the jewellery, Natasha drew her hand to her chest and pulled away from Ian. The other princes muttered under their breath.

"Ian, you insensitive wretch," Bertha said. "Make yourself useful and take that pink castle back to the foyer. The rest of you help pick up these baskets and then go back to your tasks."

"You take a break," Finn said when Natasha attempted to help with the clean-up.

"Bertha and I will finish addressing the notes," Jessica said, taking a pen from Natasha's fingers. "Your hand is shaking."

"I'm sorry," Natasha said.

"There's nothing to be sorry about," Landon said from his seat. "James warned us to expect mischief. Can I see the card that sparked the drama?"

"This card?" asked Zed, retrieving a basket from the desk and handing it to Landon. "Is that what upset Natasha?"

"Do you recognise the handwriting?" Landon asked, offering the card and envelope to Natasha.

She glanced at the envelope, closing her eyes as she nodded. "Yes, it's from Cassie, but..."

"But Cassie couldn't have delivered the card," Landon said.

Natasha opened her eyes and stared at Landon. "You know?"

"What does Mr Greenville know?" asked Daniel.

"I know why Cassie's name isn't on the guest list."

"So do I," said Finn. "At least, I think I do. Somebody else brought the card. Cassie couldn't, because she's dead."

"Cassie's dead?" Joah asked.

"What secrets have I missed," Ian said, returning to the room.

"Natasha hasn't said anything," Finn said. "I asked if she'd seen a ghost, and I recognised the truth in her eyes."

"That doesn't explain her reaction," Daniel said. "One of Cassie's relatives could have delivered the card."

Shaking her head, Natasha sighed. "Pass me the letter opener."

Zed retrieved it from the desk.

Placing the dinosaur letter opener on the envelope, Natasha held the two up for the others to see. "Cassie traced around the letter opener to decorate the envelope. She showed me the envelope on the day she died. The card should have been in her pocket, but it was missing when I found her."

"How did Cassie die?" asked Daniel.

"When would be a better question," said Finn.

"That's enough," Bertha said. "Jessica's finishing the last note."

A few minutes later, the two female Directors ushered Natasha from the study. Landon remained to oversee the remaining tasks.

"If they can't be trusted to install a couple of display boards in the foyer," Bertha said, "they don't deserve to be considered for any further advancement within the Corporation."

"But the gift bags—"

"Stop fussing. It's almost eleven and your father will be wondering where you are."

"Do I need to repair my makeup?" Natasha asked.

"You're pale," Jessica said, "but you turned off the tears before your mascara ran. I doubt anyone other than Edith will notice anything amiss."

26

Intuitiveness

At eleven, the chef wheeled in a castle-shaped cake. There were twenty-five turrets of varying heights, each crowned with a hissing sparkler. While guests applauded the confectionery masterpiece, the photographer took centre stage, snapping photos from multiple angles.

The chef handed Natasha a beribboned carving knife.

Someone shouted, "Don't forget to make a wish."

While the guests sang the traditional birthday song, Natasha plunged the knife into the cake. The "hip hip hoorays" faded, but the photographer wasn't satisfied. His camera flashed again and again. Luke and Edith were summoned for a "few" family photos with the "Birthday Girl".

It was a relief when Natasha surrendered the knife to the chef. She stepped back so the team of servers could distribute the cake.

"You get the first piece," the chef said, handing Natasha a plate and a silver fork. He studied her face as she sampled a mouthful.

"It's delicious," she said.

Beaming with pride, the chef clapped his hands. The serving team spread through the room.

Natasha searched for a quiet place to sit. Her father, deep in conversation with Ian, had his back towards her. Natasha changed direction, going to the furthest corner. But she had barely settled on a chair when she was surrounded by the other princes.

"What did you wish for?" Joah asked.

"It won't come true if she tells you," Zed laughed.

"If you must know," Natasha said with a sigh, "I wished for ten minutes without anyone bothering me. Please go away and let me enjoy my cake in peace."

"Your wish is my command," Finn said, bowing low and backing away. The other men glanced at each other before they retreated.

Oleander appeared behind her. "Masterfully done."

"Where have you been?" Natasha asked, too weary to glance at him. "Did Landon tell you about Cassie's card?"

"Freeman went back through the security footage, but it's impossible to tell who was responsible."

"So you don't have any answers," Natasha said, handing her empty plate to a passing server.

"I've talked to the security guard. He moved the castle at your father's request, in a message delivered by Delores, which Luke has confirmed."

"What about Ian?"

"What about him?" Oleander asked.

"I have a feeling," Natasha said.

"Go on."

"Oh, I wish Cassie were here. She had a saying." Natasha closed her eyes and tried to imitate her friend's Scottish accent. "Nessie, your intuitiveness is infallible."

"Do you think of Cassie often?"

"Not as often as I used to," Natasha said, glancing around. "Keeping busy helps. When Cassie died, it was as if part of me died too. I was numb... but since the kidnapping, it hurts here." She pressed her hand to the centre of her chest and closed her eyes. "It's been seven years, Oleander, and I miss her more tonight than I ever did."

Oleander didn't respond immediately. A heavy silence settled over Natasha like a cloak, as she fought tears. Then Oleander's hand brushed against the back of her head. "I'm sorry, Natasha. I cannot remain any longer. It looks as if those young men took you literally, and your ten minutes are up. Don't dismiss your intuitiveness. Perhaps Freeman is right, and God is guiding you?"

Before she could reply, Oleander was gone.

"Who would you like to dance with first?" Daniel asked, already reaching for her hand.

Half an hour later, Natasha curtsied to Finn, the last of the five red princes to claim a final dance before midnight. Lacking enthusiasm for another dance, she was relieved nobody waited to claim her. Retreating to the refreshment table, she sipped fruit punch as she surveyed the room. Across the crowd, she spotted Delores waving to her.

"I have a message for you," Delores muttered when she arrived. "I was worried I'd forget – I've been busy all evening." The girl searched the pockets of the black apron tied around her waist. "I wrote it down. I hope you can read my scribble."

"Who is the message from?" Natasha asked.

"He said you'd know. Here it is." The girl spun around and disappeared among the crowd.

Natasha frowned at the crumpled paper in her hand.

MERMAID FOUNTAIN

BEFORE MIDNIGHT

TIMELINESS NECESSARY

The final phrase captured Natasha's attention, causing her heart to race. Taking a deep breath, Natasha pushed against the rising flood of emotions. This message did not – could not

– come from Cassie. Yet only Cassie had ever used "timeliness necessary" to summon her.

Where was Oleander when she needed him? Natasha threaded her way around the crowded room, but he was nowhere to be seen. An explanation for the note hit her like a blast of Antarctic wind. Of course! Oleander knew about Cassie's word games. That cryptic message matched this evening's sneakiness. He must have important information and didn't want anyone to overhear.

Approaching the doorway that accessed the garden, Natasha expected her stomach to stop churning. She had a logical explanation, so why was that tingling sensation running up and down her spine? Oleander had told her to trust her intuitiveness. If he hadn't sent the message, who waited at the fountain?

Her foot tapped to the music to cover her restlessness. Who wanted to catch her alone? Her mind immediately identified six candidates. She retraced her steps to check the ballroom. Was one of them missing? No. Ian remained at her father's side, and the other princes were in plain view.

Who else knew about Cassie's code words? Would Oleander have shared his knowledge with Landon? Natasha shook her head. Oleander liked to keep secrets to himself. Delores hadn't seemed concerned about delivering the message. It had to be someone trustworthy. Perhaps it was

Freeman? Her stepbrother already knew about the code words, *and* he was on duty in the security hub.

Grasping this new possibility like a lifeline, Natasha slipped into the side room. Before her courage failed, she crossed to the open French doors and stepped out of the house. A guard emerged from the shadows.

"I need some fresh air," she said with a smile. "I'm going to the mermaid fountain on the other side of that hedge."

"Other guests are in the garden," the guard said. "Would you like me to organise an escort, Ms Jacobson?"

"That won't be necessary. I know where the cameras are, and I'll stay on the path where I can be seen."

"Shout if you need assistance," he said.

She nodded, walking briskly as she followed the illuminated path, hoping the guard couldn't sense the alarm his parting words inspired. A few seconds later, the guard's radio clicked and hissed as he informed the security hub of her whereabouts. His voice ceased, but the night was not silent. Orchestral music floated across the landscaped gardens on a gentle breeze.

With each step, her anticipation intensified. Freeman had never invited her to a secret meeting before. What would it be like to be alone with him in the darkened garden?

Her imagination took an unexpected detour. What if he had something other than her security on his mind? *This could be a romantic midnight rendezvous.*

Where had that thought come from? Natasha halted as a memory unfolded with alarming clarity. Transported back to her Summerlands University days, Natasha watched helplessly as Cassie prepared for that fateful party.

"You're eighteen tomorrow, Nessie," Cassie had said. "A little romance won't ruin your future. Won't you leave your assignment for a few hours? I've found you the perfect boyfriend. I've already told him you've never been kissed, and he's promised to be gentle."

Natasha shuddered at her past self's reply. "I'm sorry, Cassie, but this assignment is important." If only she could unsay those words.

"More important than spending time with your only friend?" Cassie grabbed her coat and stormed towards the door. "One day, you'll come to your senses and find yourself alone." The door slammed, but a few minutes later, Cassie burst into the apartment. "Please grant me your forgiveness, Nessie. That was so, so, so unkind. I'd rather be dead than hurt you."

Those words pierced Natasha's heart, yet she was unable to stop the recollection.

"You stay here and work on that assignment, sweetness," Cassie had said. "I'll talk to your secret admirer. I'm sure he'd love to commemorate your birthday with a romantic midnight rendezvous."

With a jolt, Natasha returned to the present, trembling in the middle of the path. Her fingers tingled, and she felt faint. It was seven years since Cassie had made that terrible prediction, and it had come true. Natasha was alone...

And facing another midnight rendezvous!

Her imagination took charge. Was history repeating itself? Was she about to meet *him*? The secret admirer Cassie had said she'd bring home. That would explain how Cassie's card came into the house. The police had never identified the man Cassie left the party with...

What foolishness was this? Fighting the urge to flee back to the ballroom, Natasha resumed her progress. The mermaid fountain was in the next garden room.

Another memory awakened from a conversation when Cassie had been fourteen.

"Timidness won't win you any prizes, Nessie."

With a sigh, Natasha increased her pace. "Timidness no longer defines me," she whispered into the evening air. "But this would be easier if you were here."

27

Madness

Romans 10:10
For with the heart, one believes
resulting in righteousness;
and with the mouth confession is made
resulting in salvation.

The mermaid statue was brightly lit, but the outer corners of the garden room were in shadow.

"Hello?" Receiving no reply, Natasha approached the fountain. The water splashed into the circular pond, drowning out the distant music.

Circumnavigating the fountain several times, Natasha trailed her fingers in the water, waiting for her nerves to settle. Just as she made the decision to return to the house, approaching footsteps crunched on the gravel beyond the hedge. Ian Norris stepped through the gap in the hedge.

Natasha retreated until the fountain's concrete rim pressed against her legs. "What are you doing here?"

"I asked you to meet me."

"I didn't know the message was from you. I shouldn't have come."

"But you did," he said, walking towards her. "Don't you want to hear what I have to say?"

"What could you have to say that couldn't be said in the ballroom?"

He laughed, holding out a small, blue velvet box. "Your father asked me to give you this."

Natasha eyed the box suspiciously. "Why didn't he give it to me himself?"

"He's been surrounded by admirers, and he wanted to spare you a large audience."

"He could have asked Edith to give it to me."

"You'll understand when I show you." Ian flipped open the lid. A gold ring studded with diamonds nestled on a white satin pillow. "This ring belonged to your mother."

"My mother?" Natasha swayed on her feet, battling the warm fuzziness flowing over her. Flashes of bright light disrupted her vision.

"Careful," Ian said, catching her around the waist. "You almost fell in the fountain." He helped her to a bench seat.

"We'll sit here until you recover. Understandably, you're shaken after receiving a gift from beyond the grave."

The dizziness eased, but the visual flashes continued to haunt her. She blinked up into Ian's face. "This ring belonged to my mother?"

"Yes. Luke wants to see you wearing it at midnight." Ian removed the ring from the box and placed it in her right palm.

"Midnight?" Natasha asked, examining the ring.

"You were born five minutes past midnight, so it's not officially your birthday until then."

Nodding, Natasha balanced the golden band on the tip of her left index finger to examine it in the light. "What did he tell you about my mother?"

"Apart from mentioning he secretly married her, he's said nothing. He's spent more time talking about his hopes and dreams for you."

"He doesn't talk about her to me either. Someone told me he was heartbroken when she died. I can't believe he's giving me her ring. Are you sure he wants me to wear it?"

"May I?" Ian asked, catching her left hand. Before she could pull away, he had the diamond band on her ring finger. "It's a perfect fit." He continued to hold her hand as he leaned closer.

Reading his intentions on his face, Natasha's eyes widened with understanding. A romantic midnight rendezvous? Ian was claiming her with a kiss. Her mind screamed, but her foolish tongue remained silent. Even worse, she could not banish the stupid smile she had worked so long to perfect.

As he pressed his mouth over her smiling lips, another wave of dizziness threatened to drag her into oblivion. She grabbed his jacket with both hands, pressing against his chest to shove him away.

"Perfect," said another voice. "Hold that pose while I get some close-ups."

Natasha flinched, realising the bright flashes weren't hallucinations. The photographer had been lurking in the background, capturing every moment of this humiliating encounter. Ian continued to kiss her, ignoring the intrusive photographer. Using her waning strength, Natasha pushed Ian away. Her words came in short gasps, as she struggled to her feet.

"Ian... stop... kissing me... I-I'll... tell... my... fath—"

Rising with her, Ian pulled her into his embrace, trapping her hands against his chest. "Luke knows everything, Nessie." He silenced her with another kiss.

As the implications of Ian's words exploded in Natasha's mind, darkness claimed her.

With her heart dancing to a crazy rhythm, Natasha fought a strange floating sensation. What was causing this burning agony in her chest? Why couldn't she take a deep breath?

A chill washed over her. Something pressed against her face...

Her body was bound in tight wrappings; she couldn't move...

The soft scrunch-crunch of gravel rose towards her from below...

Her arms were trapped, but her lower legs were unrestrained. Natasha kicked her feet, but they became entangled within her heavy skirts.

Pushing against the solid object beneath her hands, she encountered resistance, like firm muscles beneath silken fabric.

The slow intake of breath, the throbbing of a second heart...

Someone was carrying her like a slumbering child, crushing her upper body against their chest. Strong arms tightened around her...

"Stop there. Adjust the angle of her head."

The disembodied voice was behind her. There were two captors! Whoever was carrying her stopped moving forward and applied pressure to her chin.

"That's good," said the voice. It sounded like the photographer. "Perfect. Yes, yes, keep looking down."

Bright flashes disrupted the darkness as the final piece of the puzzle dropped into place. Memories of the encounter with Ian flooded her mind.

"I think she's coming round," the first man said. "Natasha, are you awake?"

"Urrmmm?" she murmured, wriggling her head until she could stare up into his face. "Ian? Ian! This is madness! Put me down!"

"Stop struggling," Ian said, adjusting his grip to squeeze tighter. "We're almost at the house."

Turning her head, Natasha confirmed the veracity of his words. The French doors were a few hundred metres away. She glimpsed the security guard standing in the middle of the path before the photographer loomed into view again.

"I can walk the rest of the way," she said, turning from the flashing light to glare at Ian.

"It would be *madness* to release you now, Nessie," Ian said, lightly kissing her forehead. The camera continued to flash. "I wasn't expecting you to faint." He punctuated his words with more kisses as his lips worked their way down her face. "But I'm going to take full advantage of the opportunity you've presented me."

This time, Natasha's growing anger drove back the dizziness when Ian's mouth claimed her own.

Flash, flash, flash...

Turning her head away from the bright lights, Natasha ended the kiss. "No more photos. Make the photographer go away."

The photographer chuckled, circling the pair as the flashes continued. "The camera loves you, sweetheart. You don't need to be looking at the lens for me to get a great shot." *Flash, flash, flash, flash.* "A few more, and then I'll head inside." *Flash, flash...*

When the brightness finally faded, Natasha risked a glance. The photographer was grinning as he checked the camera's viewing screen. He looked up but not at her. "I've got what I need, Ian. Do you have any final instructions?"

"Be discreet," Ian said. "Warn Jacobson I'm carrying his daughter, and tell him to proceed with the plan.

"I'll do better than that," the photographer said, waving his camera. "A picture's worth a thousand words. I've captured the moment when she swooned in your arms. That front-cover-worthy shot should have her father issuing the wedding invitations tonight."

"Wedding?" Natasha asked. "Ian, why would my father think I'm marrying you?"

Ian's attention focused on the departing photographer. The security guard spoke briefly to the man before reaching for his radio.

"Ms Jacobson," called the guard. "Are you okay?"

"There's no reason for concern," Ian shouted. "Her father sent me to collect her."

The guard spoke into his radio again and then strode towards them. A distant shout from the darkness echoed through the garden.

"Be careful what you say, Nessie. I'm counting on you not to make a fuss." Ian tightened his grip. "Your father's announcing our engagement. Don't embarrass him in front of his guests."

"I never agreed to marry you."

"You're wearing my ring," Ian said, glancing sideways across the garden as he hurried forward to meet the guard.

"You said it was my mother's ring," Natasha said, staring at the precious diamonds. "Why did you lie?"

"I didn't lie. Your father gave me that ring so I could propose tonight."

"Propose? You didn't—"

"Shhh, Nessie. No one needs to know that. You didn't protest when I placed the ring on your finger, and my photographer's evidence supports my claim."

"Ms Jacobson," the guard said, stopping in the middle of the path and blocking her view of the open French doors. "Is this man bothering you?"

"I'm acting under her father's instructions," Ian said with a charming smile. He took a step closer. "It's Rhys Kennedy, isn't it? You heard what Luke Jacobson said at the security briefing. I have his full authority tonight. Now, go back to your post."

From a side path, the sound of running feet grew louder.

"I don't answer to her father," the guard said, refusing to budge. "Help is here, Ms Jacobson." His head jerked left. Matthew Wallace, the commander of Sentinel City Security, was only a few metres away, with four guards running in formation behind him.

"Ms Jacobson doesn't require any help," Ian said. "Listen, Nessie, that's the trumpet. It's gone midnight, and your father is waiting."

"Put me down, Ian," Natasha said, shoving against his chest with renewed determination.

"Do as she says," Matthew Wallace shouted, coming to a halt beside the first guard. The other men moved behind Ian to create a secure perimeter.

"If you insist," Ian said, releasing Natasha without warning.

A scream caught in Natasha's throat. Matthew lurched forward, but Ian was closer. He recaptured Natasha before she struck the ground, dragging her upright against him. "As you can see, Ms Jacobson is very unsteady on her feet this evening," Ian said as he held her trembling body in his arms. "Wallace, step aside. Luke Jacobson is at the door, summoning us."

28

Anxiousness

Matthew 6:33
For the LORD is good.
His loving kindness endures forever,
His faithfulness to all generations.

Matthew Wallace signalled the guard to step aside. The head of security accompanied Ian and Natasha along the path towards the house. When they were close enough to see Luke's unsmiling face, Matthew caught Ian around the shoulders and pulled him back. "Ms Jacobson will walk the rest of the way alone."

Free from Ian's grasp, Natasha ran through the French doors into the house.

"Father," she cried, throwing her arms around Luke and burying her head against his shoulder. The stiffness of his posture quashed her fragile sense of relief.

Luke drew her further into the room. The door to the ballroom was closed, and they were alone. "I'll talk to you in a moment, Natasha. First, I need to deal with the security concerns your actions have triggered."

His words planted a seed of anxiousness in her heart. Natasha glanced over her shoulder. Matthew stood in the doorway, preventing Ian from entering the house.

"Wallace," Luke said. "I have everything under control. Let Ian inside and close the door behind you. This is a private matter."

"Ms Jacobson?" Matthew asked. "Would you like me to stay?"

Natasha glanced at her father and shook her head.

The outer door closed, leaving Natasha to endure her father's scrutiny. She stepped back and waited for him to speak.

Luke studied her face. "I've been watching you all evening. You almost convinced me Ian's concerns were unfounded. But now this little melodrama has confirmed everything he's told me tonight. He said you wouldn't be able to resist an opportunity to play out your twisted fantasies—"

"Ian said what?"

At the mention of his name, Ian appeared beside her.

Her anxiousness blossomed. "Father, make Ian go away. I need to talk to you—"

"Ian's staying, Princess," Luke said, shaking his head sadly. "There's no excuse you can offer that will diminish my deep disappointment in your behaviour. I had hoped you would avoid the kind of trouble that destroyed your mother, but you're just like her. Are you still wearing her ring?"

Natasha looked at her hand. "It really is my mother's ring?"

"She bought it for herself," Luke said, his lips curving into a sad smile. "It symbolised her commitment to give up her past lovers and stay true to me. I thought my dreams had come true the day she married me, but my love was not enough to heal her brokenness."

"Is... is that why you... never talk about her? I thought she loved you."

"I should have talked about this before," Luke said, staring into Natasha's eyes. "Your mother stayed true to her promise, and I never doubted her love. Neither should you." He shook his head. "You look more and more like your mother each day. I'm sorry not to have told you about her character flaws. We wouldn't be in this situation if I had spoken earlier."

"I don't understand."

"Before I married your mother, she surrounded herself with acolytes who fed her voracious appetites and encouraged her excesses. Beauty and wealth were her weapons for destroying reputations, wrecking marriages and ruining lives. Your mother had everything money could buy, except happiness. After you were born, she gave it all away and lived like a saint, but it was too late to save her. The secret burden of guilt and shame was too great."

"But I'm not—" Natasha said.

"I know," Luke said. "Compared to your mother, you're an innocent child. You've kept your little games under wraps, and not even I suspected what you were doing until Ian confessed everything tonight. But I know now and I cannot allow you to make your mother's mistakes. That's why I asked Ian to give you this ring, to remind you happiness comes only with commitment. It's not too late, Princess, and we're determined to save you."

"Save me? Ian's the one—"

Luke spoke over the top of her. "I've suspected for months that he was your lover, and he's proven his loyalty by keeping your secrets. It took courage for him to tell me that he discovered you organised your own kidnapping."

"What? No! Ian's lying."

"Sweetness," Ian said, placing a hand on each shoulder and stroking her bare skin. A shiver ran through Natasha. Her father's approving smile towards Ian silenced her protest. Ian brushed his lips against her neck. "Calm down. You're not helping this situation by getting upset."

"Listen to Ian, Princess – he'll look after you," Luke said, releasing her hand. "I'm returning to the ballroom. Take a few moments to compose yourself, and then I expect you to appear before your guests."

Natasha held her breath, torn between the urge to escape her tormentor and the desperate need to make her father understand. She took a deep breath and caught hold of Luke's sleeve. "Please listen, Father. Ian's not—"

"Natasha." Luke's stern expression took Natasha's anxiousness to a higher level. "Don't make this any worse. You're lucky to have Ian – a lesser man would have walked away, but he's been patient. You promised to marry him months ago. We're making the announcement tonight."

Without waiting for a reply, her father abandoned Natasha. She stepped towards the closed door, and Ian pulled her back to him.

"Not yet," Ian said, continuing to massage her back with one hand. The other arm wrapped around her waist. "Your smile has disappeared. Take your time finding it again. There's no hurry. Your father will ensure we aren't disturbed, and I'm only getting started."

The agitated young woman froze. The familiar tingling in her extremities was back, but the pulsating darkness refused to claim her.

Numbness awoke at the centre of her being, and she fell into an ancient nightmare. To escape her present danger, her mind transported her back to the day her mother died. That was the day Natasha fell into the swimming pool. She relived the sensations, floating beneath the shimmering ripples as the icy numbness separated her from her emotions.

Time ceased...

"You're no longer reacting to my touch," Ian said, spinning her around to face him. He traced her lips with a fingertip. "I'm a little disappointed to see that perfect smile again. I was looking forward to kissing you into submission."

Natasha blinked, pulling away from Ian. "I'm ready to go into the ballroom."

He laughed, catching her hand and hurrying her towards the entrance. As the door opened, the orchestra played a loud fanfare, and the guests began to applaud. Natasha blinked again. Ian led her across the dance floor to where Luke and Edith were waiting

Behind her father, photographic images from her garden encounter flashed across a massive digital screen. That was her face, smiling as Ian slipped the diamond ring on her finger. The following image showed her smiling as he leaned closer to kiss her...

A lifetime of pretending kept her moving forward.

"I knew your smile wouldn't fail you, Nessie," Ian whispered as he wrapped his arm around her waist.

When she arrived in front of her father, Ian turned her around to face the room. Natasha aimed her smile at a spot on the furthest wall. Not even the photographer's camera flashes could distract her.

"A toast to the happy couple," Luke declared. "To Natasha and Ian, may you have a long and happy marriage."

"To Natasha and Ian," echoed the crowd.

"Congratulations," Luke said. He spoke loud enough for his voice to boom across the room as he shook Ian's hand. "Welcome to the family, Ian. If my daughter brings you half the happiness I found with her mother, you'll not regret this decision."

Luke stretched an arm around Ian before pulling Natasha into a group hug. Her father lowered his voice. "Thank you, Princess, for honouring my wishes." He slapped Ian on the back. "A word of advice, Natasha. I'm not blind. There's darkness in Ian's soul, the same ruthless ambition Stephen Spendor saw in me. Trust your instincts. Make your grandfather proud."

Her father stepped away, leaving Natasha puzzling over his comments. The numbness that deadened her emotions began to ease.

After Edith offered them her blessings and left, Ian signalled to a nearby couple. The man was of a similar age to her father. He had come to the ball dressed as a well-known American president. The much younger woman beside him wore a figure-hugging Marilyn Monroe costume.

"Natasha," Ian said, "may I introduce you to my father, Absalom Norris."

"It's a pleasure to finally meet you, Natasha," the portly, red-faced man said. "Please call me Abe. I've been following your career with interest. I look forward to getting to know you better."

Natasha inwardly cringed as he pressed in for a hug. His clammy hand caressed the bare skin on her back as he aimed an alcohol-laden kiss towards her lips.

"That's enough, Mister President," said the Marilyn-lookalike, pushing Ian's father aside. "You will have to excuse my husband, Natasha dear. He can't resist a pretty face, and when he's had too much to drink, he thinks he's irresistible. Abe, go and talk to Natasha's father before your son has to teach you some manners."

"This charming creature is Yolanda Sanderson-Norris," Ian said. "She holds the distinction of being my father's third wife."

Yolanda air-kissed both sides of Natasha's face. "Delighted, I'm sure."

The words lacked sincerity, and the expression in the woman's eyes was reminiscent of the spiteful girls Natasha remembered from boarding school. The stepmother turned to Ian, ruffling his hair with her red manicured nails. Her behaviour seemed more suitable for an older sister.

"I wish you'd stop introducing me like that, you naughty boy. You know your father can't afford to divorce me, so there'll be no fourth wife." Yolanda paused, glancing at Natasha. "I hope you're not marrying my charming stepson for his inheritance, Natasha dear, because there won't be one." Snatching Natasha's hand to examine the engagement ring, the woman spoke again. "Oh, that's right. I remember reading somewhere you've inherited money. That explains everything. Ian wouldn't tie himself to anyone for less than a million."

Yolanda pouted. "The wicked boy kept his relationship with you a secret. But it's not too late for you to give me the juicy details. Apart from your money, what did you do to capture his wandering eye?"

Ian smiled at his stepmother before pulling Natasha closer and running his fingers along her shoulder. He traced patterns on the skin above the bodice of her dress. "Natasha, don't fall for her tricks. She'll lure you in with hints about my past affairs to make you jealous, but half of what she says will be untrue. I'm trusting you to keep our secrets closely guarded. Anything you say to Yolanda will be embellished and spread all over town."

Natasha blinked in surprise at the expression that flashed across Yolanda's face. Ian's stepmother leaned in and gave Ian a lingering kiss.

Yolanda smirked as she brushed away a trace of red lipstick from his mouth. Natasha's stomach churned as she recoiled, revising her assessment. Definitely not a sister-brother relationship.

"Behave," Ian said to Yolanda. "Remember where we are and whose daughter you're insulting."

"It was a little harmless fun," Yolanda said as she smirked at Natasha. "Please forgive me for teasing you both, my dear. Perhaps I've had too much of your father's excellent French champagne. But Ian has to take his share of the blame for my indiscretions. The despicable tease can't announce a surprise fiancée and expect no mischief in return. That reminds me, Ian. Why wasn't Giselle invited? The poor girl will be so-o disappointed to have missed her only brother's engagement party."

Yolanda's expression switched to a calculating smile. "But at least my stepdaughter can console herself as a bridesmaid." She paused, surveying the room. "I don't see any other candidates, so perhaps Giselle will be the only one. Of course, she wouldn't be seen dead in that outrageous shade of pink."

Grabbing Natasha's skirt, Yolanda sneered at the handful of layers. "Who chose your costume? I hope you're not letting them anywhere near your wedding dress. I'll get my designer to send you some fabric swatches and sketches." Yolanda nodded as if that settled the matter. "Giselle is away at St Catherine's – someone said you're a St Catherine's girl, too? We have so-o much in common."

The woman paused, resting her hand on Ian's shoulder. "We must do lunch soon, Natasha."

After another round of air kisses, Yolanda darted across the room and disappeared among the crowd.

For the next hour, Natasha endured a constant stream of well-wishers without allowing her smile to fade. Apart from making the occasional token response, she left Ian to answer the guests. There was a sameness in the questions.

"When did you meet?"

"After Natasha entered the Spendor Corporation Graduate Program."

"Weren't you both at the same university?"

"I was preparing for my final exams when she arrived for her first semester. I admired her from afar, but she never attended any of the parties I went to."

"Did she fall in love with you at first sight?"

"That only happens in fairytales."

"But isn't this a fairytale?"

"More like a business merger." That answer always inspired a nervous laugh.

"When is the wedding?"

Ian grinned. "Tomorrow would not be soon enough..."

Nobody questioned Natasha's quietness.

Not every guest ventured across the ballroom to congratulate them. Jessica, Bertha and Landon watched the proceedings from a distance, and the rejected suitors sat in a drunken huddle near the refreshment table. Matthew Wallace stood near the main exit, his arms folded across his chest as he surveyed the room. Oleander had not shown his face in hours.

The conductor announced the final dance, inviting the "Happy Couple" onto the dance floor. Ian guided Natasha into the centre, draping her hands around his neck. The guests applauded, and the ever-present photographer voiced his satisfaction as his camera clicked and flashed.

"Your father's watching," Ian said, shuffling in time to the slow music with both arms around her waist. "He's expecting a performance. Try not to faint this time unless you want me carrying you upstairs in front of everyone."

"Wh— Mmm–grrwmm..."

Ian silenced her protests with a kiss. Natasha clung to him, battling the familiar dizziness.

29

Business

Psalm 100:5
For the LORD is good.
His loving kindness endures forever,
His faithfulness to all generations.

Smothering a yawn, Natasha glanced towards her father, who mingled with departing guests in the forecourt. One of the parking attendants drove up in a car, and another round of farewells began. Edith stood on the other side of Luke, smiling and nodding, the perfect hostess. Included in the conversation, Ian held Natasha captive at his side.

Smiling and nodding were draining, but Natasha clung to a glimmer of hope. If she could stay awake until the guests had left, she would ask her father about his remarks...

"Natasha's exhausted," Ian announced before the next car arrived. "I'm taking her upstairs to bed."

It seemed as if every eye flew to Natasha. Her cheeks flushed. But another yawn smothered her protest.

"Goodnight, Princess," Luke said, enfolding her in his embrace. "Don't worry about work tomorrow. I'll clear your schedule so you're fresh for the afternoon Directors' meeting." Her father released her into Ian's waiting arms. "Goodnight, Ian. I'll see you both in the morning."

While her feet propelled her towards the house under Ian's direction, Natasha's mind scrambled for a way out of this predicament. Halfway through the main entrance, Natasha grabbed the doorframe and called out to her father. "Ian's not—"

"Natasha," Luke said, frowning in her direction. "It's late, and your fiancé is ready to retire. Go. To. Bed!"

"Your father's made his expectations clear," Ian whispered. "Shall I carry you?"

Pulling from his embrace, Natasha raised her heavy skirts and ran for the stairs.

Ian laughed and gave chase, passing her on the third step. He leaned against the banister, barring her way.

"Why are you doing this?" Natasha asked, attempting to dodge past him. "You don't love me."

"Think of this as a mutually beneficial business deal, Nessie," Ian said, snagging her around the waist and lifting her into his arms. He resumed his ascent. "Your father's desperate to see you married for reasons he's promised to reveal tomorrow. I'm not sure I believe what he said about your mother. But whatever his motives, we all know you'll do anything to please him. In return, I'll enjoy the benefits of his patronage."

"I'm not marrying you."

"After tonight, you'll change your mind. I know you've been saving yourself for your future husband…"

Natasha flinched, and words flew from her mouth. "Who told you that?"

Ian chuckled. "I'm not going to reveal my sources."

The upward climb continued as Natasha considered that remark. Not even her father knew about the vow she'd made at Summerlands University. It had proven an effective shield against the temptations that had distracted Cassie from her studies and contributed to her death.

"One night won't change my mind," she said.

"I'm not trying to change your mind, Nessie," Ian said, "I'm giving you a choice. One night, and then I'll leave you alone if you tell your father to bring forward the wedding. If you don't agree, then I'll come back tomorrow night – and every *other* night until you're pregnant."

"Put me down. I'll scream—"

"I doubt that." Ian laughed, reaching the top of the stairs. "You've done nothing but surrender all evening. You're mine. There's nothing anyone can do to take you from me."

Stepping onto the spacious gallery, Ian turned towards Natasha's bedroom.

"That's far enough, Mister Norris."

Natasha spun her head. Wallace stood in their way.

"Please lower Ms Jacobson to the floor. My men have Tasers; I've authorised them to shoot if you don't comply."

"You wouldn't dare," Ian said, glancing over his shoulder. Two uniformed men blocked his retreat. "Natasha would also be zapped."

"That would be preferable to the abuse she's about to endure."

"You've misunderstood the situation," Ian said, stepping closer to the team leader and lowering his voice as if imparting a secret. "Natasha likes to play *games*. She's the 'unwilling virgin', and I'm the ardent lover who can't control himself."

"That's a lie," Natasha said.

"Ask her father," Ian said.

"I've already explained," Matthew said. "Luke Jacobson isn't the client I'm working for tonight. Release Ms Jacobson, and you can walk away without further inconvenience."

"Ian, put me down," Natasha said.

"If that's how you want to play this, sweetness." Shaking his head, Ian dumped Natasha onto the floor. "Wallace, I told you she likes to play games. If you won't talk to her father, ask the servants."

Matthew helped Natasha to her feet. She stood trembling at his side.

"Why should I talk to the servants?" Matthew asked.

"I had Luke warn the household staff," Ian said. "I didn't want anyone panicking if they heard her scream."

"What?" Natasha stared at Ian.

"I knew your father expected me to stay tonight, sweetness, and I didn't want him caught unawares by your bedroom games."

"You told my father..." Natasha covered her face with her hands. "He–he *believed* you?"

"Of course," Ian said, shaking his head. "You heard him say that you take after your mother."

"Go to your room, Ms Jacobson," Matthew said. "Norris won't bother you again tonight."

"I'm not leaving, Nessie," Ian said. "Luke assigned me the blue guestroom on the other side of the gallery. I'll leave the door unlocked and I'll be waiting."

The other guards followed Ian as he walked past her suite. At the end of the walkway, he turned the corner and opened the closest guestroom door. He blew a kiss towards Natasha before disappearing from view. The guards remained outside Ian's room.

Matthew opened Natasha's door.

"I took the liberty of asking Freeman to hide inside your suite," Matthew said. "After you retire, lock the door. If Norris returns, I doubt he'll make it past your bodyguard, but keep your phone beside your bed as extra insurance. I'll be removing my men from this floor, but they will take turns in the security hub until morning."

"Thank you. I'm sorry for the trouble."

"I should be apologising to you. I'm sorry your birthday celebrations were marred by this unpleasant business. I'll pray for you to have an undisturbed sleep."

The door closed behind Natasha. Greg Freeman rose from one of the sitting-room armchairs and waited in the middle of the room. He hadn't changed from his formal black trousers and white shirt, but his jacket and tie lay across a second chair.

"A fine mess you've landed yourself in, Queenie. Why did you go outside? When I saw you leave the house, I knew there'd be trouble. You were like Red Riding Hood wandering in the forest while the Big Bad Wolf licked his lips, preparing to eat you."

"If you knew Ian was the Big Bad Wolf, why didn't you come out and chase him away?"

"Oleander assured me you'd run away when the wolf started huffing and puffing. Why did you allow Norris close enough to pounce?"

"You've mixed up your fairytales," Natasha said. "Red Riding Hood's wolf doesn't huff and puff. And I wasn't wandering in the wolf's forest. I was in my father's garden in view of security cameras. I thought I was safe."

"You would have been safe if you'd stayed inside."

"Do we have to discuss this now?" Natasha asked, moving past him. She paused with the bedroom door open, rubbing her forehead.

"You've got one of your headaches?" Greg asked, closing the distance. He stared into her eyes, and she could not avert her gaze.

Natasha recognised something in his eyes that reminded her of Ian. She shivered as jumbled lines from Red Riding Hood's story popped into her head.

What big eyes you have?
All the better to eat you with, my dear…

If Ian was the Big Bad Wolf, what role did Greg envisage for himself? Was she safe, or was her stepbrother another dangerous beast?

Although Greg didn't touch Natasha, her every nerve screamed for her to barricade herself in her bedroom.

Retreating a short distance, Greg looked down at his feet as he shoved his hands into his jacket pockets. "I'm sorry. I shouldn't take my frustration out on you. I'm having trouble with my anger—"

"Your anger is justified. I acted foolishly."

"Oh, Natasha," Greg said, looking at her. "I'm not angry with you. I failed you when you needed me most."

"You're not failing me now." Natasha stepped into her bedroom. "Ian won't get past you if he comes back."

She shoved the door closed, leaning against it. Her heart raced as she thought about how the evening might have ended. If Ian had succeeded with his plan...

"You shouldn't need a guard outside your bedroom, Queenie." Greg's voice came through the door. "When Matt and Ollie ordered me here, I told them your father would never allow Norris to rob you of your innocence."

"My father doesn't believe I'm innocent. He thinks Ian and I are lovers."

"He what? I'll go and talk to Luke—"

"Please don't. I tried. He refused to listen." Sliding down the door to the floor, Natasha began to weep.

"Queenie, don't cry. You're breaking my heart." Greg's voice sounded as if he was also on the floor. Only the door separated them. "Oh God, I don't understand why this is happening, but Lord, I know You are a just God. Please help Natasha gain victory over her enemies...

30

Hopelessness

Every doubt Natasha had about whether she was safe with Greg evaporated as she listened to him petitioning God on her behalf. She rested her head against the door as his words soothed her wounded spirit.

Ten minutes later, she dried her eyes on the hem of her ballgown and struggled to her feet. "You can stop praying now. I'm going to try and get some sleep."

"Sweet dreams, Queenie."

Unable to respond without risking more tears, Natasha dragged herself to her dressing room.

After putting away her high heels, she removed her jewellery. Each piece had a special box. She was careful to store them correctly.

As she tugged the jewelled hairpins from her hair, she thought about Cassie's card and the dinosaur pendant she had left downstairs in the study. Shaking her head, Natasha raked her fingers through the twisted blonde tendrils to loosen them.

A few strands snagged on her mother's golden band. The sight of the diamonds on her wedding finger made her nauseous, but switching the ring to the other hand didn't help. The association with Ian's treachery was too strong. What was she to do with it?

Natasha wrenched the golden band from her hand and strode to the window. She reached for the catch and then hesitated.

Her father's assurance the diamonds belonged to her mother kept her from tossing the ring into the darkness. Storing it with her other jewels was not an option.

It was her father's house, and he'd send someone to retrieve it.

Pacing her room, Natasha dismissed a hundred hiding places. The dressing room seemed too obvious, and she didn't want the diamonds in her bedroom.

Entering the bathroom, she placed the ring on the marble ledge beside the basin. Perhaps a solution would come while she removed her makeup?

Opening a drawer, she collected the supplies she needed and arranged them in order along the bench. After tying her hair back from her face with an old blue ribbon, Natasha set to work.

When the task was complete, she frowned at her reflection, checking for any trace of her party face in the illuminated mirror. If only her problems were as easily erased?

Her smile had disappeared along with the makeup. What had Ian meant when he taunted her about her perfect smile? The hopelessness of her situation intensified her headache.

Would it be easier to obey her father's wishes? He wanted her to marry Ian. She should put the ring back on. Ian had promised to leave her alone if she agreed to marry him—

Natasha shuddered. Ian could not be trusted. He had convinced her father she liked violent fantasies – which revealed more about her tormentor's intentions. Ian expected her to scream.

Horrified, she dropped her head into her hands, and the ribbon fell into her lap. Retrieving the ribbon, Natasha undid the knot and dropped the blue satin onto the bench beside the ring. This simple action triggered two separate memories.

On a high shelf in Natasha's study, there was an antique porcelain doll wearing a blue dress. The doll had belonged to her grandmother, Esmeralda Spendor, and was stored in a glass case on a high shelf.

The second memory was from her boarding school days. One of the students had tied a ribbon around her neck to hide a ring under her uniform.

Threading her mother's ring onto the blue ribbon, Natasha tied a secure knot and looped the satin around her hand.

Crossing her dressing room, she entered her study, where she wrestled with her pink skirts to climb a stepladder. Balancing her bare feet on the top step, she opened the protective case and removed the doll.

After slipping the ribbon around the doll's neck, she tucked the ring inside the frilly dress.

When she returned the doll to the transparent case, Natasha frowned at the fingerprints on the glass.

Polishing the outside with her skirt, she cast a critical eye along the dusty shelf for other signs the case had moved. Satisfied, Natasha began her careful descent. Her full skirts made this simple task difficult, and she almost fell.

Safely on the floor, Natasha tugged at the offending dress. It was the last reminder of her disastrous evening. She twisted and contorted, holding her breath against the tightness of the stiffened bodice.

Not one of the tiny pearl buttons was within reach.

Running to her dressing room, she tried again in front of the full-length mirror. Nothing worked. How had she forgotten she needed Edith's help?

Frustrated, Natasha threw herself onto her bed, but the tight bodice made sleep impossible. She tossed and turned, tears pricking her eyes as she stared at the ceiling.

Snippets of conversation reached her from the sitting room.

Tiptoeing to the door, she pressed her ear against the painted surface. Only one voice? She couldn't make out what Greg was saying.

Cautiously, she opened the door and peered around the edge.

"What are you doing awake?" Greg asked, leaping from his armchair. He placed his smartphone face down on the coffee table.

Stepping into the room, Natasha gestured to her outfit. "I can't get out of my dress. I tried sleeping with it on, but I couldn't breathe."

Greg reached for his phone and tapped the screen. "I'll summon my mother—"

"No! My father will want to know why you're here. I'm supposed to be with Ian."

Greg's frown deepened. "Call Edith from your phone. I can hide."

"Can't you help me?" Natasha asked.

"I'm not sure that's a good idea."

"Please, Greg. I only need you to undo a few buttons."

Greg sighed. Natasha turned her back and held the front of her dress. He took a deep breath, and his hand brushed her bare skin. Natasha squeaked and leapt forward.

"This isn't going to work, Natasha. You're too nervous, and my fingers weren't made for tiny buttons."

"Try again." Natasha closed her eyes. "Please?"

Greg muttered under his breath, "God give me strength."

He tugged and pulled as his fingers wrestled with the first button. "That's one, Natasha. How many more?"

"I'll tell you when you've undone enough."

A few minutes later, he paused. "That's the top ten buttons. Are you sure you can't manage the rest yourself?"

"Close your eyes, and I'll check."

"Close my— Oh, God help me. Natasha, are you wearing anything under that dress?"

Natasha hesitated, glancing over her shoulder.

Greg faced the other way.

She wriggled and twisted, but the buttons evaded her fingers. "I'm still stuck."

"You didn't answer my question," Greg said, resuming his task.

"Ask me something else," Natasha said.

Silence reigned for several minutes as his fingers worked on the buttons.

"That's enough," Natasha finally said, wrapping her arms around the loosened bodice. She turned, backing towards the open bedroom door. "Thank you, Greg. I'll leave you in peace."

"You said I could ask you another question."

She stopped moving. "Okay."

"Why did you meet Ian in the garden?"

"I was expecting someone else."

"Who?"

"That's a second question. I'm tired, Greg. Can we talk about this in the morning?"

"I'm tired too, Natasha. I can't stop thinking about what happened. I need to know who you were expecting."

"Have you seen the message?"

"Oleander fished it out of the bin."

"Only four people knew 'timeliness' would trigger a reaction: Oleander, Goose, Amanda and you. Goose and Amanda weren't there"

"You thought you were meeting Oleander?"

"No," Natasha said. "Not Oleander. I was hoping it would be you."

Greg retreated a step. "Are you crazy? Why would I ask you to meet—"

His eyes widened, and he shook his head. "I don't believe this. You put yourself at risk because you thought..."

"I'm sorry." Natasha turned her head to hide her tears. "I wasn't thinking straight. The whole evening was horrible, and I – I needed a – fr-friend."

She disappeared into her bedroom and closed the door.

31

Earnestness

It seemed as if Natasha had barely closed her eyes when she heard someone calling her name. Torn from a terrifying nightmare, she lurched upright with the bedclothes clutched to her chin. The rational part of her mind declared she was safe in her bedroom. But her imagination refused to be silenced.

The sitting-room door was open.

Backlit by warm light, a monstrous silhouette loomed at the foot of her bed. The shadowy figure wielded a white light that flashed around the room. Natasha screamed, drawing the beam to her face.

"Natasha?"

The monster had stolen Greg's voice.

"Greg? Greg!" Natasha pulled the bedcovers over her head. "Turn off that light. You're blinding me."

The bright torch snapped off.

Natasha peeked out from behind the quilt. "What are you doing in my bedroom?"

"You screamed, and I was checking everything was okay. I didn't mean to wake you."

"I must have been dreaming. You can go. I'm fine."

Greg's silhouette retreated towards the door. "I'm sorry I disturbed you."

As he reached the threshold, Natasha's terror resurfaced. "Greg, wait. I'm not fine. I've had a terrible nightmare, and I can see monsters in the shadows. Please don't leave me alone. Come and sit beside me."

His figure paused in the doorway. "I can't, Natasha. Would you invite Ian into your bedroom to watch you sleep?"

"Of course not. Why are you comparing yourself to *him*? You're nothing like Ian."

Surely the earnestness of her declaration would reach him. "I know I can trust you."

"I'm not immune to temptation." He closed the door, leaving her alone with the darkness. "Goodnight."

Temptation? Natasha switched on the bedside lamp. Her reliable, trustworthy friend was tempted? Everything that had passed between them this evening took on new meaning. She groaned.

What must he think of her? Perhaps her behaviour had been so shameful, he couldn't stand to be anywhere near her? Was Greg still there?

Natasha threw herself out of bed, dragging the bedcovers with her. Wrapping her body inside the generous quilt, she staggered toward the closed door. Wrenching it open, the young woman stormed into her sitting room.

"Natasha, what are you doing?" Greg asked.

She choked back a sob, fighting the urge to drop to the floor and weep with relief.

Of course he was there. What was she thinking? Her mind scrambled for an excuse.

"I can't sleep, so I'm going to listen to music." Natasha wrestled with the quilt as she circumnavigated the coffee table.

Reaching the stereo, she flicked a switch. A lively classical concerto flooded the room. She sighed, increasing the volume until her body resonated with the music. She dropped onto an armchair and closed her eyes. "Pretend I'm not here."

After a few minutes, the music diminished. Natasha peeked through her lashes.

Greg stood beside the stereo with his arms crossed over his chest. "Are you trying to wake the whole house?"

"Humph!" Natasha wriggled to find a more comfortable position.

Returning to his sofa, Greg stared at her across the coffee table. "Tell me what's bothering you."

A desperate need to confess the fear that he'd abandoned her burned within, but a lifetime of secrets kept Natasha silent.

Reaching for his phone, Greg tapped the screen. "While you were sleeping, I've been praying and meditating on Scripture."

Natasha pulled the quilt over her head. Why was he tormenting her? Six years of attending daily chapel had done nothing to ease her inner turmoil. Neither had the Scriptures her friend Cassie had encouraged her to memorise.

"I'm not listening," she said. Yet she couldn't drown out the earnestness of his voice.

"'Cast all your burdens on Him, because He cares for you.' I've claimed that promise for both of us." *Click, click.* "And this one is perfect for tonight. 'You will not fear the terror of night… no harm will overtake you, no disaster will come near your tent.'"

Footsteps approached her. Natasha held her breath as Greg pulled the edge of the quilt from her face. "You said you trusted me, so prove it. Bring your pretty little head out of that 'tent', and start unburdening yourself." He dropped to the floor beside her chair.

"You make everything sound easy."

"I never said it would be easy," Greg said. "But I'm hoping you'll find the courage to go back to bed after you've talked about your fears."

With a sigh, Natasha nodded. She would tell him about the dream. "I've had the same nightmare before, and I don't know why it won't let me go."

"Start at the beginning. Perhaps the answer will become clearer."

"Cassie and I are walking along a darkened street. She's wearing her new party dress, the one she wore the night she died. The blue sequins catch the light, all shimmery and sparkling as the streetlamps flicker into life."

Natasha wriggled within the folds of her quilt. "I'm watching Cassie, aware it's a dream. I know she's dead, and nothing that's about to happen is real. Yet I'm still desperate, trying to persuade her to return to our apartment. I look back at the way we've come, certain someone is following us. The streets are empty. She laughs at my nervousness.

"I huddle inside my heavy winter coat. There's a wild storm coming, and I'm freezing. But the icy wind doesn't bother Cassie. She sings as she dances up the middle of the road in her skimpy dress. She's so alive. I reach for her hand, and she darts away. Everything turns black, and I'm falling. That's usually when I wake up."

"But not tonight?" Greg asked.

"I'm falling, and then Cassie grabs my hand. She pulls me back onto the pavement beside her, and we run through the city streets. 'Timeliness necessary,' Cassie says.

"I ask her what she means. Instead of answering me, she runs towards a huge castle on top of a hill. The castle looks like my dollhouse, but it's made from crystal instead of wood.

"As Cassie draws nearer, the shiny walls catch the reflections from her dress. The blue shimmering intensifies until it's brighter than the floodlights at a sports arena. I shield my eyes as I follow Cassie."

Natasha squinted at the memory. "Cassie doesn't hesitate, sprinting across the drawbridge and disappearing through the archway.

"I stare up at the towering castle walls. They're carved from a frozen glacier that stretches as far as I can see in both directions. I step onto the drawbridge, and it starts to lift. I run for the archway, slipping and sliding the last bit until I tumble into the castle. The drawbridge slams shut behind me, melting into the walls. I'm trapped in a tower.

"I hear Cassie calling me, but she's nowhere to be seen. Silvery-blue light dances within the icy walls, rippling like moonlight on the ocean. I run around the circular room, searching for a door. The temperature is dropping. My coat has vanished, and I'm shivering in the pink princess dress I wore this evening. Music begins to play, and the sparks within the wall spiral around me. I approach the translucent barrier, watching the lights as I stretch out my hand. From the outside, an arm reaches toward mine like a reflection in a mirror.

"Cassie! She's standing on the other side. I'm so pleased to see her. We remain there, our hands pressed against the wall, talking, laughing, and crying as we gaze at each other. Then a figure appears from the darkness behind Cassie."

Natasha took a deep breath. "I point to the man, and Cassie turns her head to look at him. She smiles, stepping away as she beckons me to follow her.

"I beat upon the icy walls, but she won't listen. She goes willingly into the shadows with him. I can't look away. When she falls to the ground at his feet, I know she's dead. The man laughs as he turns and walks towards me. I scream, and then I'm in my bed, and you're in my room."

32

Blackness

Natasha groaned. Why was sunlight shining on her face? Blackness flickered before her eyes. She pulled the pillows over her head.

"It's time to get up, Natasha," her stepmother said, snatching away the pillow.

"Edith? What time is it?"

"It's almost eleven. I've asked for your breakfast to be delivered to your suite."

"Eleven!" Natasha threw off the covers and dropped her feet to the floor. "Is Father waiting—"

"Luke and Ian left for the city hours ago."

"Ian?" Memories from the previous evening came crashing back. "Oh, no. What did Ian say... about... last night?"

"We'll talk later. You need to shower and dress. I want you wearing more than that negligee when Gregory returns with your breakfast."

"Gregory?"

Edith rested her hands on her hips, a disapproving look on her face. "How much champagne did you drink last night?"

"You know I don't dr—"

Edith opened a drawer in the bedside table and rummaged through the contents. "After hearing your father's revelations about your recent behaviour, I don't know you at all."

Bowing her head to hide her tears, Natasha asked, "What are you looking for?"

"A second stash." Edith searched the next drawer. "Your father's already confiscated the pills from your laptop case downstairs."

"What pills?"

"Little blue ones with a black stamp on them," Edith said.

"Blue pills? They're not mine!"

Natasha closed her eyes as another memory from her university days flashed into her mind. The police had discovered blue pills in the handbag beside Cassie's body.

The police believed Natasha's testimony that she had never seen them before. The blue pills were mentioned during the coronial inquest. The Coroner determined a cocktail of drugs and alcohol had contributed to Cassie's death.

"Ian's already confessed he saw you purchase them," Edith said, "so don't try to convince me of your innocence."

Staring at her stepmother, Natasha swiped at the tears rolling down her cheeks. The distraught young woman rushed to the bathroom, slamming the door behind her. She turned on the hot water in the shower and began her daily rituals to reorientate her mind.

Ten minutes later, Natasha sat before the dressing room mirror, pulling her hair into a severe bun. Her solemn reflection appeared unimpressed when she applied clear gloss instead of her trademark pink lipstick.

"Breakfast is here," Edith said, appearing in the doorway.

Natasha followed Edith through the bedroom into the sitting room. The aroma of freshly brewed coffee wafted towards her.

Greg smiled as he put down his mug and rose to his feet. "I hope you're hungry," he said, raising the cloche from a tray on the coffee table. "Mrs C sent up a mountain of pancakes with all your favourite toppings."

Waiting until Natasha had perched on the edge of a chair, Greg passed her a loaded plate and a fork. After confirming Edith had already eaten, Greg served himself. Returning to his seat, he bowed his head over his breakfast before dedicating himself to his meal.

Natasha's throat closed, and blackness flickered at the edge of her vision. Dropping her plate onto the table, she went to the coffee machine. Back in her chair, she wrapped both hands around the mug and stared at the dark brew.

"You've forgotten your smile this morning, Queenie," Greg said. "And you didn't add milk or sugar to your coffee. Is that headache still bothering you?"

"My headache is the least of my worries. Your mother searched my room for drugs."

Shovelling more pancakes into his mouth, Greg chewed while he stared at his mother. "You should have asked me first, Mum. I make a security sweep twice a day, and apart from two bottles of champagne someone left last night, there's not been anything to find."

"Your mother won't believe you. She's accepted Ian's lies and already passed judgement about the blackness of my soul." Natasha stood, abandoning the mug on the table. "I'm going to brush my teeth."

"Sit down, Natasha," Greg said, discarding his plate and striding around the table.

Natasha retreated from his frown, falling back onto her chair.

"You're not going anywhere," Greg said. "Not until you've eaten something. Pick up your plate and make a start, or I'll feed you."

Edith sprang upright. "Gregory Leonard Cross, stop bullying your sister!"

"It's Freeman, Mum. Free-MAN. I've already reminded you Natasha is NOT my sister. She pays me to look after her, and how I fulfil my duties is none of your concern."

"While you're living under this roof—"

"Don't say anything more," Greg said. "If you refuse to accept nothing happened between Natasha and me last night, start packing her bags. I've warned Luke I'll take her away if this house is no longer safe."

"Stop arguing!" Natasha cried.

Falling to his knees, Greg wrapped his arms around Natasha. "I'm sorry, Queenie. Please don't cry."

"Natasha dear," Edith said, appearing beside them. "It breaks my heart to see you like this. Running away from home won't bring you happiness."

"I don't want to run away," Natasha said, drying her tears with her black silk sleeve. "But I can't stay if you won't believe I'm telling the truth."

"Gregory, go back to your breakfast," Edith said, giving her son a gentle shove. "I'll sit with Natasha. Dear, you'll feel better once you've had something to eat."

After studying Natasha's face for a moment, Greg retreated to his side of the table.

"You don't have to sit with me, Edith," Natasha said. "I'll eat." She picked up her plate and moved the fork towards her mouth. "Perhaps you could get me a clean shirt? I've smeared makeup on this one."

"That's the other thing we need to talk about, Natasha," Greg said. "You've dressed for a funeral. Unless you've conceded defeat to your enemies, you should rethink your outfit."

"There's nothing wrong with my suit," Natasha said, glancing down at her tailored shirt and knee-length skirt.

"Black on black, with black stockings and shoes, and not a trace of that shocking pink you love."

"Is there anything else you don't like about my appearance?"

"Now that you've asked, you need to do something different with your hair. You've pulled it back even tighter than usual. No wonder your headache won't go away."

"I can't eat any more," Natasha said, rejecting her meal. Moving to the bedroom door, she beckoned to Edith. "Come with me. I need you to choose me something else to wear."

After Edith closed the dressing room door, she steered Natasha towards the chair in front of the dressing table. "I'll gather what we need while you take off that outfit and repair your makeup. You need waterproof mascara today. Gregory didn't mean to hurt you with his remarks, but something had to be said. Stop trying to blend in with the other executives."

Natasha blinked in surprise when Edith returned with pink fabric draped over her arm. "I can't wear—"

"Hush, Natasha. Trust me."

A few minutes later, Natasha studied her reflection in a full-length mirror. The pink dress came to her knees and featured a scooped neckline and three-quarter-length sleeves.

"I knew that dress would suit you," Edith said, looping a black leather belt around Natasha's waist and tightening it. "Those suits were sending the wrong message. You're a beautiful woman, and you shouldn't have to pretend otherwise to succeed in business."

Edith ran her nimble fingers through Natasha's blonde hair. "Stop fidgeting and pass me those hairpins. I've been longing to try a double Dutch crown braid. Sit still, and tell me about you and Gregory."

"There's no *me* and Gregory," Natasha said. "He spent last night on the sofa, and he was only there to keep Ian away. And before you ask, there's no me and Ian, either…"

The words flowed without restraint. By the time Natasha had finished unburdening herself about Ian's deception, the braided hairstyle was complete. Edith stared into the mirror, a troubled frown furrowing her brow. Natasha turned away, slipping her feet into a pair of medium pink heels.

"I'll get you a light jacket in case the afternoon turns cold," Edith said. "This tailored bolero will be perfect. Change those gold studs for the diamond drop earrings. Your father commissioned them to match your— Oh, you're not wearing your engagement ring!"

Natasha shook her head. "Oh, Edith, I thought you understood. There is no engagement. My mother's ring is safe, but I refuse to have it anywhere near me. I won't be bullied into marrying Ian." She snatched the pink jacket and fled.

33

Unnecessary

Natasha massaged her temples. She watched the traffic, an isolated passenger in the rear of her pink car. Greg was driving and Edith occupied the front passenger position. The car stopped at a red light four blocks from the Spendor Corporation Headquarters.

Greg drummed his fingers on the steering wheel. "Come on, come on. We've got fifteen minutes to get to that meeting."

"I'm sorry I've made us late, Gregory," Edith said for the umpteenth time. "I can't understand why Luke forgot to tell me about this meeting. Did Oleander say anything else? I've left Luke several messages, but he's yet to get back to me."

"Only that the Trustees called a special Shareholders' Meeting, and it was important for you to be there." Greg frowned at Natasha in the mirror as the lights changed. The car surged forward. "I didn't know you were a shareholder, Mum. I thought Stephen Spendor had his shares tied up so tight only the Directors were entitled to any."

"Are you sure Oleander told you I was a shareholder?" Edith asked. "A decade ago, I signed a document authorising Luke to manage my portfolio. He's always assured me my presence at meetings was unnecessary."

Natasha leaned forward, keeping silent as her heart raced. Edith was a Director? There was no mention of her stepmother's name on the Corporation website.

"You've been a secret Director for a decade?" Greg asked. "And Luke Jacobson has control of your vote? I can't believe you gave him that power—"

"It was a relief when Luke offered to take charge," Edith said. "I didn't know what to do when Stephen made provision for me in his estate. I'm a humble English and Drama teacher. I'm not qualified to be a Director. Luke assured me I was helping him secure Natasha's future."

"Natasha's future," Greg said, decelerating as the entrance to the underground parking garage came into view. "The same future where she marries a monster?"

"Please don't bring Ian into this conversation," Natasha said. "You're worrying your mother unnecessarily. It wouldn't matter if my father controlled dozens of proxies. All the major decisions have to be unanimous."

"It would matter if my mother is a dissenting vote," Greg said, driving past the security checkpoint and heading towards Natasha's designated parking space.

"We're out of time," Natasha said. "Please, Greg, could you say a quick prayer? Oleander's waiting near the elevators, and I'm not ready."

"Do you have a specific prayer request?"

"I've got a growing list. There's the argument you've just had with your mother – I hate seeing you both upset. Then there's my father and the fake engagement. I've got the shakes thinking about being in the same room with Ian. I could do without this unexpected summons..."

Oleander tapped on Edith's window and reached for the door. As he assisted Edith from the car, he was already opening the rear door. "Sorry to hurry you, Natasha, but the meeting can't start without you."

"You've heard Natasha's requests, Lord," Greg prayed aloud, exiting his side of the car. "I'll add amen to that. Please go with us into the lion's den."

"Amen," said Oleander, taking Natasha's arm and propelling her towards the elevator. "I'm sorry to rush you, Natasha, but the 'lions' were snarling when I left them. Some of the Directors didn't appreciate the abrupt summons from the Trustees."

"That's why Luke didn't tell me about the meeting," Edith said. "He's been preoccupied—"

"Don't forgive Luke too easily," Greg said. "Ollie, the Directors already had a lunch meeting scheduled for one-thirty, and they're the only shareholders. Why couldn't the Trustees wait?"

Oleander used his electronic card to access the executive elevator. "The revised agenda for the one-thirty meeting was sent out at nine. Landon called the Shareholders' Meeting half an hour later. Edith and Natasha could have arrived with time to spare, except their invitations never left the CEO's office."

"What kind of accusations are you making, Oleander?" Natasha asked when they were inside the elevator with the doors closed. The shiny metal walls seemed to press in on her, and her chest tightened. "You've worked for my father for decades. The Corporation always comes first."

As the express elevator ascended, Oleander shook his head. "I'm sorry, Natasha. There's no time to explain. But if you don't stand up to your father, an abusive relationship with Ian Norris will be the least of your problems."

Edith gasped, and Natasha took a step back.

Sadness tempered Oleander's smile. "I've loved you since before you were born, Natasha, and I'd do anything to spare you this pain, but you can't escape your destiny."

"Stop talking like this," Natasha said. "You're frightening me."

Edith embraced Natasha, and Greg placed a hand on the trembling young woman's shoulder.

"Do not let fear define you, Queenie," Greg whispered. "God has not given you a spirit of timidity. Instead, He has promised to prepare a table for you in the presence of your enemies."

"Listen to Freeman, Natasha," Oleander said. "Lean on him – if that gives you strength. Keep him close, and he'll watch your back. But you're the only one who can fight this battle. You're a talented, determined and hardworking businesswoman. Hold your head high when you walk from this elevator and don't let anything convince you that you don't belong here. I know you're ready."

"Ready for what?" Edith asked.

"Shh," said Oleander. "The elevator doors are about to open. It's time for Natasha's most convincing performance. She's already thrown off her middle-management disguise by wearing that stunning dress. Now she has to march into that meeting and convince everyone she was born to rule."

There was no time for Natasha to react to Oleander's remarks. The doors swished open to reveal a tall thin woman.

"Mrs Jacobson, Ms Jacobson! At last." The woman waved away the security guard as he stepped forward to intercept them.

The woman peered at Oleander over reading glasses perched on her long nose. "I was beginning to think James had led you astray. I'm Victoria Pepperwood. Please follow me."

Speaking rapidly, Victoria marched them across the foyer. Her sensible black pumps made a distinctive sound on the marble floor. "I'm the Executive Secretary to the Board of Trustees."

Natasha and Edith hurried to keep up with the Executive Secretary, with Oleander and Greg a few steps behind them. Victoria led them away from the Directors' Board Room and the other executive offices. They approached a pair of frosted glass doors Natasha had never passed through before. The Spendor Corporation crown-and-palace logo stretched across the panels in glistening gold paint. The automatic doors opened, revealing a generous wood-panelled reception area furnished with three desks and enough luxury chairs for an important delegation. The room was empty.

"Welcome to my domain," Victoria said, pausing before a portrait of Natasha's grandfather, smiling down at them from the wall. "For fifteen years, I had the privilege of serving as Executive Secretary to our late Chairman." She paused as if she had something important to say. Natasha held her breath.

A muffled shout floated across the reception room from behind a closed door to the right, bringing Victoria out of her reverie. "Alas, there's no time to reminisce. This way, the Shareholders' Meeting is in the smaller conference room."

When Victoria opened the door, every eye turned towards the new arrivals. The room fell silent.

"I must leave you," Victoria said, hurrying towards a long table in front of a wall of windows.

"Oleander!" Luke bellowed, striding to meet them. "What is the meaning of this unnecessary interruption? Natasha's meeting isn't until one-thirty."

Oleander bobbed his head in acknowledgment and backed away.

"Curse that man," Luke said. "I don't know why I keep him. He doesn't follow orders, and he never explains himself." He turned to Edith. "Why are you here?"

"I apologise for our tardy arrival," Edith said. "There was some miscommunication, and we didn't receive the summons from the Trustees until it was almost too late."

Natasha trembled as a dark look passed across her father's face. Mindful of Oleander's advice, she spoke before her courage abandoned her. "Good afternoon, Father. We're here now. Why don't we find a seat?"

"Happy Birthday, Princess," Luke said, wrapping Natasha in a quick embrace. After yesterday's party, it was a shock to be reminded that today was her actual birthday. He glanced at her bodyguard. "Freeman, there's no need for you to stay. Go downstairs, and I'll summon you when the afternoon meetings have concluded."

Withdrawing from her father's embrace, Natasha edged toward her bodyguard. "Freeman stays."

Her father ignored her.

"Freeman, I told you to go," Luke said, waving to where Ian stood with a group of men. "Natasha's fiancé is the only protection she needs."

One of Ian's companions grinned and whispered something into his ear. As Ian separated himself from the group, the other man slapped him on the back. Ian crossed the room with his eyes locked on Natasha. The grin on his face didn't waver.

From behind Natasha, Greg said, "No."

Burying the impulse to bow her head and submit, Natasha gazed into her father's eyes. "Freeman stays."

Luke inhaled sharply, his eyes darkening. Natasha braced herself for his heated response, but intervention came from an unexpected source.

"Luke Jacobson," Edith said. "This is neither the time nor the place for this discussion."

The look Luke bestowed on his wife alarmed Natasha, but Edith's smile didn't waver. "You're a good man, Luke, and there's no doubt you love your daughter more than life itself. But you're too accustomed to people bowing to you when you roar at them."

Luke blinked, his expression softening. "Always the peacemaker, Edith." He focused on Greg, and his dark eyes narrowed. "We'll talk later." Then his attention returned to Natasha. He leaned closer and lowered his voice. "I'll concede to your wishes, Princess, but there will. Be. Consequences."

Without waiting for a response, Luke took Edith's arm and led her away. He paused to talk to Ian, and Edith glanced back. After a brief conversation, Luke directed his wife to a seat in the front row. Ian continued towards Natasha.

As the gap diminished, Ian's wolfish gaze focused on Natasha's curves. She squirmed, checking for the closest exit. When there was only a metre between them, her bodyguard stepped forward.

"Stop there," Greg said.

Ian halted, studying Greg before addressing Natasha. "I've been eagerly anticipating our reunion, Nessie, and I see you've dressed for the occasion. Tell your bulldog to step aside so I can show you my appreciation."

"Don't come any closer," Natasha said. "I've told my 'bulldog' about the threats you made last night."

"I don't recall making any threats, Nessie," Ian said. "Only sweet promises I'm impatient to fulfil, but that pleasure will have to wait. The meeting is about to start. Come, your father has reserved you a seat in the front row where everyone can admire your beauty."

"You can sit with my father," Natasha said. "I'm staying here."

Turning away, Natasha dropped into a chair in the last row. Her knees were weak, and she was dizzy. From the corner of her eye, she could see Ian watching her. He waited for a few moments before rejoining her father.

Greg appeared beside her. "Round one to you, Queenie."

Closing her eyes, Natasha waited for her heart rate to settle. If that was only the opening salvo, she was in serious trouble.

34

Awareness

Psalm 112:4
Light dawns in the darkness for the upright,
gracious, merciful, and righteous.

Natasha surveyed the conference room. A rectangular table, covered with a red cloth, dominated the open space between the floor-to-ceiling windows and the rows of seats that would accommodate approximately fifty people. There were five chairs at the table, each equipped with a microphone. Landon Greenville occupied the central chair. He was talking quietly with Victoria Pepperwood. There was an open laptop in front of Victoria.

Leaving his chair, Landon approached a carved wooden lectern to the right of the table. It was embellished with the Spendor Corporation logo. He adjusted the microphone. "Ladies and gentlemen, please take your seats."

Conversations ended. The standing executives sought seats closer to the front. With more than enough chairs for the assembled shareholders, Natasha and Greg were the only ones in the back two rows.

Frowning, Natasha whispered, "I can't see Oleander?"

Scanning the throng, Greg replied, "There are more shareholders than I expected. There must be thirty people here."

"Most of them are the Directors' deputies."

"Thank you, ladies and gentlemen," Landon said, signalling to Victoria. The secretary aimed a controller at the ceiling. A massive digital screen descended, one corner coming to rest a few centimetres above Landon. Victoria tapped her keyboard, and the gold Spendor Corporation logo filled the screen.

"My name is Landon Greenville. As the Public Officer for the Stephen Spendor Trust, I welcome you to this Shareholders' Special Meeting. Before I introduce the other Trustees, Victoria will display the agenda."

A buzz of voices hummed within the room. Natasha sat straighter, every nerve alert.

"What?" Greg asked, looking around.

"The identities of the other Trustees have always been a closely-guarded secret."

The screen flickered, and printed text appeared. A long list of names appeared beneath the heading: The meeting attendees with their designated titles. Greg nudged Natasha.

"Look, there's your name," Greg said, "I didn't know you owned any shares."

"I—"

The screen blinked, and an additional name appeared at the end of the list: Gregory Freeman. Natasha looked at Landon. He nodded when she made eye contact with him.

"Item one on the Agenda," Landon said. "The Stephen Spendor Trust and the Trustees; relevant clauses from Stephen's Last Will and Testament..."

For the next few minutes, Landon read from his copy of the document without pause or explanation. Then he put down the paper, leaned upon the lectern and scanned the audience. "To summarise, Stephen appointed four Trustees, granting them authority to intervene in the governance of the Spendor Corporation, which includes all subsidiary companies, if and when key conditions are met."

Pausing, Landon retrieved the document from the podium. "I now invite my fellow Trustees to come forward." He returned to his chair at the table and adjusted the central microphone. "Bertha Doncaster, one of the founding Directors, and Jessica Becker-Tompkins, appointed as a Trustee a month ago to fill a vacancy."

The two women came from one end of the front row. Bertha and Jessica filled the two chairs beside Landon.

"The final Trustee is James Dubois."

A man in a grey suit entered through a side door. A ripple of awareness spread through the room as Oleander strolled towards the seat beside Victoria.

"What?" Luke leapt to his feet. "Oleander, I DEMAND an explanation."

"Please sit down, Luke," Landon said. "You will have an opportunity to address the meeting at the appropriate time."

Edith, beside Luke, pulled at his sleeve. The businessman sat as an excited murmur spread among the other executives.

Leaning closer to Greg, Natasha whispered, "I almost didn't recognise Oleander without his uniform. I can't believe he's James Dubois. I've seen that name in historical documents, but he disappeared from the public record while my mother was a teenager."

"I'm sure those 'historical documents' are fascinating," Greg said, "but don't miss the bigger picture. Oleander's a Trustee. That gives him more authority than your father."

"We will proceed to the next agenda item." Landon's amplified voice was louder than the speculation. "Item 2: A proposed amendment to the Spendor Corporation Constitution. This motion was scheduled for discussion at the meeting later this afternoon. The Trustees need this resolved before addressing the main item of business. I invite the Chief Executive Officer to the lectern."

Without hesitation, Luke strode forward.

Victoria handed Oleander a printed document, which he delivered to the lectern. Oleander and Luke faced each other, but neither spoke.

Fighting the urge to flee from the growing tension, Natasha grabbed Greg's arm. Her bodyguard glanced down at her white fingers before studying her face. He sought her hand and squeezed it. "Don't worry about Ollie. He deliberately created this scenario."

At the front, Oleander nodded to Luke before retracing his steps to the table.

Facing the audience, Natasha's father shrugged his shoulders. He glanced at the document before beginning his address. "The existing Constitution permits a maximum of twelve Shareholder-Directors. Last month, there were nine, but with Horatio Ironbark's recent death, that number has dropped to eight."

Pausing, Luke addressed the Trustees. "Landon, you mentioned Jessica was new to her role. I'm presuming Horatio was the Trustee she replaced. You acted without delay to restore your number because three Trustees did not fulfil your charter.

"I put to you that eight Directors are not enough for an expanding twenty-first-century corporation. We need new Directors, and the mechanism for appointing them is defective. That's why it's imperative to amend the Constitution."

Turning back to the audience, Luke continued. "Why are there only eight Directors? Under the Constitution, there are two pathways to being appointed as Director. An existing Director may pass on their shares as an inheritance. In recent years, four Directors have made such a bequest. In three cases, those beneficiaries, including Horatio's heirs, opted to surrender their shares in favour of a financial payout.

"Only Max, our newest Director, accepted his father's mantle. The other provision in the Constitution is for a Director to be appointed by the Chairperson. Regrettably, under the same Constitution, the Chairperson's powers belong exclusively to the Majority Shareholder. The Trust controls eighty-four per cent of the issued shares but you've heard Landon outline the Trust's responsibilities."

Taking a breath, Luke shook his head at the Trustees. "The Chairperson's role is not one of them." The CEO dropped his shoulders, lowering his voice as if making a heartfelt confession to a few favoured confidants. "When Landon nominated me as Acting Chair, I didn't foresee the problems that would come because I lacked the authority to appoint Directors..."

"The amendment's on the screen," Natasha whispered.

"I move the following motion," Luke declared. "To amend the Constitution to allow Directors, in the absence of the Chairperson, to nominate candidates for a vacant Director position on the Board, at a General Meeting, and for the decision to be decided by majority vote."

"Who seconds the motion?" Landon asked.

"I second the motion," the newest Director said, raising his hand. The middle-aged businessman had been the only Director absent from Natasha's party yesterday.

"The motion has been moved and seconded," Landon said. "I invite a response from the floor."

"Can the deputies speak?" someone asked.

When Landon gave permission, Luke moved sideways, and that deputy hurried to the lectern. The young man delivered an impassioned speech lauding the excellent qualities of the CEO and the wisdom of his proposal. No sooner had the man finished than another deputy also availed himself of a similar opportunity.

"Yes–men," Greg muttered.

"My father's proposal is not without merit," Natasha said.

Absalom Norris, Ian's father, spoke next. He acknowledged the other speakers and then launched into a lengthy complaint about the increasing workload for the remaining Directors. He insisted there were worthy candidates among the gathered deputies. Some of the younger audience members shouted their agreement.

When order was restored, Jessica raised her hand.

"Landon," Jessica said, "I would like to move an amendment to the motion. I propose the decision be determined by secret ballot."

"I'll second that motion," Bertha said.

"I put Jessica's amendment to the vote," Landon said. "Only Directors are eligible to vote. Those in favour of amending the motion, raise your hand."

Holding her breath, Natasha fastened her eyes on the Trustees. All four hands went up. She glanced towards Edith in time to see her stepmother's hand rise. Luke frowned at his wife before raising his hand. The remaining Directors followed his example.

"Eight votes," Landon said. "The amendment is carried. Now we will vote on the amended motion..."

A few moments later, a unanimous vote approved Luke's amended change to the Constitution.

"What's happening?" Greg asked Natasha. "I thought the Trustees were trying to limit your father's power?"

"If Edith hadn't been here, my father's supporters would have voted against the amendment," Natasha said, awareness awakening. "In a tied decision, the Acting Chair gets the casting vote. A secret ballot was important because it makes it possible to vote against my father without fear of retribution."

35

Calmness

"Moving on to the next item of business," Landon said. "Nominations for the position of Director. I converted the email list Luke circulated into a ballot slip. While James distributes the voting papers, Victoria will publish the list of nominees on the screen. Directors will vote for five candidates. The four candidates with the highest votes will become Directors. The first runner-up will be the reserve..."

The screen flashed, and as Natasha read the first name, the colour drained from her face. Her father had nominated Ian Norris. Maximilian Romonovski the Fourth had seconded the nomination.

"I will call the nominees to the lectern to make a brief address," Landon said. "Ian Norris, you're first..."

Closing her eyes, the last vestige of calmness abandoned Natasha. "I think I'm going to be sick."

"Take some deep breaths," Greg said. "I'll get you a drink from the water cooler behind us." He was back in moments, and she grasped the cardboard cup with trembling hands. Greg dragged his chair closer. "You've been preparing for this moment since you were born."

"What?"

He nodded towards the screen. "It's no secret your father wants you to be a Director."

Running her eyes down the list, Natasha came to the tenth and final nomination. She blinked at her name. Absalom Norris had nominated her and the seconder was Maximilian.

"I'm praying for you," Greg said. "Try to reclaim your legendary calmness before it's your turn to speak. I don't think you've got any reason to worry. Your father must be confident you'll be elected, or he would have put your name higher on the list."

"I'm not ready—"

"You keep saying that. Would you rather have Norris take your place?"

"No!" Natasha's cry echoed across the now silent room. Everyone stared at her. Ian scowled from the lectern.

"Be quiet, Natasha," Luke called from his seat, before

sending Edith to the back row.

"Please continue, Ian," Landon said. "Before the unfortunate interruption, you were expressing your gratitude for Luke Jacobson's mentorship and looking forward to becoming his son-in-law."

"I must apologise for my fiancée's thoughtlessness," Ian said to Landon. "I can assure you, under ordinary circumstances, Sweet Nessie is renowned for her calmness. This rashness has been in evidence since the recent kidnapping." He paused and shook his head. "The timeliness of this illness is regrettable. I hope the Directors will excuse this temporary weakness and not let it affect their judgement about her fitness for promotion..."

Dark thoughts flooded Natasha's mind.

"Let it go, Queenie," Greg said, wrapping his arms around Natasha to keep her on her chair. "You'll get your chance to respond, but if you can't control that anger, you'll only give power to his lies."

"Listen to my son," whispered Edith, adding her arms to the huddle. "Please don't let anything Ian says ruin your chances. I know how hard you've been working, and I'm confident you can prove him wrong."

While the other nominees for promotion came to the lectern, Greg and Edith continued encouraging Natasha.

"And now," Landon said, "it is time to hear from the final nominee, Natasha Jacobson."

With Greg on one side and Edith on the other, Natasha took a route that kept her far from her father.

"God, give Natasha the words she needs to vindicate her right to be here," Greg said as they reached the front.

Edith and Greg sat in the chairs Jessica and Bertha had vacated earlier. Oleander nodded as Natasha walked through the gap between the Trustees' table and the lectern. She didn't glance toward the seven male and two female candidates who waited on the far side.

"Thank you, Mister Greenville," Natasha said. "I must confess I was surprised by this nomination. I apologise to Mister Norris for the unintended interruption."

Pausing to scan the room, Natasha checked her smile was in place. "To quote Shakespeare: 'What's in a name?' I cannot deny doors open when people discover I am Luke Jacobson's daughter, but I've been careful which opportunities I've embraced. I've had aspirations to follow my father into business since childhood, but there's more to me than my family connections."

Another pause to smile at her father. "I'm clever and ambitious. I'm financially independent, starting my first company when I was fourteen. I have multiple degrees and I've served as an intern across every division."

Moving from the lectern, Natasha put her hands on her hips and posed like a fashion model. Back at the microphone, she made eye contact with those seated near her father. "Appearances can be deceiving. I'm not a 'ditsy blonde' who spends other people's money, nor am I a party girl. The Sisters at St Catherine's Academy taught me well. I'll leave you with a quote I learned from Sister Mary-Thomas. 'Charm is deceitful, and beauty is vain, but a woman who fears God is to be praised. Give her a share in the fruit of her hands, and let her works praise her at the city gates.'"

After nodding to Landon, Natasha directed her eyes towards Greg as she joined the other nominees. The voting process was swift. Oleander circulated among the Directors with the ballot papers, returning to collect them in a sealed box. Victoria collated the results and then swung her laptop towards Landon.

"The following nominees are elected," Landon said. "Natasha Jacobson, eight votes, a unanimous decision..."

Applause broke out across the room. Natasha struggled to hide her emotions. She blinked away tears, unable to concentrate on the rest of Landon's announcement. When her vision cleared, only the other three new Directors remained beside her. Ian was not among them.

The tally of votes was on the screen, Natasha's name at the top. Only three votes were recorded for Ian.

"...commiserations to the unsuccessful candidates," Landon said before he dismissed the new Directors.

Shaking her head when her father beckoned her to sit with him, Natasha headed towards the back row.

She was halfway down the aisle when Landon spoke again. "There remains one item on the agenda."

A collective gasp arose from the shareholders. Spinning around, Natasha stared at the large screen: "New Chairperson."

Luke was almost to the Trustees' table when Oleander intercepted him. The room fell silent. Whatever transpired in the muttered conversation between the men was brief. When Luke returned to his seat, Ian leaned across to him and asked, "What's going on?"

Luke shook his head, folding his arms across his chest and glaring at the Trustees. "We'll find out soon enough."

"Thank you, ladies and gentlemen," Landon said. He nodded to Victoria, and lines of text appeared on the screen as he spoke. "This is another section from Stephen Spendor's Last Will and Testament. '...When the aforementioned conditions have been met, the Trustees will call a Shareholders' Special Meeting and make the following announcement: I, Stephen Spendor, bequeath my share portfolio, with the full responsibilities as Majority Shareholder, to my granddaughter, Natasha Stephanie Spendor Jacobson...'"

36

Hugeness

Lamentations 3:22b-23
His mercies don't fail.
They are new every morning.
Great is Your faithfulness.

"Oh, Grandfather." Natasha's voice faltered as the hugeness of Landon's statement exploded in her mind.

The scowl on Ian's face transformed into a look of triumph. He leapt up and rushed towards her. Adrenalin surged through Natasha's body, activating a desire to escape – to run and keep running.

Greg propelled Natasha away from the conference-room uproar. Loud voices diminished as a door closed and another opened. Her bodyguard stopped urging her forward yet his arms remained around her. It was a few moments before

Natasha could make sense of his words. Greg was praying aloud.

"Mighty Redeemer and Defender, You know all things, understand all things, have victory over all things. Nothing ever takes You by surprise…"

The comfort Natasha had experienced when Greg prayed over her in the early morning returned.

"You have already defeated the plans of her enemies. There's nothing they can do to steal Natasha's inheritance. Open her eyes. Help her to understand that You have been preparing her for this opportunity. She needs Your reassurance because she doesn't understand the length, and depth, and breadth of the blessings You have bestowed on her. Show Natasha how safe and secure she is in Your presence. Help me to convince Natasha she is Your precious child…"

Taking a deep breath, Natasha pushed herself free from Greg's embrace and away from his whispered prayers. But physical distance didn't quieten the confusion inside her.

Greg spoke as if her future was secure, so why could she foresee nothing but trouble?

What did he mean by saying she was a child of God? Wasn't it bad enough that both her father and her grandfather had put impossible expectations upon her? What would God demand?

Pacing the room, Natasha surveyed her new surroundings. The door leading to the outer office was locked. The silhouette of a guard was visible through the frosted glass panel beside this exit. Natasha crossed to what must be the conference-room door. It was also locked.

The furnishings seemed familiar, yet she was sure she had never been in this office. Taking in the paintings on the wall, Natasha stopped in front of another portrait of her grandfather. In it, he was seated behind the same desk that dominated this room.

This sanctuary was her grandfather's executive office. While she processed that revelation, there came a quiet knock. Greg went to the outer door, listening for a moment before he opened it wide enough for Edith to slip inside. He shoved the door shut and relocked it, and his mother glanced across at Natasha.

"Gregory, I don't understand what's happening," Edith said. "Did either of you know Natasha was about to inherit everything?"

"No," Greg said. "Ollie probably thought it was safer that way."

"Safer?" Edith asked.

"You saw the reaction. This inheritance gives Natasha incredible power."

"What kind of power?" Edith asked.

"As Majority Shareholder," Natasha said, resuming her pacing, "I could disband the Board of Directors and start afresh."

"But you won't, Queenie," Greg said. "You'll keep your enemies close so you can watch them."

"What enemies?" Edith asked. "The loyalty of everyone on the Board is beyond question."

"Don't be so sure," Greg said. "Ian Norris's motives are questionable, and Luke's involvement in the fake engagement makes him suspect."

"Luke hasn't had an opportunity to respond to those allegations," Edith said. "There's sure to be a logical explanation."

"You were there when Luke told everyone Natasha was emotionally unstable," Greg said. "It doesn't matter whether he was conned by Norris or if he's part of the conspiracy—"

"Why are you talking about a conspiracy?" Edith said. "Natasha was elected unopposed."

"I know," Greg said. "I think the plan was to make Norris and Natasha Directors. Then Norris could fulfil his threats, leaving Natasha too traumatised to attend meetings, effectively handing him control of her vote."

"Her father would never—"

"Norris boasted he had Luke's approval," Greg said. "They weren't expecting the Trustees to get involved in the election. Norris missed his opportunity, but I don't think he'll give up. He'll be even more determined to marry her now."

"Oh," said Edith, dropping onto a chair. "Oh, no."

"What?" Greg asked.

"I overheard Ian and Luke discussing an insurance policy. I didn't think anything of it until now. After breakfast, I witnessed a document Luke and Ian signed. It was a pre-nuptial agreement empowering Ian to act on Natasha's behalf if anything happened to her..."

"Natasha is not marrying Norris," Greg said.

His declaration sent a tingling through Natasha from the tips of her toes to the top of her head.

"She doesn't have to," Edith said. "They made provision should an accident or illness prevent the marriage from taking place."

Edith's words unsettled Natasha's stomach. Striding to the desk, the heiress sat in her grandfather's chair. Bowing her head, she used the intense emotions to drive away every doubt and fear. When she reopened her eyes, she gazed across the desk. "Greg, see if the guard in the outer office is someone we trust. If you know him, invite him in."

Greg crossed to the door and disappeared outside. Natasha waited until the door closed before raising her eyes to the ceiling.

"Okay, God," Natasha said. "This might be foolishness, but I'm ready to believe You chose me for this role. I have a plan, but we both know the mess I got myself into last night. I'm sorry it's taken me so long to ask for Your help. Please stop me if this is another mistake."

Smiling at Edith, Natasha chose one of her grandfather's pens. "Right, let's see if this pen works. If it doesn't, that will mean 'No'."

"I don't think that's how God works—" Edith began.

"Shh!"

Selecting a notepad, Natasha tested the pen. The rich blue ink left a satisfying mark. She waved the pen towards the ceiling. "Thanks. Now help me with the right words."

Opening a drawer, she found paper bearing the Spendor Corporation letterhead. She stared at her name beneath the logo for a moment, and then she began to write.

Greg returned with a guard Natasha had met yesterday. After confirming the newcomer understood the need for secrecy, Natasha invited them to sit as she continued with her document. When the task was complete, she smiled at her witnesses.

"First, Greg, I expect no argument. This is a temporary measure. I know enough about inheritance law to draft the basics. 'I, Natasha Stephanie Spendor Jacobson, bequeath all my worldly possessions to Gregory Leonard Freeman. If Gregory Freeman does not survive me, then my estate will be distributed...'"

After Natasha signed the document, she invited Edith and the guard to witness it. Natasha went to the scanner in the corner and made four copies. When she returned to her desk, Greg presented her with a similar document. Natasha raised an eyebrow.

"If they come after you, Natasha," Greg said, "I'll be with you. My previous Will left everything to Mum, so I've changed it. I'm hoping they won't go after Goose and Amanda before Matt Wallace gets them the protection they need."

While Greg copied his document, Natasha addressed three envelopes: one to Matthew Wallace, as the head of Sentinel City Security; one to her corporate lawyer at her company, NASSJA Enterprises; and one to Landon Greenville, as the Stephen Spendor Trustee. She passed the remaining envelope to Greg.

"Send a copy to someone you trust."

Greg wrote on his envelope.

Gathering the four envelopes and stuffing each one with copies of the two documents, Natasha spoke to the guard. "I've summoned a courier. When they arrive, escort them from the floor before you hand over these letters."

"Is that precaution necessary?" Edith asked.

"This is our insurance," Greg said. "I can't tell you what to do, Mum, but I'd appreciate it if you didn't tell anyone about the letters until they've been delivered.

37

Unpleasantness

Isaiah 35:1
The wilderness and the dry land will be glad.
The desert will rejoice and blossom like a rose.

The phone on Stephen Spendor's desk rang. Natasha stared at it, unwilling to deal with further unpleasantness.

Greg snatched the receiver, listened for a moment and then hung up. "That was Ollie. They're waiting for you to join them for lunch. We'll go through the outer office."

Edith led the way to the largest of the executive meeting rooms. Natasha followed close behind, with Greg at her side. When they entered the room, Landon appeared before Natasha.

"Congratulations and welcome, Natasha. As the Chairperson, it is your prerogative to be served first."

A moment of panic awakened. The clock on the wall proclaimed the lateness of the hour. It was almost two o'clock. Keeping everyone waiting for lunch was not an ideal start to Natasha's first official duty.

Landon seemed unconcerned. He gestured to a team of wait staff standing behind a side table draped with white linen. Steam rose from the covered, stainless-steel trays spread along the table. A waiter in his pristine uniform stood to attention, ready to pass Natasha a gold-rimmed black plate.

A path through the executives opened for Natasha. After checking Greg was behind her, she stepped forward. No sooner had she advanced into the opening than the crowd closed the gap behind them, pressing in like the waves of a surging tide.

A flash of memory transported Natasha to the St Catherine's Academy dining hall. One of the earliest lessons impressed upon new students was the timeliness of meals. How often had she endured tense unpleasantness because someone else was late? The Headmistress refused to begin the formal mealtime prayers before everyone was present. Natasha's heart pounded as she glanced around the room.

Her father's expression was not dissimilar to the Headmistress's stern disapproval.

You're ruining everything, her critical inner voice began.

"What are you waiting for?" Greg murmured.

"For you to say the blessing, Freeman," Natasha said.

Greg stiffened, and then he shrugged. "You're the boss." He raised his voice. "Dear Heavenly Father, Gracious Provider and Sustainer of Life. We thank You for Your bountiful provision. Your Word says You furnish a banquet table in the presence of our enemies. May these executives eat together as friends so they can enjoy the blessings of health and security. We ask these things in Jesus' name, Amen."

"Amen," said Natasha, opening her eyes.

When the server offered Natasha the heated plate, she handed it to Greg. "You'll eat with us, Freeman."

The waiter provided Natasha with a replacement plate. None of the other executives moved toward the buffet table. Together the new Chairperson and her bodyguard walked along the serving line.

Accepting the smallest portion of each offering, Natasha encouraged the servers to pile Greg's plate high with roast meat and vegetables. When she reached the end of the buffet selection, Landon was there to usher them towards the polished table dominating the room. Natasha paused to admire the cityscape through the floor-to-ceiling windows.

When Natasha rested her plate on the placemat at the head of the table, Landon pulled out her grandfather's wing-backed chair.

As soon as Natasha was seated, everyone began to applaud. That was the signal for the others to queue for food. Natasha watched the proceedings. The Directors went first, in order of seniority, except for Edith. Her stepmother stood with Luke near the front of the line. After the Directors came Hamish Baxter, her father's PA, then Victoria and Hilary, the Minutes Secretary.

The deputies brought up the rear, seeming to favour a less formal approach, pushing and shoving to claim their place. Natasha matched their faces to the names in her memory. As service continued, some of the waiters disappeared through a side door to replenish the food supplies.

"Eat," Greg said from behind Natasha. He remained standing as he devoured his food.

After loading her fork, Natasha glanced at her bodyguard. His plate was almost empty. Uncomfortable under his gaze, she surveyed the seating arrangements. Her chair was in the centre with Victoria on her left and Hilary on her right. At the opposite end, there were four chairs. Luke, Edith and Oleander were joined by Hamish, her father's PA.

"Why are you standing?" Natasha asked Greg. "There's room for another chair."

"I prefer to stand," Greg said, waving his fork. "You said I'm more intimidating on my feet, and I'm not averse to using my cutlery to make you eat."

"There's no need for your bodyguard to remain," Luke said. The Boardroom acoustics carried his command to the far corners of the room.

Every conversation ceased. Natasha tightened her grip on her cutlery. Only a lifetime of guarding her tongue prevented a sharp rebuttal.

"A gentle answer turns away wrath," Greg said under his breath.

Natasha recognised the quote. She smiled, bringing her loaded fork to her mouth as she nodded to her father as an invitation for him to continue. Silently she prayed she wouldn't choke.

Luke picked up a lapel mike from the table and attached it to his collar. His amplified voice continued. "Matters of security come under Oleander's portfolio. His presence is more than adequate to cater for your *many* insecurities."

Natasha glanced to Oleander, who gestured towards the open laptop before him. Natasha set aside her plate, reaching for the laptop near her placemat. When Luke leaned forward and frowned at his computer, the other Directors also studied their screens.

The electronic document in front of Natasha was the agenda for the upcoming meeting. It included an annotated diagram matching the attendees to their seat assignments. The recently elected Directors' names had not yet been updated from their deputy positions. As Natasha watched, a yellow highlighter swept across one name: Gregory Freeman, deputy to James (Oleander) Dubois.

She checked the appointment date: the day after the last executive meeting. Confirmation of his appointment was one of the agenda items. Clicking on Greg's name, Natasha smiled. Oleander had thought of everything. There were reports, including subsidiary company share purchases, to support the claim he'd been active in the position for a week. Natasha clicked back to the main document.

"This is a day for surprises," Natasha said to Greg.

Pointing to the vacant position around the corner from Victoria, Natasha issued an order. "Freeman, that's your chair."

Greg stiffened, and for an instant, Natasha feared he would defy her. It was a relief when she sensed him moving from behind her. When Greg settled in the designated seat, Victoria leaned toward him. Greg opened the laptop before him and focused on the screen.

Clipping her lapel mike to the neckline of her dress, Natasha addressed the opposite end of the table. "Father, I am grateful for Oleander's foresight. I didn't want to begin my first Directors' meeting with unpleasantness between us. I'll need your guidance as I take over the reins of my grandfather's companies. However, I reserve the right to disagree with you when the occasion demands it."

The final deputy settled in his chair. Natasha checked the buffet table. The servers were collecting their trays and preparing to exit the room. The other executives cast glances towards her as they ate. Only the Directors wore lapel mikes, but there were cordless microphones on the table within reach of every deputy.

A flashing icon appeared on Natasha's computer screen. It was a message from Victoria:

> This is our private chat.
>
> Any questions? Just ask.
>
> Open the meeting when you are ready.

Natasha typed a quick response:

> Thanks

Laying aside her cutlery, Natasha reached for the glass of water beside her plate. Another chat window popped up.

The banner at the top identified the new sender as Greg. Natasha resisted the urge to look at him as she read it:

Don't forget to pray.

Smiling over the rim of the glass, Natasha took a sip and then replaced the tumbler. It was time to begin her first official address as Chair.

"Ladies and gentlemen, fellow Directors and Deputies, welcome to today's meeting."

Natasha moved her eyes around the table to include everyone, although she passed over Ian with haste. If Greg had been referencing that predatory expression when he described Ian as the Big Bad Wolf, then her enemy's hunger had grown.

Pushing that dread towards a tiny bubble of peace that remained after her conversation with God in her grandfather's office, Natasha fortified her smile. She projected calmness as she continued.

"I'm mindful the task my grandfather, Stephen Spendor, has set me surpasses anything I would have chosen for myself. My father, Luke Jacobson, is correct. I have 'many insecurities', and taking charge of the Spendor Corporation is an immense responsibility. But I'm also aware of the timeliness of this appointment. I may appear young and inexperienced, but I can assure you I am not ill-prepared."

38

Newness

Pausing in the middle of her welcoming speech, Natasha folded her hands on the table. "My grandfather told me never to start anything without the necessary resources to complete the task. He set up the governance for his business empire before entrusting the maintenance of his legacy to each of you. It will be an honour to serve alongside you."

That would be the perfect place to end her speech, but Natasha's heart thumped with an urgency she couldn't ignore. She closed her eyes for a moment, but Greg's reminder to pray was there, like a pop-up message behind her eyelids.

Perhaps the newness of her situation inspired her boldness? "A dear school friend once said God gave me many gifts, but timidness was not among them. If I am to succeed as the head of the Spendor Corporation, I cannot forget I owe what little strength I have to God. That is why I intend to open every meeting with a short prayer."

A murmur ran around the table. Natasha caught a look of surprise on Greg's face. Bowing her head against the distractions, she silently asked God to keep her from fumbling this opportunity. A warm sensation began in the middle of her chest, and words danced across her mind. Natasha chased after them, speaking them into life.

"Our Father in Heaven, we humbly come before You. Please hear our prayers. Forgive us for our pride and selfishness. Absolve us from past mistakes, and teach us to forgive those who have offended us."

Pausing, Natasha silently acknowledged the hurts she still clung to. "Keep us from causing harm within the relationships among us, and prevent us from perpetuating evil in the businesses we manage. We ask for Your peace. Please mediate our discussions."

A gentle tapping on the keyboard beside her confirmed Hilary was typing this prayer into the meeting minutes. Natasha risked a peep at her father and her eyelids snapped shut to block out his disapproval. The next sentences poured out in a rush. "Help us make wise decisions. May we pursue justice, mercy and compassion instead of chasing self-serving ambition."

Taking a breath, Natasha regained control. "We ask for increased productivity – not because we want more money – but for the people who depend on our financial success for their livelihood. Help us to appreciate what we already have and show us how to put our resources to good use."

The inspiration ceased abruptly. Natasha could remember only one formal prayer ending. "I ask these things in the name of the Father, in the name of the Son, and in the name of the Holy Ghost, Amen."

A couple of Amens floated upward from around the table. Natasha reached for her laptop. "Next, we need to confirm the minutes for the last meeting. Please familiarise yourselves with that document..."

Everything progressed predictably until the Business Arising agenda item: Appointing New Directors. Landon was first to speak, tabling the election results from the Shareholders' Special Meeting. His motion to accept the results was received without discussion.

Luke raised his hand for permission to speak. Natasha nodded.

"It is not for me," Luke began, "to question why the Trustees allowed Natasha to be elected as a Director when they knew she was about to become the Chairperson."

Pausing, Luke aimed a dark look toward each of the Trustees. "Her ascendency has created a new Director vacancy. I invite Natasha to invoke her authority and appoint her fiancé—"

Natasha's stomach cramped, and she clutched the edge of the table.

"No."

The word was out before she could stop it. She stumbled to her feet, drawing every eye back to her. "I'm sorry to interrupt you, Father. I will not appoint Ian as a Director. There was a fair election, and he didn't win enough votes. A reserve was elected, and it's only fair to give them the position."

"What about your obligation to your fiancé?" Absalom Norris demanded. "Is it *fair* to deny my son a Directorship over something as *inconsequential* as a lover's TIFF?"

"This is not an appropriate forum for this discussion," Natasha said, addressing Ian's father. When Absalom opened his mouth to respond, she held up her hand. "Stop!"

Restless energy hovered over the table. Whatever Natasha said next would have serious ramifications. She sighed, moderating her voice. "I said I did not want to discuss this, yet you refuse to let the matter drop. I expect you to take full responsibility for the consequences."

Addressing her father, Natasha asked, "Have I understood my constitutional powers correctly? As Majority Shareholder, it is my right to make Board appointments without requiring a vote?"

"Yes," Luke said. "But—"

"Thank you, Father," Natasha said, turning to Absalom. "*Director* Norris, you seem to be under the impression someone promised Ian a Directorship. If that is correct, the promise was not mine. If you cannot accept your son will not become a Director today, I *invite* you to tender your resignation."

Absalom pushed back his chair, but Ian's hand pressed on his shoulder, keeping the incensed Director in place. Whatever his son said to him had a dramatic impact. The anger drained away, replaced by a cunning smile. Absalom spread his palms upward, his eyes lingering on each Director before he answered Natasha.

"Madam Chair, it's regrettable you have misunderstood my concerns. I was only doing what any father would do, speaking from the heart on behalf of my son. It's understandable you deem it necessary to honour the election results. As Ian has reminded me, some concession must be made for your newness to a position of power. For that reason, I'm willing to set aside this regrettable incident."

Absalom concluded, "Let the Minutes state that I offer you – and my fellow Spendor Corporation executives – my full support."

Resuming her seat, Natasha nodded to Hilary to record the decision before asking, "Is there any further discussion?" Nobody spoke. "Good. Congratulations, Asher Goldmann, on your appointment as Director." She dropped her eyes to the laptop. "The next item on the agenda is 'New Deputies'..."

Different candidates were proposed, and their merits debated by the Directors without any input from Natasha. It was not surprising Joah, Blaze, Zed, Daniel and Finn, the red princes from last night's party, were at the top of her father's recommendations.

The deputy who had been managing Edith's responsibilities was among the newly elected Directors. Luke offered his wife first choice from the candidates as replacement. She selected Joah. Bertha claimed Finn and added one of the female candidates Jessica proposed, to fill her second vacancy. The remaining red princes were each assigned to a new Director. When all the vacancies were filled, Luke instructed Victoria to email the newly-appointed deputies before suggesting a brief recess.

At Luke's signal, the wait staff returned to clear the table and serve coffee and cake. Natasha didn't move from her seat and was grateful nobody approached her.

Another message from Greg appeared on the screen.

Need anything?

Natasha's reply was swift:

No thanks. Do you think the danger has passed?

Greg tapped on his keyboard.

Ollie's still on high alert. I'm not going to relax until you're safely home.

While she contemplated her reply, the other Directors returned to the table.

"I feel sorry for your new deputies, Bertha," Absalom said. "They don't last long, and when they resign, you've ruined them for any other position within the Corporation."

"It isn't my fault the younger generation are afraid of a little hard work," Bertha said.

"Having more Directors will lighten the load," Maximilian said. "It will be a relief to release some of my reporting responsibilities."

Absalom reinserted himself into the conversation. "The next item on the agenda is Luke's proposal for redistributing the portfolios."

"Thank you for calling my attention to the agenda," Natasha said. "I was waiting until everyone returned to their seats before reconvening."

Clicking on the attachment, she studied the rows of data filling her screen, long lists of names and company descriptions. She couldn't pinpoint what troubled her, but the hair on the back of her neck was bristling.

Luke asked for permission to speak. "Allocating portfolio responsibilities is a complex matter, Natasha. Because of your newness to your position, I recommend you leave the decisions to the more experienced Directors. I've prepared a preliminary document..."

After her father spoke for five minutes, Natasha interrupted him. "Thank you for providing that information. I agree with your opening remark. This is a complex matter. The recently-elected Directors and I haven't had time to study the attached document. We will defer further discussion until next week's meeting."

"An excellent suggestion," Bertha said.

Luke folded his arms and glowered at Bertha, yet he maintained his silence.

"This meeting is already an hour and a half behind schedule," Jessica added. "I agree with Bertha and Natasha. Any decision we make now would be rushed."

"Is there anything further you want to say, Father," Natasha asked, "before we move on to the reports?"

"With your permission, Natasha," Luke said, "I'll generate a link to an online forum where Directors can discuss these portfolios in depth before the next meeting. That way, we'll be ready to make the necessary decisions without further delay."

39

Lateness

Psalm 136:26
Oh give thanks to the God of heaven,
for His loving kindness endures forever.

"Are we ready to move on to the Directors' reports?" Natasha asked.

"Madame Chair," Maximilian said, raising his hand. "Jessica has already referenced the lateness of the hour. Regrettably, I have family obligations, and I must leave at four-thirty."

A message from Victoria flashed on Natasha's screen:

Widower, 3 daughters, lateness = BIG trouble

"Why don't we reschedule some of the reports?" Jessica suggested. "Each Director can give a quick overview of the companies on today's rotation, and we'll reserve discussion for anything urgent."

"I'll second that recommendation," Absalom said. "I've only one matter requiring a vote."

The other Directors agreed and, by consensus, Maximilian spoke first. When he finished his summary, Maximilian asked the Directors to ratify a decision relating to a retail complex refurbishment. He nominated accepting the lowest tender, which undercut the other quotes by fourteen million dollars.

Maximilian's recommendation favoured an interstate contractor over two local ones with longstanding connections with the Corporation. Reluctant to contribute to the lateness of the meeting, Natasha didn't participate in the extended debate. When it came time to vote, a window opened on her computer, accompanied by a message from Victoria:

Subsidiary Company conditions apply.

60% = majority decision

Nodding, Natasha clicked the red "No" button. Thirty seconds later, "Carried by majority decision" flashed across the screen. Keeping her expression neutral, Natasha announced the result. Perhaps the Directors who had spoken against accepting the lowest quote didn't have sufficient votes? She made a mental note to analyse share distribution before the next meeting.

The following Director to offer his report was Landon. Halfway through his summary, a message from Greg flashed on Natasha's screen.

The Trust isn't always majority shareholder?

She typed a quick reply:

No, maximum 40% permitted for subsidiary companies

His reply was swift.

Look at Silverstone Industrials shares

Glancing at the list of subsidiary companies on Landon's list, Natasha couldn't find that name. She typed "Silverstone" into a search bar. A separate window opened with the relevant information. That company came under Absalom Norris's reporting responsibilities and was not scheduled for today's meeting. At the bottom of the page was a list of shareholders. Natasha stared at the screen before clicking the "Calculate Percentage" option. The list rearranged itself: Absalom Norris 40%, Ian Norris 35%, Stephen Spendor Trust 15%, Luke Jacobson 5%, Edith Jacobson 5%.

Was this an anomaly? Hadn't the conditions governing the Trust recommended maintaining the maximum forty per cent share across every subsidiary company?

A few clicks took her to the history tab, where she tracked the ownership of Silverstone shares. Additional shares were issued six months ago. None were purchased by the Trust.

Natasha blinked. That explained the drop from forty to fifteen per cent ownership. At the same time, Absalom added to his portfolio to sustain his maximum quota. The remaining new shares were purchased by Ian, taking advantage of a ruling, made three weeks earlier, granting deputies share-purchase privileges. With seventy-five per cent between them, father and son had become majority shareholders of Silverstone.

Raising her eyes to her father, Natasha considered the implications. Had Ian and Absalom acted alone or was Luke complicit in this scheme? Perhaps he sensed her scrutiny because Luke shifted his attention from Landon to Natasha. Checking her smile, Natasha refocused on Landon as that Director came to the end of his report.

For the remainder of the meeting, Natasha fulfilled her obligations without contributing to the discussion. There were five more voting opportunities. Two went against her decision.

Impatient to return to her new office to begin her investigation, Natasha remained seated to avoid being drawn into conversation as the other Directors left. When only her bodyguard and the two secretaries remained at her end of the room, Natasha's father called from the doorway.

"If you can spare a few minutes, Natasha, I'd like a private word in my office."

Luke didn't wait for a reply, ushering Edith from the room.

Natasha closed her computer, thanking Hilary and Victoria for their contributions.

Hilary smiled. "If I hurry, I've enough time to check for typos before I leave this afternoon. I'll have the Minutes ready for your approval in the morning, Ms Jacobson. Is ten-thirty agreeable?"

"I've already added a meeting with Hilary to your schedule, Natasha," Victoria said.

The phone in Natasha's pocket vibrated.

"That will be the schedule," Victoria said when Natasha retrieved the phone. She ushered Natasha and Greg towards the door. "In ten minutes, you have a meeting with the Trustees."

"But my father—"

"He should have checked with me first. I've allocated Luke five minutes and sent him confirmation. I'll phone his office if you don't appear on time. Any questions?"

Natasha looked at the schedule on her phone. "You've allocated *six* hours for the meeting with the Trustees?"

"That includes dinner at the Pink Star restaurant and a tour of your city apartment."

"What city apartment?"

"Your father is waiting." Victoria indicated the time. "Run along. Don't make lateness your trademark."

"You heard her," Greg said, guiding Natasha to her father's office. He knocked and entered without waiting for a response.

"There you are, Princess," Luke said, crossing to meet Natasha and pressing a glass of champagne into her hand. "Congratulations. You look tired after chairing your first Directors' Meeting."

"Natasha only has five minutes," Greg said.

"Wait outside, Freeman," Luke said, reaching for Natasha's arm to lead her towards the sofas in front of the windows. Edith was already seated, with Ian and his father, Absalom, standing nearby.

"If Greg leaves, I'm going with him," Natasha said, shaking free and backing into her bodyguard. "The Trustees are waiting. What did you want to discuss?"

"The Trustees can wait," Luke said, not hiding his animosity. "You're *my* daughter. That should have been taken into consideration before they sprang this afternoon's surprise."

"You're in charge now, Natasha," Absalom said. "Don't let the Trustees order you around. You need time to celebrate with your family."

Natasha glanced at Absalom before refocusing on her father. "Please take back this drink. I don't want any champagne. I need to keep a clear head. I have more questions than answers, and the Trustees can give them to me."

When her father refused to accept the glass, Natasha held it towards Greg.

Ian appeared, snatching the glass from her hand. "Oh, Nessie, is there no limit to your selfishness? It's not enough you've corrupted your stepbrother with your reluctant-bride fantasy, but now you're tempting him with alcohol."

Greg took a step forward. Natasha raised her hand to caution him into silence.

"I didn't come here to talk to you, Ian," Natasha said. "Father, you had something to discuss with me?"

"I'm worried about you, Princess," Luke said. "I fear the Trustees have foisted too much responsibility upon you, too soon. If I'd known what they intended, I'd have acted earlier to advance the marriage negotiations. You need someone dependable to help carry the load." He produced a bundle of folded pages from his pocket. "I have documents for you to sign."

Shaking her head, Natasha refused to look at the pages. "Deliver them to my secretary. I'm not signing anything unless my legal team give me approval."

"The Corporation lawyers prepared this document," Luke said. "Ian and I have already signed, and we only need your signature to finalise the agreement. And this is the Marriage Licence Application. All the details have been completed."

Brrrp brrrp. Brrrp brrrp... The desk phone began to buzz.

"That will be Victoria, admonishing me for my lateness," Natasha said. "Is there anything else before I leave?"

"Nothing that can't wait until you're home this evening," Luke said.

"I'm not sure what time I'll be home. The Trustees have invited me to dinner."

"Then Ian should accompany you. As your fiancé, he must be included—"

"Ian is not invited."

"Natasha," Luke said. "Don't let the Trustees come between you and your fiancé."

"The Trustees don't approve of me," Ian said, smiling at Natasha over the rim of his glass. He sipped his champagne before he spoke again. "But that's of no concern to me. Nessie knows I'll be waiting in her bed when she gets home."

"Father, how long is Ian staying at the Estate?" Natasha asked.

"I've told him to consider it his home," Luke said.

40

Homelessness

Bursting through the door into her grandfather's office, Natasha threw herself onto the nearest chair. Her head dropped into her hands. The gathered Trustees paused in their conversation.

Victoria appeared beside Natasha with a glass of water. "Your meeting with your father didn't end well?"

"I've added a new word to my lexicon," Natasha said, accepting the glass and surveying the room. "Homelessness. But you already knew this would happen. That's why you mentioned a city apartment."

Rising, Natasha approached the desk to sit in her grandfather's chair. Victoria followed, stopping to sit in a chair positioned at right angles to the desk. The executive secretary tapped the keyboard on her laptop. Greg appeared at Natasha's side, standing to attention. Oleander, Landon, Bertha and Jessica claimed the visitor chairs arranged before the desk.

Frowning at the Trustees, Natasha sorted through the confusion in her mind. The unpleasantness in her father's office had temporarily blinded her to the problems revealed during the Directors' Meeting. Were the Trustees aware control of Silverstone had slipped from their hands? She was desperate to know the extent of the problem and whether her father was involved. But now was not the time to raise those concerns. Her highest priority was to discover why the Trustees announced her inheritance today.

The Trustees remained silent.

Greg shuffled his feet. Natasha glanced up at his unsmiling face. His sober presence was an unwelcome reminder that naming him as heir had been a drastic decision. For the briefest moment, a desire to be wrapped in his arms pushed aside every thought.

Startled, Natasha squashed the impulse. Anger at herself tainted her words. "Don't stand so close, Freeman. I don't need your constant reminder that I have enemies."

A flash of emotion appeared in Greg's eyes, but he masked his hurt well.

Natasha softened her tone, placing a hand on his arm. "I'm sorry for my harshness. I value your devotedness, but could you save your intimidating scowl for the Big Bad Wolf? I want to see your smile. Why don't you find a seat where you can pray from the sidelines?"

The grin transforming his face was the answer Natasha needed. She turned to Victoria. "That exchange had better not appear in your meeting notes."

The executive secretary rested her fingers on the keyboard as the corners of her mouth twitched.

Natasha considered the waiting Trustees. "You've gone to a lot of trouble to alienate me from my father. I hope you're satisfied?"

"We've only done what we thought necessary to protect you," Oleander said.

"No more meddling, James Oleander Dubois. I'm tired of being a pawn in other people's games."

When Natasha could no longer concentrate on the documents before her, she ended the discussion. "Enough. It's past six o'clock and you promised me dinner."

"We'll reconvene at the Pink Star in an hour and a half," Landon said. "In the meantime, James can take you to your apartment."

"If only your other problems were as easily resolved as your homelessness," Jessica said.

"How far is the apartment?" Greg asked. "Can we walk, or will we need the car?"

"It's only two blocks," Oleander said, "but people will be watching for your departure. The longer we keep Natasha's whereabouts a secret, the happier I'll be. I'll fetch her car. Do you remember where I collected you last time?"

Greg nodded, and the other Trustees left the room with Oleander.

Victoria closed her laptop. "I asked your downstairs secretary to pack up your office before she left this afternoon. Housekeeping will deliver the boxes overnight, and Amanda will come at eight to begin her formal induction. I'll bid you good evening. Enjoy your dinner."

Natasha joined her bodyguard near the door. "I'm sorry you're caught in my melodrama, Greg. Don't feel obligated to stay. I'll understand if you've had enough."

"Queenie, I'm not leaving while the Big Bad Wolf's around. But I must confess you took me by surprise when you chose homelessness as this evening's code word. When did you decide you weren't going back to your father's estate?"

"It isn't safe, with Ian living there."

"I agree," Greg said, his hands tightening into fists. "When I saw the way Norris looked at you—"

"I don't want to think about Ian," Natasha said, reaching for his hands. "Will you stay with me in the apartment?"

Greg pulled his hands away and stepped to the door. "That might not be necessary. Let's find Oleander. I'm eager to discover the plans he's made for your security."

Another long-forgotten memory awakened for Natasha as she followed him into the hallway. Not long after arriving at St Catherine's, twelve-year-old Natasha had been escorted to the chapel and ordered to stand before the Academy's cleric. Sister Augustine admonished the child before leaving her with the priest. "You are here to make your Confession. If you don't acknowledge the sinfulness reigning in your heart, you will spend your eternity exiled from Heaven."

Exiled from Heaven? Shaking free from the memory, Natasha reflected on the immensity of that kind of homelessness. She increased her pace.

"Have I done something wrong?" Greg asked as the elevator doors closed.

"It's me who did something wrong," Natasha said. "I shouldn't have asked you to stay in the apartment."

"That's not the problem. You can't afford to spend too much time alone with me. People will presume I'm taking advantage of you."

"Oh."

"Oh?" Greg said. "I still can't read you well enough to discern what you mean. Is that 'Oh', you're disappointed I'm not tempted? Or 'Oh', now you're thinking about the other men who *have* tried to take advantage? Or—"

"It's not fair. You've been honourable, and I'm ruining your reputation again."

The elevator doors opened. Natasha set off toward the sky bridge. The hallways were empty, and only dim security lights marked the way.

"Ruining my reputation again, Queenie?" Greg asked. "I'm capable of destroying my life without your involvement. You weren't overseas with me."

"If I hadn't behaved like a Jezebel, you would have remained with your mother, living a good life—"

"Whoa!" Greg caught her arm, pulling Natasha to a stop. "Who's been comparing you to Jezebel?"

Blinking away another fragment of school-days memories, Natasha shook off his hand and walked on. "We need to hurry. Oleander will be waiting."

"This is not finished, Natasha." Greg appeared at her side again. "You were twelve, not even old enough to know how to behave like Jezebel."

"I was old enough to know you wanted to kiss me." Natasha stepped onto the sky bridge. "Old enough to know you found me physically attractive. You're still attracted to me."

She rushed into the shopping centre, hoping to lose herself in the crowd, but most shops were already closed for the evening. The few remaining shoppers were hurrying towards the exits.

"You heard what my father said," Natasha said, lengthening her steps. "He was *disappointed* with you, but he was so very, very *angry* with me."

"Why are you talking like this?"

"My father sent me to a girls-only Catholic school. The priest warned me not to corrupt anyone else."

A chilly breeze ripped through the gloom when they arrived at the car park entrance where Oleander had previously collected them. Natasha shuddered.

"You're shivering," Greg said. "Here, take my jacket."

"No, I won't allow you to suffer because I left mine in the car. Oleander will be here any minute."

"If you won't take my jacket, share my warmth."

"Haven't you been listening?" Natasha asked as Greg wrapped his arms around her from behind. "You need to keep your distance."

"The Trustees will have my head if you freeze to death. Stop changing the subject. Why do you believe your father holds you responsible for what happened? You were a kid."

"Six years at St Catherine's, and he never came to visit me. Your mother said he was busy, but I understood the real reason. I vowed I'd never do anything to anger him again. When I went to university, Cassie was my only friend. I avoided public places because men kept asking me to go out with them. That's why I didn't go to the party with Cassie and why I never drink alcohol. Cassie said I 'lived like a saint'. I've worked hard to prove there's more to me than my appearance. I made one stupid mistake last night by going into the garden, and now my father's angry again, and I've been contaminated by the Jezebel spirit. He believed Ian's lies because he knows to expect the worst from me."

41

Warmness

Natasha waited for Greg's response to her confession. The muscles in his arms and chest hardened as he held her even tighter against his torso. The silence lengthened.

Oleander finally arrived. Greg wrenched the pink car's door open and shoved her inside. Natasha retrieved her jacket from the seat, shuffling across until she was behind the driver.

"Turn up the heater," Greg said, throwing himself beside her and slamming the door. "What took you so long?"

Oleander shot Greg a questioning glance before putting the car into gear. He accelerated toward the street exit. "It took longer to get rid of the people watching for Natasha's car. The bright pink paintwork is too conspicuous."

Greg checked the traffic behind them. "Are you sure we're not being tailed?"

Resting her head against the upholstery, Natasha welcomed the air-conditioned warmness wafting over her.

"Don't get too comfortable, Natasha," Oleander said. "We don't have far to go."

A few minutes later, he steered the car into a narrow alleyway, approaching a rising roller door at the end. Oleander drove into an enclosed space, turning left as another barrier opened into a small parking garage. There were eight spaces, and only one was occupied.

"We're the only residents who can access this garage," Oleander said.

"Where are we?" Greg asked, already out of the car looking for security cameras.

"Esmeralda Towers," Oleander said, opening Natasha's door. "This is Tower Four South. You'll be staying in one of the penthouses."

"My grandfather was a major developer of this complex," Natasha said, already missing the car's warmness.

Oleander opened a storage cupboard. Bringing out a swathe of cream-coloured canvas, he gestured to Greg. "Help me cover Natasha's car. Even though I'm confident this building is secure, I'm not taking any chances."

Five minutes later, the trio were inside an elevator, heading to the top of the tower. Oleander led them across a carpeted foyer serving two apartments.

Approaching the right-hand door, he brandished a key card. After opening the door, he handed the card to Greg. Natasha and Greg followed Oleander inside. Halfway across the luxurious lounge room, Oleander called out: "Mrs Trencher?"

A short, silver-haired woman appeared in a doorway, wiping her hands on her white apron. "Mister James! Welcome. Would your guests like refreshments before I show them to their rooms?"

"Natasha," Oleander said, "let me introduce you to Miriam Trencher, our longsuffering housekeeper."

"A pleasure, my dear," Mrs Trencher said. Up close, her face was lined with wrinkles, but her busy hands never stopped moving.

"Turn around and let me look at you. Mister Stephen always boasted his granddaughter was a beautiful child."

Natasha complied, and when she completed the spin, Mrs Trencher swept her into a tight embrace. When the housekeeper released her, there were tears on the older woman's face which she dried upon the apron.

"What a stylish young woman you are. You have your poor mother's blonde hair and blue eyes, but I can detect none of her rebelliousness."

"Thank you, Mrs Trencher."

"Call me Miriam," Mrs Trencher said. "Only Mister James calls me Mrs Trencher. I'm sure he only does it to annoy me." The housekeeper frowned at Oleander for a few seconds, before shifting her attention to Greg. "Young man, stop scowling at me." The housekeeper flipped the skirt of her apron at the bodyguard and then waggled her finger at him. "Save your menacing glare for someone else. I'm no threat to your sweetheart."

"I'm not his sweetheart," Natasha said, warmness rising on her face. "This is my bodyguard, Gregory Freeman."

The housekeeper studied Natasha before taking Greg by the arm and leading him across the room. "Bodyguard, how will I address you?"

"Freeman."

Natasha and Oleander followed behind them.

"Here is your bedroom, Freeman," Miriam said, "right next to mine. I'm a light sleeper, so don't think you can sneak upstairs in the middle of the night. Unless Miss Natasha changes her mind and names you her sweetheart, your place is downstairs. Is that understood?"

"Perfectly," Greg said, grinning down at the petite older woman.

"There's a shared bathroom there." Miriam moved on before Greg could look behind the door. The housekeeper beckoned to him. "Come along. For a young person, you're slow. Here's the kitchen."

The spacious open-plan kitchen was immaculate, with gleaming stainless-steel fixtures and white marble benchtops. The cupboards and the door to the well-stocked pantry were Tasmanian blackwood with gold handles.

"I keep an orderly household. It was that way with Mister Stephen, and I expect no less from you." Miriam fluttered around the room, opening and closing doors.

"Help yourself to whatever's in the pantry or the refrigerator, Freeman, but don't leave the house in disarray. There's the dishwasher, and I've put a laundry hamper in your room. Your job is to take care of Miss Natasha, and the cooking and cleaning are my domain.

Abruptly, Miriam turned to Oleander. "That applies to you too, Mister James. The old house rules apply. Just because you've been an occasional visitor over the years doesn't mean I have to put up with any bad habits you've brought back from the other household. Now get yourself to your apartment. I've laid out your tuxedo in your dressing room."

"I'll be back in forty-five minutes," Oleander said before he left.

"Mister James has the apartment next door," Miriam said, ushering Natasha towards a set of stairs. "Come along, Miss Natasha. I have your city home to show you before you change for dinner.

Natasha glanced at Greg, who was standing in the middle of the lounge room.

Smoothing her apron, Miriam nodded. "This once, Freeman, you can come upstairs and familiarise yourself with the layout. I'm half your size and likely twice your age, but I won't put up with any mischief. I'll take after you with my rolling pin if you don't show Miss Natasha the proper respect."

"Yes, ma'am," Greg said, his eyes bright with suppressed laughter. "Queenie, I told you Ollie would take care of security."

Greg bounded up the stairs ahead of them. His laughter carried down. "Only a reckless fool would tangle with a determined housekeeper and her trusty rolling pin."

At the top of the stairs, Miriam hurried them along the right-hand hallway, opening and closing doors. "Here's the guest wing. I'll only show you the first bedroom, a generous twin double with an ensuite bathroom. The other three have the same layout; the only difference is the colour scheme. Here's the guest sitting room." Retracing her steps, the housekeeper entered the left hallway. "Here's Mister Stephen's study – your study now, Miss Natasha. That's the library, and through this door is your suite."

With a flourish, Miriam opened the door, and Natasha entered. The room was even larger than her bedroom at home, furnished with dark wooden furniture that included a king-sized bed.

"Not a hint of pink anywhere," Greg said, scanning the room before approaching a glass wall. He rapped on the window with his knuckles.

"Reinforced one-way glass," Miriam said. "Nobody can see in, and there's no chance anyone can get through that window without a tank, so stop leaving great paw prints everywhere."

Resting his hands behind his back, Greg laughed as he gazed over the city. "You have a great view of your headquarters, Queenie. I can see why your grandfather chose this apartment."

"This was Mister Stephen's city retreat," Miriam said, drawing herself up to her full height. "He also had a country estate and a beachside mansion, but he sold both when Miss Stephanie..." Shaking her head, the housekeeper rushed to open a pair of double doors. "The bathroom is accessed through your dressing room. Unfortunately, your luggage has yet to arrive, so your options for this evening's dinner engagement are limited."

Miriam opened a wardrobe and ran her hands along a row of colourful dresses. "Mister James found these in Miss Stephanie's room after one of her visits, and he's kept them all these years. He thought you might like to have them, so I've laundered them for you."

"What's this?" Greg asked, reaching over Miriam's head and pulling out a shimmering red cloak. He raised the hood and smiled at Natasha.

Miriam snatched the cloak from his hands and draped it over a chair. "Miss Stephanie wore that to a costume ball. She looked stunning, but it was the costume she wore under the cape that set people talking."

Returning to the wardrobe, the housekeeper considered and dismissed several dresses, shaking her head and muttering.

Greg pulled out a tiny gold cocktail dress. He grinned at Natasha, who fanned her face and remarked about the warmness of the room.

Grabbing the dress from Greg's hands, Miriam shoved him toward the door. "Out! Miss Natasha does not need you putting ideas into her head. Shoo! You need to get changed. There's a new suit waiting for you in your room."

"A new suit?" Greg asked from the hallway. "I don't remember ordering one."

"Mister James made the arrangements. Now, go."

Alone with Natasha, Miriam shook her head as she held up the gold dress. "I don't know what Mister James was thinking. A respectable girl like you wouldn't wear something like this in public."

Natasha swallowed, unable to look at Miriam. She shut her eyes, trying to forget the look in Greg's eyes as he held the gold dress.

"Here," Miriam said, thrusting fabric into Natasha's arms. "This will have to do."

When Natasha looked, she was holding a dark blue gown. She stood before a full-length mirror.

The sleeveless silk dress had a high neckline and flowed to the floor. Only when Natasha held the dress at arm's length did she discover the back was scooped to below the waist. Her eyes widened. Shaking her head, Natasha watched Miriam rummaging through a dresser drawer.

The housekeeper nodded. "I know what you're thinking. You won't be able to wear conventional underwear."

42

Costliness

Psalm 62:12
Also to You, Lord, belongs loving kindness,
For You reward every man according to his work.

Miriam fussed, adding accessories from among the treasures hidden in the dressers. The ruby-encrusted bracelets adorning Natasha's arms and the heavy pendant hanging low on her chest had belonged to a grandmother she had never known. As the young woman fastened the matching ruby earrings, her business mind calculated the costliness of the ruby collection. Yet the stories Miriam told added priceless value to these jewels.

If Miriam was correct, the rubies were evidence of the love and devotion Stephen Spendor had lavished on his wife, Esmeralda. That kind of love and adoration was a treasure beyond measure.

Checking her appearance in the mirror, Natasha frowned. She could not forget the sensual undergarments hidden beneath the flowing silk gown. Her long hair hung loose, helping to conceal her feminine curves, but when she adjusted her pose, there was no denying this dress belonged to a temptress.

"Queenie, Ollie's here," Greg called up the stairs.

Miriam smiled as she draped the red cloak about Natasha's shoulders. The blue dress disappeared, hidden within the folds. "You're beautiful tonight, my dear," the older woman said with tears in her eyes. "I'll be praying you stay safe from the temptations that ruined your mother."

After flipping the hood up to cover Natasha's hair, Miriam pulled the young woman into a quick embrace. "The world will throw itself at your feet, but don't give in to temptation. Your soul is too high a price to pay."

Natasha froze.

"I remember when your mother was innocent," Miriam said, leading Natasha along the hallway towards the stairs. "My mother was the housekeeper then. Miss Stephanie and I grew up together. Don't look so surprised, I'm much younger than I look. I told you temptations come at a cost. But we're not talking about me. Now where was I? That's right, your mother – it was heartbreaking when Miss Stephanie realised she could use her beauty and power to get whatever she wanted. I wasn't going to say anything, but my conscience won't let me alone. Your mother wore that dress for her engagement to Mister James. It was a tragedy when she cast him aside."

"My mother and Oleander?" Natasha asked, stumbling at the top of the stairs.

"Oleander?" Miriam asked, catching Natasha and waiting until she regained her balance before they started to descend. "That's the name Miss Stephanie gave Mister James while they were at university. He refused to tell anyone what happened, but when they came home after her first semester, there was no more talk of marriage. Mister James still accompanied your mother everywhere, but he wore a chauffeur's uniform and stood with the servants. It must have broken his heart to see how she behaved, yet he always waited until she was ready for him to drive her home."

"My mother and Oleander," Natasha said again, spying Greg at the foot of the stairs. She rushed the final steps, stumbling to a stop as he caught her. "My mother and Oleander were *engaged* before he became her chauffeur."

Oleander's voice called from across the lounge room. "Mrs Trencher, I asked you not to tell Natasha."

"I had no choice," Miriam said, marching to meet her employer. "I won't stay silent and let history repeat itself."

"What does she mean?" Greg asked. "How is history repeating itself?"

"I've inherited more than my blonde hair from my mother," Natasha said, moving out of Greg's arms and hurrying to the external door. She exited, crossed to the elevator and pressed the only button.

"You're nothing like your mother," Oleander said, appearing beside her as the elevator doors opened.

Stepping inside, Natasha moved to the furthest corner, bowing her head until the hood hid her face. "I don't want to talk about this."

Two pairs of men's legs wearing matching black trousers and polished shoes appeared in her narrow field of vision. A swoosh signalled the door's closure, and the elevator descended.

"But I do," Greg said. "Ollie, why didn't you tell us you were engaged to Natasha's mother?"

"The James Dubois Miriam remembers ceased to exist long ago," Oleander said. "He was young and foolish, not yet eighteen when he fell for Stephanie Spendor."

The elevator stopped on the eighth floor.

"Come this way." Oleander led them to a door marked "No Admittance". He tapped keys on the electronic lock, and the door opened. Signalling them to remain silent, he directed them into a shadowy space. After navigating a narrow, twisty maze, they passed through another locked door, emerging into a bright hallway. "We're now in Tower Three."

Although the hallway was empty, Natasha adjusted her hood as they approached a pair of elevators. Upon arrival, Oleander glanced around.

"We can't be too careful," he said, pressing the up and down buttons. When the empty downward elevator arrived, Oleander leaned inside and pressed multiple floors but stopped his companions from entering. He held the doors open until the other elevator arrived. That, too, was empty. Ushering Natasha and Greg into the second elevator, he released the first one before punching the button for the eleventh floor in the second.

Natasha's heart rate increased with the rising elevator.

Greg spoke to Oleander, but not about their unknown destination. "Does Natasha's father know about the engagement?"

"Stephanie told him everything in the months before she died. She was haunted by ghosts from her past."

"What happened?" Greg asked. "Why didn't you marry Stephanie?"

"I've already told you I was young and foolish," Oleander said. "I should never have believed a teenager's declarations of undying love."

"How old was my mother?" Natasha asked.

The elevator stopped, and the doors opened. After checking the hallway, Oleander fell into step beside her, with Greg behind them.

"Stephanie made the engagement announcement on her sixteenth birthday, but that's not what you're asking. The relationship was consummated when she was fourteen."

Natasha gasped.

"Don't look at me like that," Oleander said. "Stephanie ran around with a fast crowd, looking and acting as if she was much older. I knew the truth, but she wouldn't leave me alone. I woke up after a drunken party, and she was in my bed."

"Being drunk is no excuse," Natasha said.

"I'm not excusing my behaviour," Oleander said, directing her to the left of the hallway as a couple approached from the other direction. He waited until the strangers had passed before he spoke again. "I accepted full responsibility. Years later, Stephanie told me she'd spiked my drink. She was a brilliant actress, convincing me I'd seduced her. It was a trick she'd previously used successfully, but it backfired with me. I went to her father, and after confessing what had happened, I requested permission to marry her."

"What did my grandfather say?"

"He prepared a betrothal agreement for us both to sign, and then he packed Stephanie off to St Catherine's until she was old enough." Oleander pointed ahead. "Take a left at the next junction and head for the stairs. If I proved faithful while she was away, we would marry when she turned sixteen."

"And if you broke the agreement?" Greg asked.

"My father countersigned the document because I was underage. He vowed I would forfeit my inheritance if I dishonoured the family name. I'd been preparing for a career in the family business empire, so that was a serious disincentive."

Entering the stairwell, the trio kept their thoughts private. Their footsteps echoed ominously in the cavernous space. When they exited the stairs on the tenth floor, another elevator delivered them to the second floor. Oleander directed them to another locked door. "We're about to cross into Tower One Central...

What should have been a brief, effortless walk to the Pink Star restaurant took much longer because of the meandering route Oleander chose. Entering an alleyway lined with rubbish skips, he approached an unmarked door, ushering Natasha and Greg into a darkened storage bay.

A large figure emerged from behind a tower of cardboard cartons, a single beam of light in his hand.

Oleander asked him, "Is everything secure?"

"I've followed your instructions," said Matthew Wallace, head of Sentinel City Security. "The other Trustees are already seated. I'll signal my operative, and she'll escort you to their table."

43

Sinfulness

A slender waitress escorted Oleander across the dining room towards an ornately carved screen. Natasha and Greg followed in single file, avoiding the other tables by remaining close to the wall furthest from the grand entrance.

Curious whispers followed them as some of the diners speculated about the identity of the woman hiding beneath the red hooded cape.

The heiress dropped her eyes and followed Oleander's heels.

At the screen, the waitress gestured to a round table concealed behind it. Bertha was the first to notice the new arrivals. A welcoming smile appeared on her face.

"At last, Natasha," Bertha said. "Has James been leading you a merry chase? I can see he insisted you come in disguise, but why he thought a red cloak was the best option is beyond me. Landon, be a gentleman and relieve Natasha of that cape."

Landon leapt to his feet from beside Bertha. He reached for the cape while nodding towards the chair on his left. "Natasha, please do me the honour of sitting beside me this evening."

Natasha jerked back, bumping into Greg. She mumbled an apology as she struggled with the cloak's top fastening.

"I recognise that cape," Jessica said from the other side of the round table. "It belonged to Stephanie. I didn't realise you inherited her wardrobe."

"Some of my mother's clothes were in the apartment," Natasha said, removing the cape.

The waitress stepped forward, collecting the garment. "I'll be back to take your drink orders."

Greg followed Natasha to her seat.

"Is that the dress—" Bertha asked, and Natasha glanced up at her tone.

Oleander was halfway into the chair on Natasha's left, alongside Jessica. His eyes widened as he gazed at the blue dress. "I'd forgotten I'd kept that."

Then Oleander smiled. "Don't worry on my account, Natasha. Time heals old wounds."

Greg stood with his hands on the back of her chair as Natasha settled onto the seat. As he pushed the chair in, his hands brushed the skin on her back, and a rush of heat warmed her face.

Natasha folded her trembling hands on the table and inhaled slowly. After checking her smile, she nodded to each Trustee. There was an empty chair opposite, between Bertha and Jessica.

"Your bodyguard is sitting next to me," Jessica said. "It will make a nice change for him. Freeman must tire of having his eyes glued to your back."

Oleander muttered something under his breath, and Landon coughed. Greg appeared in the appointed seat and kept his eyes lowered.

An awkward silence settled over the table.

Bertha frowned at Jessica, but the corners of her mouth twitched.

"What?" Jessica asked.

"Natasha is wearing one of *Stephanie's* dresses," Oleander said. "I shouldn't need to say more. Everyone knows she never wore anything that didn't attract the male gaze."

"Oh," said Jessica, tilting her head and smiling at Greg.

"It was a mistake to give Natasha her mother's dresses," Greg said. The words were directed at Oleander, but then Greg fixed his eyes on Natasha as she hid her face with her hands.

"Explain yourself, Freeman," Bertha said. "If there's any suggestion of inappropriate behaviour, I'll order James to throw you out."

Peering through her fingers, Natasha caught the beseeching look Greg threw to Oleander. It seemed her bodyguard didn't find whatever help he was expecting from the older man.

Shaking his head, Greg tightened his jaw and picked up a menu card from the table.

The waitress reappeared, accompanied by a middle-aged man wearing a chef's white uniform that strained to contain his generous waistline.

"Welcome, welcome," the chef said, rubbing his hands together. "It is an honour to have you in my humble establishment. This evening, I have created a six-course degustation menu..."

When the chef finished his prepared speech, he hurried away.

The waitress produced a notebook, her dark eyes bright as she surveyed the table. "Good evening. My name is Zhou Li-Wei Min. Please call me Li-Wei. I am assigned to serve you this evening. Can I get anyone a drink before I bring you the first course?"

Before Natasha could flip the menu card over and look at the drinks selection, Oleander removed it from her hand and passed it to Li-Wei. "Sparkling mineral water for Freeman, and a non-alcoholic Pink Starlet cocktail for Natasha. The rest of us will share a couple of bottles of..."

When the cocktail arrived it resembled pink lemonade. Tiny strawberry pieces floated among star-shaped iceblocks that whizzed and fizzed within the long-stemmed glass. Bubbles tickled Natasha's nose as she sipped the beverage, and the tip of her tongue tingled.

"Are you sure that's non-alcoholic?" Greg asked Li-Wei.

"I made it myself," the waitress said.

"I have my orders, Mister Freeman," Li-Wei continued. "No harm will come to Miss Jacobson while she is under *my* care."

Greg stared at the woman for a few seconds. The waitress bowed at the waist like a martial arts warrior greeting an opponent, before retreating from the table.

Li-Wei returned a few minutes later, carrying a laden tray. In her wake came a second waitress with a similar tray.

Li-Wei served Natasha first and then Oleander, placing freshly baked sourdough rolls on the side plates. The other waitress worked her way around the rest of the table.

Natasha leaned forward and inhaled the delicious aroma wafting upwards from the fish broth. Her stomach rumbled, complaining about how little she'd eaten today.

Dipping her spoon into the steaming liquid, she closed her eyes to taste it. As she savoured the broth, the conversation around the table fell silent.

Natasha's eyes flew open. Everyone was watching her, their soup spoons lying untouched on the tablecloth. Releasing her spoon, she waited for someone to reveal what she'd done wrong.

"Shall I say the blessing?" Landon asked quietly, and Natasha's face flushed again.

How could she have forgotten, after making such a public statement about prayer at the lunch meeting? That was further proof of her sinfulness. When Landon finished his brief prayer, Natasha glanced around the table.

Greg was breaking his bread roll into rough pieces and dunking each morsel in the broth before it disappeared into his mouth.

Hunting for crumbs on his plate, Greg said, "This serving is tiny. I don't know what a 'degustation menu' is, but if the other five courses are of a similar size, I'll still be hungry at the end of the meal."

"'Degustation' is a tasting menu," Jessica said. "The chef's trying to impress us."

Natasha glanced at her untouched bread. "You can have my roll."

"Why aren't you eating, Queenie?" Greg asked.

"I'm not hungry."

He frowned but accepted the roll when she offered her plate to him. Greg ripped the bread in half, dropping one portion onto his plate. "You haven't been hungry since your garden encounter with Norris."

Picking up her spoon, Natasha bowed her head.

"Punishing yourself won't change anything," Greg said.

"Freeman, what makes you think Natasha is punishing herself?" Bertha asked.

Natasha raised her eyes, silently pleading with Greg not to say anything.

Her bodyguard dropped his spoon into his empty bowl. "Natasha thinks she's inherited a Jezebel spirit from her mother."

Oleander swore.

Startled by his reaction, Natasha's pulse raced. Oleander's rare loss of self-control added to her sense of shame. As an early victim of her mother's sinfulness, he knew better than anyone what must be lurking within the daughter's heart.

Jessica flapped her napkin at Oleander. "I've never heard you use that kind of language. What's a 'Jezebel spirit'?"

Wrapping his fingers around his wine glass, Oleander kept his face neutral as he drained the contents. He beckoned to Li-Wei, who approached the table with a laden trolley.

After removing the bowls and placing them on the lower shelf, the waitress served the second course. Natasha played with her fresh salad, chasing variegated heritage tomatoes around her plate.

When his salad plate was empty, Oleander refilled his wine glass and nodded to Bertha. Natasha frowned, lowering her fork to watch their silent exchange.

After what seemed like forever, Bertha turned to Landon and asked, "Why me?"

"You're our expert on religious fanaticism," Landon said, patting Bertha's arm. "Countless tortured young women have turned to you for help."

"Is this another of those talks, Bertha?" Jessica asked. "You've got that look. Am I about to be lectured about not attending a religious school?"

"You asked about Jezebel," Bertha said. "If you've lost interest because she's a religious figure, I'll keep silent."

"Oh, no," Jessica said. "That trick no longer works on me. I hate being the last to know what we're talking about."

"Jezebel was a wicked woman." Bertha straightened in her seat. "Impressionable young girls are often threatened with eternal damnation for imitating her sinfulness."

"What kind of 'sinfulness'?" Jessica asked.

"Jezebel used her beauty and power to seduce people," Natasha said, staring down at her plate. "Nobody was safe from her corruption."

"When was the last time you attended the Confessional?" Bertha asked.

"N-not since I left St Catherine's," Natasha said.

"Aha!" Bertha said. "No wonder you're burdened by sinfulness."

"That's irrelevant," Oleander said. "Confession did nothing to cure Stephanie."

"Did she know about Jezebel?" Natasha asked, a sharp pain stabbing her chest.

"What Stephanie thought is irrelevant," Bertha said. "We're talking about you, Natasha. As your mother's Godmother, I command you to confess everything."

44

Bluntness

Jeremiah 18:12
But they say, "It is in vain;
for we will walk after our own plans, and
we will each follow the stubbornness of his evil heart."

Stunned by Bertha's bluntness, Natasha retreated behind the barriers in her mind. There she considered the lengthy list of sins the Sisters had warned her to avoid. She was old enough now to understand what those sins entailed. Natasha's stomach threatened to revolt, confirming her belief something deep within waited to be revealed.

From across the table, Jessica brought Natasha back to the present by the harshness in her tone.

"If this same Jezebel spirit controlled Stephanie," Jessica said, "we know what to expect. Why waste time waiting for Natasha to start her confession? What we need is specific information to reveal the depth of the problem. I'm going first."

The other Trustees stared at Jessica.

Taking a deep breath, Natasha placed her folded hands in her lap and gazed at her inquisitor.

"Natasha, I want a full list of your lovers. Don't hold back even one name. I'm especially interested in every marriage you've destroyed."

Even though she was innocent of these sins, Natasha could not look away from the unspoken pain etched on Jessica's face.

Beside Natasha, Landon tapped the table, drawing attention to his outstretched hand. "Can I see your little black book? Like your mother, you know not to leave a digital footprint."

Staring at him in confusion, Natasha's tongue refused to work.

"Her bodyguard must have the book," Jessica said, reaching toward Greg. "Hand it over. We need the names of her blackmail victims."

Greg raised his empty palms, shaking his head.

"I'll have to take steps to protect Corporation funds, Natasha," Landon said. "I want the names of your drug suppliers and distributors."

"You've excelled in concealing your crimes, Natasha," Bertha said. "James increased the scope of investigations after Freeman arrived, yet he's found nothing to incriminate you. May I see your phone?"

Natasha fumbled for her clutch purse.

Bertha waited for Natasha to unlock the phone and then grabbed it. "If I check your contacts list, I should find the names of your co-conspirators. I'm sure James can persuade them to give us access to incriminating videos. But first, I want the name of the clinic where you go when your contraception fails, and you require an abor—"

"Enough!" White-faced, Oleander leapt to his feet. "Bertha, you have gone TOO far."

"James," Bertha said, dropping the phone onto the table and shrinking in her chair. "I'm sorry. I don't know what came over me. I was so focused on the questions I should have asked Stephanie, I forgot I was talking to her daughter."

"Oh, no," said Natasha, looking at each Trustee. Her mind made terrible connections between her troubled mother and the comments each had made.

"Natasha," said Greg, "while I disagree with their methods, I think the Trustees have made their point. If half what they're suggesting was true, your mother could have been a Jezebel, but your reaction proves you are not similarly afflicted."

"Then what's wrong with me?" Natasha asked. "There's a dark ickiness inside me."

"It's a human condition called guilt," Landon said.

"Shame and regret," Jessica said.

"Sin and condemnation is the religious term," Bertha said.

"Unrighteousness," Li-Wei said, announcing her return by advancing with her trolley. "The closer we get to God, the more we recognise our unworthiness. That is the mystery of God's grace. He loves us when we are unlovable. He forgives His children before we understand there's anything to forgive."

"How long have you been eavesdropping?" Landon asked.

Dismissing Landon's concern with a gesture, Oleander asked, "What else do you have to say, Li-Wei Min?"

"Mister Freeman has the answers you need," Li-Wei said. "While the others were attacking with words, he was doing battle in prayer."

Moving around the table, Li-Wei cleared the salad plates, replacing them with a creamy chicken and rice dish. Natasha studied the waitress. Greg was last to receive his meal. He glanced at the other portions and then grinned. There was twice as much food on his plate.

"One more thing before I go, Mister Freeman," Li-Wei said, placing a hand on Greg's shoulder.

A twinge of something not experienced since youth stirred inside Natasha: jealousy. Acknowledging the powerful feeling, she squirmed.

"God has heard your prayers, Mister Freeman," Li-Wei said. "You go not into battle alone. Fear no scheme of man, nor be dismayed by the unexpected. Be bold and courageous, and follow your heart."

"That girl is too forward to be a waitress," Jessica said after Li-Wei left with her trolley.

"She's not a waitress," Bertha said. "James wouldn't let anyone near this table if they didn't work for him."

"Did you understand the message she gave Freeman?" Landon asked.

"I'm more interested in whether he understands it," Oleander said. "But let's not get distracted. While we enjoy this tasty chicken, Freeman can tell us how to rid Natasha of her 'ickiness'."

Between mouthfuls, Greg said, "Natasha's feeling condemned because she wants to please God, and she knows she's not good enough."

"Who turned Natasha into a God-pleaser?" Jessica asked. "Have you been influencing her? Is that why religion and prayer are suddenly so important?"

Greg waved his fork at each Trustee. "Pardon my bluntness, but look at yourselves before accusing anyone." He glanced at his employer. "I stand in the background, Natasha, listening to the words spoken over you. Your father and Norris aren't the only ones trying to steer you in the wrong direction."

Stabbing a piece of chicken, Natasha created swirling patterns in her sauce. The Trustees were quiet, studying Greg as he continued eating.

"Natasha, are you going to eat that?" Greg asked.

Shaking her head, Natasha passed her plate across the table.

"That's not why I was asking," Greg said, yet he started devouring her portion. "Queenie, if I tell you what God's put in my heart, will you promise to eat more than a mouthful of whatever's coming next?"

Nodding, Natasha picked up her glass and sipped what remained of the pink cocktail. The melted ice had diluted the beverage. Natasha gulped down the watery dregs, grimacing as soggy strawberry pieces slithered down her throat. Twirling the glass stem between her fingers, she waited for

Greg to continue. He stared at the empty vessel and his ongoing silence made her impatient. "What?" she demanded.

"Pass me your empty glass." Greg added her cocktail glass to the row of unused glasses arranged before his place setting on the table. Reaching for the water carafe, he half-filled the different types of goblets. "Does it matter which glass I use for water?"

"No," said Jessica, "but these glasses weren't put here for water. Take that champagne flute: the special shape enhances the bubbles."

Greg glanced at the wine goblet in Jessica's hand and selected its water-filled twin. He swirled the liquid thoughtfully. Next, he gestured for the wine bottle and began adding the expensive vintage to the water.

"What are you doing?" Jessica grabbed the bottle and an unused wine glass. "You can't pour good wine into a glass that already contains something else."

Oleander removed that glass from Jessica's hand. "Freeman doesn't want any wine, Jessica. He's proving a point."

"What point?" Jessica asked. "I can't make sense of anything he's said so far."

That makes two of us, thought Natasha.

"The pink cocktail represents Natasha," Bertha said.

"I'm a cocktail?" Natasha asked, shaking her head.

"You're the glass," Oleander said, "and everything that encompasses your uniqueness is in the cocktail. Freeman thinks our meddling is upsetting the balance."

"But we're only meddling," Jessica said, "because her father—"

"Her father and whoever else is involved—"

"Ian Norris," Bertha muttered. "If I'd foreseen the trouble he would cause, I wouldn't have supported his deputy nomination."

"These *others*," Oleander continued, "are trying to force her to become someone she isn't."

"That's like adding ingredients that aren't in the recipe," Landon said.

"Or rushing the process," Oleander said.

"Natasha, you're created for a special purpose," Bertha said. "Even the slightest divergence seems to have awakened feelings of shame and condemnation."

"How do I find my purpose?" Natasha asked. "Greg, you said God's been preparing me to take over my grandfather's companies since I was born. I'm doing my best, but it's not enough. What more does God want?"

45

Firmness

Greg waved the cocktail glass at Natasha. "You're exhausted. Don't try to deny it. Your emotions are plain to see instead of hidden behind that smile you wear as a mask. I saw how disappointed you were as you finished your drink. What was wrong with it?"

Natasha blinked. Greg was still talking about her drink? "The ice had melted, and it was mostly water."

"Of course, the ice melted," Jessica said, snatching the cocktail glass and raising it towards the gap in the screen. "Li-Wei Min!"

In an instant, Li-Wei appeared with her notebook. "What do you require, Mrs Becker-Tompkins?"

"Please bring Natasha another cocktail."

"Does anyone else require anything?" Li-Wei asked, directing her eyes to Greg.

"I'm good," Greg said, indicating the water carafe.

"Take this away." Jessica offered the goblet containing the wine-water mix.

When Li-Wei returned, she also brought the next course. The waitress placed the fresh cocktail on the table, frowning at the void where Natasha's plate should be. Shaking her head, the waitress cleared the table, hesitating at Greg's two plates.

"Don't worry," Greg said to Li-Wei. "Natasha's promised to eat whatever you're serving. If she doesn't, you have my permission to give her my double portion for the next course."

Turning from the exchange, Natasha sipped her fresh cocktail. Li-Wei served roast turkey and smashed potatoes. Putting down her glass, Natasha stabbed a crunchy potato chunk with a fork as her eyes followed the fizzing iceblocks in the pink drink. Was there something else she was supposed to learn from Greg's illustration?

Filling her mouth with more potato, Natasha picked up a dessert fork from the table. She scooped iceblocks from the drink, dropping them into a spare glass. Next, she chased the fruit fragments, gobbling them before they lost their firmness. Satisfied she had preserved her drink, she placed the cocktail on the table before returning to her meal.

Jessica said, "Natasha, that's a strange way to drink a cocktail. Most people sip continuously before the ice melts, or drain the glass in one go and ask for a refill."

"Stop pestering the girl," Bertha said.

"The refill principle works with God," Greg said. "He pours into you what you need for the moment, and then when you're empty you return to Him to be replenished. That's why you're feeling weary. You've been trying to find strength within yourself, and the ickiness is your heart telling you that you can't do it."

"So, what do I have to do?" Natasha asked. "I feel like there's nothing left but emptiness."

"You give your emptiness to God," Greg said. "Tell Him you're sorry and ask for His help. Then wait for Him to fill you again."

"What if it doesn't work?" Natasha asked. "What if I confess and He doesn't fill me again?"

"That's where faith comes in," Greg said. "You pray while you wait. If it seems to take too long, or if that ickiness lingers, you get other people to pray with you. They'll help you discern whether there's anything else standing between you and God's purpose."

"There's a problem with your analogy," Jessica said, snatching the cocktail glass. "While she's praying and resting, she's defenceless. Anyone could rush in and carry her away!"

The glass slipped from Jessica's fingers, hitting the table and breaking into jagged pieces.

"Whoops! That wasn't supposed to happen," Jessica said. "Li-Wei Min! I've broken a glass!"

Pink liquid seeped across the white cloth. The implications made it difficult for Natasha to breathe, and darkness pressed in. How easily the glass had broken...

Greg appeared behind Natasha, pulling her to her feet. "Queenie, God will not let anyone break you."

The firmness of his arms kept Natasha upright as Li-Wei cleared away the wreckage, replaced the tablecloth and reset the table.

When everyone else was seated again, Oleander invited Natasha to rejoin them. Greg pushed in her chair.

"I'm fine," Natasha said, troubled by the anxious look in Greg's eyes. "You can go back to your seat."

"You don't look fine," Jessica said. "I'm sorry, Natasha. That was an unfortunate accid—"

"Unfortunate or not," Oleander said, "Jessica's clumsiness has provided the perfect illustration of Natasha's fragileness." He glanced sideways at Greg, still loitering behind the young woman's chair. "Return to your seat, Freeman. I'd rather have you scowling at my face than lurking beside me."

Complying, Greg folded his arms and glowered across the

table at Oleander.

"Can I serve the first dessert course?" Li-Wei asked, announcing her return. "Or would you prefer to wait until you finish your discussion?"

"Better serve it now," Bertha said. "Freeman needs a distraction."

With brisk efficiency, Li-Wei distributed the deconstructed lemon tartlet with macadamia crumb and a drizzle of raspberry coulis. Determined to prove she was "fine", Natasha shovelled the cold dessert into her mouth. When her plate was empty, she sighed, glancing around.

Bertha abandoned her dessert, dabbing her lips with a white linen serviette. "Natasha, your father has strengthened his alliance with the newer Directors. He's used his influence to force decisions prejudicial to your inheritance. For anyone other than your father, we would have acted sooner. I must confess we've been divided about how to proceed. Some of us refused to believe Luke would be part of a hostile takeover. We've forestalled his bid for power by announcing your inheritance. Yet as long as you remain under your father's control, everything Stephen Spendor worked for is at risk. We must prevent your marriage to Ian from occurring."

"My father has already signed an agreement with Ian," Natasha said. "But I haven't."

"We know about the agreement," said Landon, pulling a

folded document from his pocket. "Every legal contract passes across the desks of my deputies. When they alerted me, I inserted a clause that gives you a way out."

Landon laid the document on the table, tapping the relevant section. "If you marry someone other than Ian within forty days, this agreement is null and void."

"To avoid marrying Ian I have to marry someone else?" Natasha asked, the colour draining from her face. "Oh, no, you've already decided."

Natasha stumbled to her feet. "Greg, please take me away from here."

"Stay where you are, Freeman," Oleander said. "Where will you run to, Natasha? Can your bodyguard keep you safe from your father without our help?"

"He's right, Natasha," Greg said. "I'm only one man, and I have limited resources. But I promise I won't let them force you into a loveless marriage."

Slumped on her chair, Natasha asked, "Who do you want me to marry?"

Oleander smiled. "You don't need to fear a 'loveless marriage'. The ideal man is sitting across the table."

Natasha threw her head back in surprise, staring at her bodyguard.

At the same instant, Greg jolted upright. "Me?"

46

Trickiness

Proverbs 14:22
Don't they go astray who plot evil?
But love and faithfulness belong
to those who plan good.

Natasha's mind reeled as Bertha and Jessica presented their arguments to Greg.

His face was unreadable.

"Freeman, we know she's safe with you," Bertha said. "You're trustworthy..."

"I've been talking with your mother," Jessica said. "Edith's worried about Ian. There's no predicting what he will do..."

"As long as Natasha is single, there'll be someone..." Bertha said.

"Why do you have a problem with our request? This won't change anything..." Jessica said.

"Natasha depends on you," Bertha said. "She was ready to walk out…"

Landon leaned forward, producing a familiar envelope from his pocket. "My office forwarded this. Natasha has already made you her beneficiary…"

Oleander sipped his wine, the only Trustee not contributing to the discussion. Natasha had come to associate that particular expression with trickiness. At any moment, he would interrupt the others, issue a blunt statement and end the debate.

"You don't need to make a decision now," Bertha said. "We have forty days—"

"Thirty-nine," Oleander said.

Greg lined up his cutlery before looking at Oleander. "I'll pray about it."

The Trustees fell silent.

Before the quietness had lasted ten seconds, Li-Wei appeared. Natasha examined the tennis-ball-sized chocolate sphere she was served. A tiny jug filled with hot, pink syrup accompanied the dessert.

"The chef calls this dessert 'Cherry Blossom Surprise'," Li-Wei told Natasha. "Pour the syrup over the tempered chocolate, and don't pause until the jug is empty."

When Natasha complied, the chocolate sphere opened like a flower, revealing a layered cake oozing with pitted cherries and cream. Murmurs of appreciation arose from around the table. Hot syrup drizzled from the unfurling petals onto dense cake that doubled in size. Natasha sampled the cake, pushing down emotions and stifling her thoughts. Smiling at the others, she exaggerated her delight over the cake.

When Natasha's bowl was empty, she sighed and rested her spoon. If Greg was praying, why was she worried? A warm sensation flowed over her, and then she stifled a yawn.

"Coffee?" Li-Wei asked Oleander. "Or is it time to leave?"

"No coffee," Oleander said. "I've already summoned the car."

Li-Wei bowed her head. "I will fetch the ladies' coats."

A few minutes later, Li-Wei delivered the coats and withdrew. Landon assisted Bertha into her jacket, but Jessica dismissed Oleander when he offered the same service. Natasha draped her distinctive cape around her shoulders, adjusting the folds to cover her dress. When she reached for the hood, Oleander stopped her.

"Leave your head uncovered. I want everyone in the restaurant to notice you."

"What new trickiness is this?" Greg asked, stepping between Oleander and Natasha. "Why did you lead us through a labyrinth to get here if you're broadcasting her location now?"

"We're leaving a trail of breadcrumbs," Oleander said. "By the time her enemies respond, Natasha will be safely hidden." His phone buzzed and Oleander checked the screen. "The car is waiting."

"I can see several diners who were at Natasha's birthday party," Bertha said. "We'll head in their direction."

"I don't want to talk to anyone," Natasha said.

"You won't have to," Oleander said. "Use your acting skills to convince everyone you're exhausted. Freeman, your disapproving look is perfect. Now wrap your arm around Natasha while I walk on the other side. If there's trouble, take her outside to the stretch limousine."

The other Trustees took an indirect path across the bustling restaurant, while Natasha and her guides took the shorter route. Natasha heard her name mentioned several times before the group converged near the entrance.

"Uncle James," a voice shouted. "Un-cle Ja-a-ames!" A young man staggered towards them, his dress shirt untucked at the waist and his bow tie loose.

"One of your relatives?" Jessica asked.

"My brother's youngest son." Oleander faced the youth. "Jimmi, I didn't know you were in town. Why aren't you in Europe with your parents?"

"Came home early, ol' man, for Harry's pre-wedding celebrations." Jimmi waved to his friends. "Hey, Harry, remember Uncle James? Come have a few drinks with Harry an' me."

"Not tonight, Jimmi."

"Where are you staying, ol' man? At the Charlton or the Esmer—"

"He's staying with me," Jessica said, taking Oleander's arm. "Darling, our car is waiting."

"O-oh. Good ol' Uncle James." Jimmi backed away, but then he spotted Natasha. "Hey, you were in the paper. You're engaged to Izzy Norris's brother. What's 'is name?"

"Don't believe everything you see in the paper," Greg said, steering Natasha out the exit.

"Hey, don't go." Jimmi pursued them outside. "I wanna selfie to send to Izzy. She's not gonna believe I met her new sister."

A uniformed chauffeur opened the rear door of a white car occupying two parking spaces. Greg pushed Natasha inside, dropped onto the seat beside her and shoved her across. Oleander rested his hand on Jimmi's chest, preventing the youth from following them.

"No photos, Jimmi. Go back to your friends."

"Oh, right. Sorry, ol' man. Shoulda guessed you're involved in more trickiness. Don't worry. I won't tell anyone where you're going..."

When Jimmi had retreated, Bertha, Jessica, and Landon entered the vehicle through that same door. The female Trustees crossed the darkened interior to a row of side-facing seats. Landon advanced to the front of the car, joining two shadowy figures on rear-facing seats. Natasha squinted through the gloom, but the darkened windows blocked out too much light and the interior lights were off. The screen between the rear compartment and the front was shut.

Oleander climbed in, extinguishing the streetlights with the closing door.

"Turn on the lights, James," Jessica said, as the vehicle began to move.

A moment later, brightness revealed the identity of the hidden passengers. Matthew Wallace and Zhou Li-Wei Min remained silent as Oleander settled on the seat beside Greg.

"Freeman," Oleander said, "you asked why I was broadcasting Natasha's whereabouts. Wallace will assume your identity and, with Li-Wei Min's assistance, we'll convince everyone Natasha is staying at the *Charlton Hotel* tonight."

"Matt's not ugly enough," Greg said, as he guided Natasha across the moving vehicle to swap places with Li-Wei.

"Nobody will be looking at me," Matthew said. "Help Natasha out of her red cape, Freeman; pass it to Li-Wei."

It was easy for the two women to switch seats, but the confined space was problematic for two big men. From her new position, Natasha studied the security agents as understanding awoke. Matthew's hairstyle had changed, and he wore a tuxedo. Li-Wei's face was concealed by the red hooded cape.

Leaning against the upholstery, Natasha shivered. Greg removed his jacket, attempting to drape it around her shoulders.

"I'm not cold," Natasha said. "Li-Wei may be in danger because of me."

Shaking his head, Greg nudged Natasha forward, pulling the jacket around her and holding it in place with his arm. Pushing her back against the seat, his other hand tucked the voluminous garment around her. His actions awakened a warm sensation she could not name. After a few moments, Greg removed his arm, redirecting his attention to the people opposite.

Matthew was speaking. "...then Li-Wei removes the cape, and she's out of the *Charlton* before trouble arrives."

"Do not fear, Miss Jacobson," Li-Wei said from within the cape. "I can take care of myself. It is an honour to serve you. I welcome the opportunity to defend you."

"Tomorrow, Li-Wei Min will join your office staff, Natasha," Oleander said. "To the outside world, she's an assistant, but she's there to take on some of Freeman's responsibilities."

Greg leaned forward. "I don't need—"

His leg pressed against Natasha as Greg adjusted his position. She slowed her breathing to hide her reaction.

"Nobody doubts your dedication, Freeman," Oleander interrupted. "But we must accommodate your changed circumstances. Natasha's security away from the office becomes your primary focus."

"There's an additional benefit to employing Zhou Li-Wei Min," Matthew said. "She doesn't look like a bodyguard. Your absence will suggest we're growing complacent."

The limousine stopped. Oleander leapt out. Matthew drew Li-Wei after him.

Jessica moved to the seat beside the door and kept it ajar, peeking out. After a delay, she chortled before pulling the door shut.

"Li-Wei Min fell against Wallace in a swoon," Jessica said. "He scooped her into his arms, and she pressed her face against his chest. James drew more attention, rearranging the red cape until there was nothing of the girl to be seen. They've gone inside. We should have ten minutes to conclude our business before James returns."

47

Heaviness

Natasha flinched. "What business?"

"While James is busy," Landon said, "the two of you will sign these documents. First is your Marriage Licence Application."

"You said there was no rush for a decision," Greg said, accepting the printed document.

"The application process takes thirty days. We're running out of time."

Thirty-nine days, Natasha's inner voice whispered.

"Then we'll leave it for a few days," Greg said.

"I wanted to apply without your knowledge," Jessica said. "Forging your signatures wouldn't be difficult, but Landon didn't want to give Luke grounds for an annulment."

"Applying for a licence doesn't mean marriage is inevitable," Bertha said. "Think of it as a safety net."

"A safety net?" Greg asked.

"Only one marriage licence can be issued for Natasha. Landon wouldn't sanction forgery, but don't expect the same scruples from others."

Fighting heaviness in her heart, Natasha lied. "I-I don't understand."

Jessica tilted her head before she answered. "Your father must have access to documents bearing your signature."

"Pass me a pen," Greg said.

"Oh, Greg," Natasha said. "I don't like the pressure they're applying."

"I'd do anything to keep you from marrying Norris. If your Trustees can't find another way, I'll be grateful the paperwork is sorted."

After Greg signed, Natasha added her signature, and Bertha was their witness.

The page disappeared into Landon's jacket. "I'll lodge this before midnight. Next is the prenuptial agreement..."

Closing her eyes, Natasha listened to the terms and conditions. Greg didn't ask a single question. Quietness descended, and then a pen appeared in her hand, signalling the need for her signature.

"Anything else?" Greg asked, watching Landon pocket the pages.

"This stays between us," Bertha said.

The door opened. Oleander re-entered the limousine and settled beside Jessica on the rear seat. The vehicle resumed its journey.

"Well? What happened?" Jessica asked.

"Everything went as planned. The gala event patrons were transitioning from the restaurant when we entered. That nosy reporter, Freda Collins, was with the charity press secretary, so she had the perfect view. When Wallace planted himself in the centre of the lobby, I heard plenty of speculation about the woman in the red cloak. It shouldn't take long to make the connections to our exit from the Pink Star. Anyone looking for Natasha will think I've made a terrible blunder."

"What now?" Jessica asked.

"We're taking the scenic route, dropping Landon and Bertha at their homes on the way to your house. You told Jimmi I was staying with you, Jessica, so I'll have to come inside in case anyone's tailing us."

Oleander's eyes shifted to Natasha. "Try and get some sleep. It's going to be at least two hours before I collect you from the limo garage."

"Are you sure there's nothing else we need to do before we let Natasha leave?" Jessica asked.

"Did Freeman sign the documents?"

Jessica nodded, and Landon patted his pocket.

"Then there's nothing to worry about."

Pretending to obey, Natasha rested her head against the window. The conversation flowed around her as her mind drifted.

"Is she asleep?" Oleander asked.

"I'm not sure," Greg said.

When she sensed her bodyguard leaning over her, Natasha remained still. It took every ounce of determination not to react when his fingers lightly touched her face. A moment later, Greg pulled her against him, wrapping an arm around her shoulders. A small sigh escaped from her lips, and he froze. Natasha shifted as if she was dreaming, snuggling against him. After several seconds the tenseness in his muscles relaxed.

"Definitely asleep," Bertha said from across the compartment.

"Freeman, there are things we need to discuss," Oleander said, "and I don't want Natasha to know about the other precautions we've taken..."

The dream began in the circular room. Heaviness hovered over Natasha. Every muscle ached, and her movements were clumsy. She staggered to the familiar silvery-blue wall.

"Are you there, Cassie?" she asked, pressing against the icy barrier.

Instantly, Cassie appeared. "I'm here, Nessie."

Before Natasha could reply, Cassie glanced over her shoulder as the sinister dark figure appeared.

"Everything's happening too fast," Natasha wailed. "Cassie, don't go with him. He'll kill you."

"Nessie, this is a dream."

"I know it's a dream, but that doesn't change anything."

"It changes everything," Cassie said. "This is the last time, Nessie. Follow me if you want answers."

"I can't get through the wall."

"You're not trying hard enough, Nessie."

Cassie walked towards the waiting man. Natasha lunged at the wall and tumbled through. When she picked herself up, the man was out of the shadows. For the first time, Natasha saw his face.

With a jolt, the dream ejected Natasha. She sat up, fighting the bedcovers as she reached for the bedside lamp. Her hands encountered another pillow where the edge of the bed should be. Stretching sideways, she found the corner of a piece of furniture and followed an electrical cord. When she activated the lamp, she blinked at the brightness as she surveyed the unfamiliar room.

It was several minutes before the dream's heaviness lifted and she recognised her grandfather's city apartment. Scrambling from the bed, Natasha shivered in her too-brief negligee and threw on a robe that was draped over a chair. Her bare feet sank into the thick carpet as she paced.

Had her subconscious mind blended her past with the present? Why else would Ian Norris emerge from the shadows in the Cassie dream?

But there was a more pressing problem. How could she dispel the emotional storm the dream unleashed?

Greg's asleep downstairs—

Natasha paused mid-step. For years, she had dealt with these nightmares alone. Yet it had taken a single night for Greg to become the first – and only – comfort she wanted.

Berating herself for her neediness, Natasha took a calming breath. She didn't have a dance studio where she could turn up the music and work until exhaustion overcame her. But there was plenty of space to stretch and move until her mind stopped pursuing every stray thought.

Natasha commenced her opening stretches. Waking Greg was not an option. Even if she dared venture downstairs, what would the housekeeper say if she caught Natasha visiting Greg? Dressed like this? To save his reputation,

Natasha would have to confess the dream. Miriam would want to supervise their conversation. Telling Greg about the dream was already problematic, without having to explain to Miriam that Ian was Natasha's *other* fiancé.

Other fiancé? No! She wanted only Greg – did he think of himself as her fiancé? There had been no opportunity to ask.

The compulsion to rush downstairs became impossible to resist. Halfway to the door, Natasha stopped. *What are you doing?*

If she didn't find a way to control this craziness she would be a wreck by morning.

Taking more deep breaths, Natasha resumed her stretching routine.

Visiting Greg was not an option, but that didn't mean his kind of help was beyond reach. The previous night, he had read from a Bible app, and she had fallen into a deep, dreamless sleep. Reaching for her phone, she rocked while waiting for the screen to awaken. A "battery low" icon flashed, and the screen died. Natasha stared at the device, weariness rising from the depths of her soul. She tossed the phone onto the bed.

"I can't do this."

The post-dream heaviness dropped Natasha to her knees beside the bed. She wept as another schooldays-memory emerged from the recesses of her mind. How many times had

Cassie knelt beside her in Chapel? What would Cassie say if she could see Natasha now?

In an instant, a Scripture popped into her head, a verse Cassie had asked her to memorise long ago. "I can do all things through Jesus Christ who strengthens me."

Perhaps it was her imagination, but the heaviness eased a little with each repetition. Ten minutes later, Natasha dried her tears and returned to bed. She smiled at the ceiling. Disturbing Greg's sleep was unnecessary. Natasha would tell him of her nocturnal torment in the morning. With a yawn, she closed her eyes, no longer fearing the dream.

Breakfast was almost over, and Natasha still hadn't found the right moment to mention her dream. Greg sat across the table, enjoying buckwheat pancakes while discussing recipes with Miriam. They conversed as if they were lifelong friends.

Oleander entered carrying a newspaper and collapsed onto a chair at the kitchen table. Natasha studied him, concerned about the extra lines on his face. He seemed older this morning.

"Pre-blessed food," Miriam said, moving aside the newspaper to slap a plate of pancakes on the table. "Freeman did the honours, and then I told him not to wait. You said breakfast was at seven-thirty."

Instead of eating, Oleander waited until the housekeeper placed coffee in front of him, and then he bowed his head.

"You're carrying the world's heaviness on your shoulders," Greg said, reaching for the newspaper. He scanned the headlines before handing it to Natasha.

"The front page?" Natasha asked, trembling at the dark expression on Greg's face. She lowered her eyes to the page.

TERRORIST ATTACK ON CHARLTON HOTEL
1 DEAD, 12 INJURED

"Oh!" After scanning the opening paragraphs, Natasha returned the newspaper to Greg.

"Wallace phoned me at three-thirty," Oleander said. "He's shaken and angry. The police have copies of his surveillance footage and have agreed to keep him updated during their investigation."

"What went wrong?" Greg asked.

"Wallace's squad were on the eighteenth floor, ready if anyone approached Natasha's room. Hotel Security was keeping them updated about movements within the building. Instead of hiding their presence, the invaders shot everyone they encountered. They neutralised the security hub before attacking the lobby.

"The report says they used tranquiliser guns," Greg said.

"When the leader couldn't find Natasha," Oleander said, "he threw one of Wallace's men off the eighteenth-floor balcony."

48

Darkness

Walking to the window after signing the final document on her desk, Natasha gazed at the Friday afternoon traffic. The horizon was tinged with darkness, a reflection of her inner condition. Twenty-five days had elapsed since the "terrorist attack". Much had happened in the intervening weeks, endless meetings and documents to sign, yet her thoughts returned to the young widow. The heartbreaking funeral haunted her dreams.

Moving around her office, Natasha made minute adjustments. There had been no intruders in her Chairperson's office, but she wasn't ready to stop monitoring where everything should be.

The porcelain doll from her home study now resided on her office credenza. That was one of the few possessions her father had permitted Edith to deliver to the city.

Oleander's plan to collect essential items on Natasha's behalf had been thwarted when Luke banished his ex-chauffeur from the estate. Everything from Oleander's servant life had been thrown into boxes and dumped in the underground parking garage at the base of her office tower.

Greg's possessions were treated with more dignity. Her father believed Greg was acting out of misguided loyalty and permitted Edith to pack his bags.

What would her father say if he knew Natasha was hiding a valid marriage licence in her office? Everyone seemed to be ignoring Natasha's assurance she'd prefer to suffer the financial consequences of breaking her father's agreement with Ian than see Greg sacrifice his future. Unless the Trustees approved another way out of her dilemma, Greg would become her husband in six days.

A gentle tapping on the door signalled Li-Wei's entry. The other women who worked in the outer office had already left for the day.

"Everything is ready. Freeman is on his way from the parking garage. He asked if you had changed your mind. He's concerned a visit to your father's estate is asking for trouble."

"Edith assures me Ian has gone, and Oleander's taken additional precautions. There's been no trouble in weeks, and I need to hear my father's explanation for his actions."

"Please change into these shoes." Li-Wei offered an identical pair to the ones Natasha wore. "There's an electronic device embedded in each heel. A tracker, in case anything goes wrong, and an audio transmitter. May I suggest you exercise caution when you are alone with Freeman? Otherwise, your private conversations will be broadcast to your security team."

Natasha thought about the well-intentioned warning while swapping shoes. There had not been a private conversation with Greg since she became Chairperson.

Fifteen minutes later, Natasha and Greg entered the express elevator. Li-Wei had already signalled her readiness to follow them at a discreet distance. Other Sentinel City Security agents along the way would monitor their journey. Greg seemed distracted. Was he concerned about the impending deadline, or did her bodyguard have something else on his mind? Natasha glanced down at her shoes.

By the time their car reached the outer suburbs, Greg was concluding his conference call with Oleander and Matthew.

There had been no attempt to exclude Natasha, but she was content to remain silent as she stared out into the darkness.

After Greg negotiated the off-ramp, traffic diminished. The car sped along the familiar route towards home and Greg concentrated on the road ahead. Impatient to arrive, Natasha planned her strategy for repairing her fractured relationship with her father.

Oleander phoned again, relaying everyone's relative position via the dashboard speaker. Natasha checked the side mirror, catching a glimpse of distant light behind them. Was that Li-Wei?

A shimmering T-junction sign emerged from the darkness. There were no lights on the side road. Greg slowed before approaching the intersection. A dark shape attacked the car from the driver's side.

Greg shouted something about a four-wheel drive as he wrestled with the steering wheel. The car bucked and leapt sideways, throwing Natasha in every direction to an accompanying cacophony of sound. The airbag inflated with a whoosh, and then everything went black.

"Natasha, Natasha."

Blinking into a flickering light beam, it took a few seconds for Natasha to recognise Li-Wei's voice. Natasha was on the ground. Li-Wei pressed something wet and sticky against

Natasha's head. The pain was intense. Natasha tried to push Li-Wei's hand away.

"Keep still, Natasha. There's an ambulance coming."

Over the sound of shouted instructions, distant sirens wailed across the countryside. Li-Wei spun toward the darkness, allowing Natasha a glimpse of the cars clustered at the top of a hill. The headlights of the stationary vehicles were directed away from the road. A crumpled mass of metal lay at the bottom of the steep embankment not far from her location. Recognising the wreckage as her pink car, Natasha tried to stand, activating a burst of shimmering light. She collapsed.

When the brightness faded, there were flashing red and blue lights everywhere. Blurry shapes marched up and down the hill.

"What's happening?" Natasha asked.

"There's been an accident," Li-Wei said.

"An accident? Where's Greg? Greg!"

Someone emerged from the chaos to lean over Natasha. Matthew Wallace had to repeat himself several times before she understood what he was saying.

"We have to get you away from here."

Grabbing Matthew's arm, Natasha asked, "Where's Greg?"

Matthew turned towards the darkness, shaking his head. Another wave of light dragged Natasha into a spiralling void. This was a terrible dream. She had to wake up...

Random flashes of awareness alternated with nothingness. The storm of confusion ended when Natasha awakened in a dim hospital cubicle with the curtains drawn.

"Where am I?"

"The emergency department," a nurse said, leaning across to check Natasha's eyes and writing something on her clipboard. "You were in a car accident. The doctor stitched your head wound and you have concussion. Apart from feeling sore and sorry for a few days, you should be okay. Do you think you're ready to sit up?" The nurse offered Natasha some iced water. "I have some tablets to help with the pain."

Enduring the change of position awakened more flashing lights. The nurse appeared beside her, offering two blue pills in a tiny cup. A niggle tickled Natasha's mind, but she couldn't pin it down.

Swallowing the blue pills was difficult with her swollen lips. Natasha fell back against the pillows. The whole room was swaying in rhythm with her pounding heartbeat.

"What time is it? My father's expecting m—"

"Your parents are waiting to talk to the surgeon who's operating on your brother."

"I-I don't have a brother."

The nurse frowned at the clipboard and continued writing her notes.

A head appeared around the curtain. "Is the patient well enough to talk to the police about the accident?"

"What accident?" Natasha asked.

"There's your answer," the nurse said. "Best if they take her witness statement in the morning. Ask the officer to leave his card with her discharge papers. She's transferring to a private clinic."

A random thought popped into Natasha's head. "My phone? My handbag? Do you have them?"

"Apart from what you're wearing, all I have are your shoes." The pink shoes appeared in Natasha's arms.

Natasha's father appeared at the end of the bed. "Princess, I'm sorry I didn't believe your life was in danger. Wallace has given me an account of the attack. I'm moving you to a secure location. There's a car outside."

After helping Natasha into her shoes, Luke wheeled his daughter from the busy emergency department towards a dark car.

"Where's Greg?" Natasha asked, glaring at the unfamiliar driver. "I'm not going anywhere without Greg."

Crouching beside the wheelchair, Luke stared into Natasha's eyes. "I'm sorry, Princess. Greg died while he was waiting for surgery."

"No, no, that's not right. I'd know if he was dead."

"Please, Natasha, get in. I have to go back inside and comfort Edith. She's waiting to see his body."

Luke assisted her into the car, and she lay against the upholstery. After her father walked away, a tsunami of pain smashed over Natasha. Nothing made sense. This had to be a dream...

The driver started the engine, and the car left the hospital.

Something was wrong, terribly wrong.

Why couldn't she think straight?

Buzzing questions and phrases whizzed through her mind. A growing sense of urgency churned her stomach and intensified the pounding in her head. The shimmering blue lights returned.

49

Witness

When Natasha came out of the trance-like state, she gazed into the night. There were no streetlights, and the car headlamps flashed across unfamiliar countryside.

"Where are we going?"

The driver laughed. "You've already asked three times. I'm taking you to a motel where you can sleep off whatever pain meds the doctors gave you."

"Have we met? I don't recognise you."

"Your regular security team are busy investigating the accident."

Arriving in a small town, the driver pointed out a country motel that backed onto a dark stand of trees. Less than a dozen vehicles were in the car park beside the motel. After parking further down the narrow street, the driver kept Natasha close to the trees as he supported her arm.

"Why didn't you park next to the hotel?" Natasha asked.

"I'm minimising the chance of witnesses. Can you manage the last bit by yourself? You're booked in as Cassie Smith, spelled S-M-Y-T-H."

By the time Natasha shook herself from her daze, the driver was no longer beside her. She staggered across to the veranda. Grabbing the doorpost, she waited for the world to stop spinning. Glancing around at the shimmering blue haze, Natasha longed for a glimpse of Cassie to confirm she was trapped in another dream.

Finding no sign of Cassie, Natasha entered the motel and rang the bell on the counter. A man peered around the corner from the noisy bar.

"I have a booking."

The man stared, wiping his hands on a towel before checking an open book on the counter. "Cassie Thorborgson-Smyth? You paid for a month in advance, starting a fortnight ago. I was beginning to think you weren't coming."

"A month?" Natasha's heart raced, and her vision blurred. "I'm sorry. I've been in an accident. Everything's muddled."

"Sign here." The man tapped the page, and she scribbled "Cassie S" on the line. He handed her a brass key attached to a plastic tag. "You're in Room 25. It's back out the door and around the corner, the last one in the second wing. You've got that part of the motel to yourself, nice and quiet as you requested. Enjoy your stay."

Natasha squinted at the tag and read aloud. "Mother Macready's Motel, the best accommodation in Willowbend Creek."

"The only accommodation in Willowbend Creek," the man said, heading back to the bar.

Outside, Natasha looked for the driver, but his car was gone. She followed the barman's directions, murmuring to herself. "Room 25, mustn't forget. Why am I talking to myself? I don't know, but I think it's necessary. I do know I'm not well. Everything is shimmery and blue. I hope I wake up from this dream soon. Room 25..."

After taking several rests, Natasha arrived at her room, but it took multiple tries to fit the brass key in the lock and open the door. Inside, finding the light switch was an equally difficult challenge.

"Hello," Natasha said when the overhead light flashed on. "If this isn't a dream, someone please explain why I'm alone." She examined the tiny bathroom before switching off the light and lying on the double bed.

Drifting in and out of her blue-light dream, Natasha tossed and turned. The headache intensified, and her neck hurt. Lurching to the bathroom, she had a drink of water. Another wave of dizziness dropped her to her knees in the doorway. She directed her next question to the ceiling. "Why am I here?"

A kaleidoscope of memories brought acid to the back of her throat. Crawling into the bathroom, Natasha waited until her stomach settled and then rinsed her mouth with water.

Her father's voice echoed in her memory. "Greg died – Greg died – Greg died…"

From across the room, a metallic sound disrupted the refrain. Was that a key turning in the lock?

"Someone's here," Natasha said, staggering from the bathroom.

The outer door creaked, and the familiar dream monster appeared in the shadowy doorway. Natasha blinked rapidly, but he didn't fade away.

Alertness tingled in Natasha's extremities. "What do you want?"

Ian Norris was the last person she expected to answer. "I've come to claim my prize, Nessie."

"I'm not your prize."

The door shut, and the light came on. Crossing the room, Ian grabbed Natasha and grasped her chin as he examined her bruises. "Your face is a mess, Nessie. It's going to hurt when I kiss you."

"I'd rather be dead than have you kiss me."

"That can be arranged, but I have other things in mind before my men finish you off."

Ian carried Natasha to the bed, dumping her on the covers. When he dropped beside her, she rolled off the other side. Groaning, she crawled towards the door. He caught her around the waist, and she fought him. Her shoe connected with his body, and he wrenched it from her foot.

"I like a woman who puts up a fight," Ian said, hurling the shoe across the room. He disposed of the second one before wrestling her back onto the bed. "Your friend Cassie warned me to be gentle with you, but that was never going to happen. Unfortunately, I don't have time to enjoy your resistance tonight. I need you more compliant for what I have in mind."

From his pocket, Ian produced two more blue pills. He pried her mouth open and stuffed them in. She tried to spit them out, but his grip on her jaw was too strong. The bitter tablets began to dissolve, and she swallowed to keep from choking.

Ian held her down, grinning into her eyes as he caressed her face. "Ask your questions while you still can."

"Is this how you killed Cassie?"

"Where's the evidence I was involved?" Ian said. "No witnesses ever came forward to identify me. I didn't pour the alcohol down her throat or force her to swallow my pills. I even warned her not to take too many."

"Why were you there?" Natasha asked.

"Cassie sold you to me for a few pills. I only wanted her mellow, so she didn't interfere when I was with you. Her death ruined my plans for an easy ride to the top of the Spendor Corporation. I've waited years for another opportunity."

"Why are you confessing now?"

"Who are you going to tell? That stepbrother who's been masquerading as your bodyguard? He's dead, and I'll be dancing on his grave. I had to eliminate him after I found out you were marrying him. Or perhaps you're thinking of telling your father? He hasn't believed a word you've said in months..."

Watching her face, Ian continued his unconventional confession, boasting about his wickedness. Her first kidnapping and the *Charlton Hotel* attack were not his worst criminal offences. There wasn't one of the "seven deadly sins" that the St Catherine's Academy Sisters had warned her about that he hadn't committed. Lives ruined, family fortunes stolen, innocent victims corrupted and forced to serve him...

Every terrible revelation should have wounded her heart, but Natasha felt nothing. Was this a side-effect of the drugs? Or had she disconnected from her emotions when the blue light dropped her into this nightmare?

Eventually, Ian fell silent.

"Finished... confessing?" Natasha asked. "Ex-pect no... ab-sol-ution ... just... kill me."

"I'm in no hurry to kill you, Nessie. But I'm disappointed with your lack of response. You really are an Ice Queen. I thought my revelations about Cassie would be enough to break you, but not even the murder of your bodyguard has melted the frozenness of your heart. Is that why there's no fear in your eyes? You don't believe I have the power to reach you? Perhaps it's time I tried targeted pain—"

CRASH! The external door shattered.

A roaring mob burst into the room.

Ian leapt from the bed, shouting for his men as Matthew Wallace and his squad charged.

Li-Wei slipped through the broken door, drawing Natasha away from the brief conflict.

"You're alone, Norris," Wallace said. "Once we identified the driver who took Natasha from the hospital, locating the others was easy. They're in police custody, denouncing you as the criminal mastermind known as the Big Boss."

"My lawyers will discredit your witnesses," Ian said. "Without their testimony, you've no evidence I've done anything wrong. It will be easy to convince the judge your accusations are false."

"Natasha will stand up in court and denounce you," Wallace said.

"You can't trust anything Nessie says," Ian said. "She's suffering from concussion and taken too many pills. No judge will accept her as a credible witness."

"We don't need Natasha's testimony," Oleander said, stepping forward. He pressed play on a handheld device.

Ian's voice filled the room.

After a few seconds, Oleander switched off the recording of Ian's recent confession. "You're going to jail for a long time."

50

Thankfulness

Awakening with a blinding headache, Natasha moaned as she checked her surroundings. A dim overhead light cast eerie shadows across the interior of a speeding vehicle. She glanced left at Oleander and right toward Li-Wei as scattered recollections flooded back.

"Cassie," she croaked. "Ian."

Li-Wei offered Natasha a few sips of water through a straw. Some of the liquid drizzled past her swollen lips and ran down her chin.

"Ian can't hurt you anymore," Oleander said, dabbing the moisture with a soft cloth. "You're safe."

"I...don't...re-mem..."

"You lapsed into unconsciousness after Wallace took him away. I blame myself. I should have checked your condition before I tried to update you about what's happened."

"What?"

"Shh, close your eyes and rest."

"Frightened..." Natasha grabbed Oleander's arm. "Crazy dreams..."

Leaning forward, Oleander spoke to the driver. "Wallace, how long until we arrive?"

"Half an hour."

"When we get to the hospital," Oleander said to Natasha, "they'll give you something to clear the drugs from your system. In the meantime, we'll try to keep your mind occupied with pleasant thoughts."

"We have much to be thankful for," Matthew said.

"Indeed," Oleander said. "We shall make 'thankfulness' your next code word, Natasha. Thankfulness for safety."

"Thankfulness for justice," Li-Wei said.

"Thankfulness for an empty road," Matthew added. "And a fast car."

For the remaining journey, her three companions contributed to the growing list. Natasha silently added phrases as Greg's face appeared in her mind. Thankfulness for his smile. His kindness. His loyalty. His stubbornness. His sacrifice... Tears rolled down her cheeks in the darkness.

"Thankfulness for the hospital," Matthew said. Voices fell silent as he navigated the driveway and stopped outside the entrance.

After a brief consultation with an emergency department doctor, Natasha received an injection. She was released following an hour's observation, but they did not leave the hospital.

Oleander pushed Natasha in a wheelchair along darkened hallways. Matthew and Li-Wei followed with quiet steps. An elevator took them to the sixth floor, where the ward sister awaited them. The nurse marched them towards a small rectangular window of light in a door at the end of the ward.

"Wait here," she said, disappearing into the room.

Murmuring behind the door ended abruptly when Natasha's father burst into the hallway. He dropped to his knees, drawing his daughter into his arms as he wept. "I'm sorry, Princess, so sorry..."

Natasha's tears flowed as she rested in her father's arms.

The door reopened and the nurse said, "You can come in now. The patient is ready to see you."

Luke stepped away. Everyone gazed at Natasha, seated in her wheelchair. She looked at the handwritten sign on the door: Leonard Cross. Leonard was Greg's middle name, and his original surname was Cross...

A dream fragment resurfaced: Oleander handing her a phone in the motel room and Greg's battered face speaking to her from the digital screen. Natasha clutched the sides of the chair as shadows swirled around her.

From a great distance, she heard her own voice. "Greg's not dead?"

"I'm sorry we told you he was dead," Oleander said. "We had to spread a false report to keep him safe. Greg's been asking for you."

Leaping from the wheelchair, Natasha rushed into the room with her father's assistance. She hesitated, surveying the scene. Edith stood near the window. Greg lay in bed, a bandage around his head, tubes and wires running to a beeping machine, and his leg in plaster.

Greg beckoned Natasha closer, and Luke steered her to the side without the machine. Natasha toppled against Greg's chest and his arms wrapped around her.

"I thought I'd lost you, Queenie."

"I was told... you... were... dead." Natasha could not hold back the tears.

Pulling her off her feet, Greg dragged her onto the bed beside him. She sobbed until her emotions were spent. When she regained control, she remembered there were other people in the room and tried to pull away.

Reaching for her chin, Greg gently tilted her head and studied her face. "I'm sorry you were hurt."

"It's me who should be apologising. You could have been killed."

"Don't waste your tears on me, Queenie. My pride put you at unnecessary risk. I fancied myself as a modern-day knight, heading into battle to protect the woman I love. Wearing high-tech body armour, I thought I could handle whatever Norris threw at me. I was wrong."

"I didn't know you were wearing armour," Natasha said.

"Matt sourced it for me. But what good is armour? I'm a failure as a knight. One attack took me out, leaving you defenceless. When I think of that man touching you—"

The machine beside the bed shrieked. *Beep! Beep! Beep…*

Greg's arm tightened around Natasha, trapping her against him. The nurse rushed in to punch a flashing button and silence the alarm.

"What happened?" Luke asked.

"There was a spike in his blood pressure and heart rate," the nurse said, touching the screen and frowning at the graphs. "And his O2 levels dropped. If it happens again, I'll summon the on-call doctor." She surveyed the room. "It's late, and there are too many visitors. My patient needs his rest."

"The nurse is right," Luke said, approaching the bed. "Come, Natasha. I'm taking you home. Greg's not the only one who needs to rest."

"Natasha's not leaving with you," Greg said.

"She's my daughter—"

"She's my fiancée. We're getting married in five days."

"Wallace!" Luke bellowed. "Get my daughter away from this madman!"

"I'm sorry, but you have no authority here," Matthew said, taking Luke's arm and guiding him towards the door. "Come with me, and we'll discuss Oleander's concerns about your recent decisions."

Oleander followed Matthew and Luke from the room.

"I'll be on duty in the hallway," Li-Wei said.

"I'd better go after Luke," Edith said. "Gregory, congratulations to you and Natasha. When were you going to tell me?"

"Mum, I'm sorry we've kept secrets from you," Greg said.

"Now that Ian's arrested, I hope that's the end to the drama."

"So do I, Mum."

After Edith left, the nurse stood with her hands in her pockets, frowning at the injured pair. She squeezed one of the IV bags before retrieving a clipboard. "You're due for the next round of antibiotics in an hour. I'll come back then."

"We have an hour, Queenie," Greg said when the door swung shut. "I've been dreaming about having you in my bed, but I never expected I'd have to break my leg to make it happen."

"Are you in a lot of pain?" Natasha asked, staring at the plastered limb poking out from under the bed sheets.

"Only if I move," he said through clenched teeth as he stretched sideways towards the machine. He lay back on the pillow with an electronic device in his hand. "Now Mum's gone, I don't have to pretend. I get good meds whenever I push this." He pressed a button and closed his eyes. "That's why I'm not worried about temptation tonight. I'm in no condition to take advantage of your sympathy."

"Greg, why did you tell my father we're getting married? Now that Ian's—"

"Natasha, promise me not to think about that man when we're in bed. I don't want that monster haunting our dreams."

He fell silent, and Natasha thought he was asleep. But then he stirred, half-opening his eyes. "Don't you want to marry me, Queenie?" Greg asked. "Marrying you is all I think about. To take care of you, and keep you safe, to cherish you and be free to convince you that I love you."

"You love me?" Natasha asked, but he didn't answer. The arm around her shoulders loosened, and she snuggled against him with her eyes closed. When her breathing synchronised with the rise and fall of his chest, she smiled.

Her heart was full of thankfulness as she drifted to sleep in his arms, secure in his love. The shimmering blue wall hovered at the edge of her awareness, and she dismissed the dream with a sigh. The shadowy monsters were losing their power.

"I love you too," she murmured.

Character List

❧**Natasha's Family**❧

<u>Natasha Jacobson</u> (aka Princess, Nessie, Queenie) (25) - Luke and Stephanie's daughter, Stephen Spendor's granddaughter

Luke Jacobson - Natasha's father, Edith's husband, Spendor Corporation CEO

Stephanie Spendor-Jacobson (dec) - Luke's first wife, Natasha's mother, Stephen's daughter

Edith Jacobson (nee Freeman) - Luke's second wife, Natasha's stepmother, Greg's mother

Stephen Spendor (dec) - Stephanie's father, Natasha's grandfather, Spendor Corporation Founder

Esmeralda Spendor (dec) - Natasha's grandmother

<u>Gregory (Leonard Cross) Freeman</u> (aka Greg) (27) security officer, Edith's estranged son

❀

❧**Spendor Corporation Directors**❧

Absalom Norris (Abe) - Ian & Giselle's father, Yolanda's husband

Bertha Doncaster (aka Bertie) - Stephanie's Godmother, Trustee for Stephen Spendor Trust

James (Oleander) Dubois - Trustee for Stephen Spendor Trust

Jessica Becker-Tompkins - Trustee for Stephen Spendor Trust

Horatio Ironbark (Dec)

Landon Greenville - Stephanie's Godfather, Public Officer and Trustee for Stephen Spendor Trust

Maximilian Romonovski the Third (dec) - father to Max IV

Maximilian Titus Romonovski the Fourth (aka Max)

Character List continued

❧Jacobson Employees❧

Mrs Conneally (aka Mrs C) - cook
Delores (aka Dee Dee) - maid
Forest - gardener
Doctor Hamilton - family physician
Henry Kincade - butler
Oleander - Luke's chauffeur and bodyguard

❈

❧Other Spendor Employees❧

Amanda Donavon - Natasha's secretary
Asher Goldmann - deputy to the Board of Directors
Blaze McGilligan - executive, a 'red prince'
Daniel Pendragon - executive, a 'red prince'
Finnegan Quartermaster (aka Finn) - executive, a 'red prince'
Hamish Baxter - Luke's PA
Hilary - Board of Directors' Minutes Secretary
Ian Norris - deputy to the Board of Directors, Luke's favourite
    advisor, the blue 'prince'
Joah Vandemeer - executive, a 'red prince'
Victoria Pepperwood - Executive Secretary to the Trustees
Zedekiah Upchurch (aka Zed) - executive, a 'red prince'

❈

❧Sentinel City Security❧

Caden Gosling (aka Goose) - Spendor Corporation security
    officer, Greg's friend
Eric Walker - security officer
Jack Smith - security officer
Rhys Kennedy - security officer
Matthew Wallace (aka Matt) - Sentinel City Security Founder
Will Remington - Spendor Corporation security officer
Zhou Li-Wei Min - security officer

❈

❧Other characters❧

Axel - a minion employed by Natasha's enemy

Cassandra Thorborgson-Smyth (aka Cassie) (dec) - Natasha's
    school friend

Freda Collins - journalist

Giselle Norris - Ian's sister

Jimmi Dubois - James' great-nephew

Miriam Trencher - James Dubois' housekeeper

Nanny Sherman - Natasha's childhood nanny

Sister Augustine - a nun at St Catherine's

Sister Mary-Thomas - a nun at St Catherine's

Yolanda Sanderson-Norris - Abe's wife, Ian's stepmother

✿

❧Locations and other business names❧

Charlton Hotel

Esmeralda Towers (Tower Four South, Tower Three,
    Tower One Central)

Jacobson Estate

Mother Macready's Motel, Willowbend Creek

NASSJA (**NA**tasha **S**tephanie **S**pendor **JA**cobson) Enterprises

Pink Star restaurant

Silverstone Industrials

Spendor Corporation Headquarters

St Catherine's Academy - Catholic Girls' Boarding School

Summerlands University

Willowbend Creek

Other Titles by the Author
River Wild Series

Romantic Suspense

Book 1 (2019) White Rose of Promise

Book 2 (2019) When Promises Are Broken

Book 3 (2020) When Freedom is Promised

Book 4 (2020) Which Promise This Time?

Book 5 (2021) When Promises Are Forever

Book 6 (2022) Waiting For A Promise

Book 7 (coming in 2023) Who Pays The Piper?

These books can be read in any order. Each story stands alone, but some characters appear in every story.

White Rose of Promise

A prophetic dream she can't remember. A shameful past she can't forget. An impossible future she dare not cherish.

Maria Evangelina Fontana hopes for reconciliation with her family. Her faith challenges wealthy businessman Sebastian Romano, turning his orderly world upside down. He thought he was done with his past, but his enemies have found her. Romano watches helplessly as her destiny unfolds...

Acknowledgements

Only in a fairytale does a story write itself. I am thankful for the support and encouragement of many.

Firstly, I am grateful to God for bringing me safely through the "writer's block" wilderness. Obedience to God's direction reawakened inspiration and gave a long-forgotten 1989 manuscript new life.

I am grateful to my reader team for help with Her Perfect Smile. Your encouragement, especially when I was stuck, was invaluable. Thanks to Naomi McGlone, Suzie Pybus, Jennie Del Mastro and Eva Bitterova for reading the first draft; and to Belinda McGuire, Donna Bullen, Glenda Charles and Gillian Perrett for responding to my questions.

A special thanks to Belinda Pollard, publishing mentor and editor. It was great to talk to you face-to-face to discuss this new story. I treasure your encouragement and professional advice.

Last but not least, thanks to my patient husband, Tony, for overlooking the messy house and late dinners; and responding thoughtfully to the random questions without notice. Your constant encouragement and ongoing support are greatly appreciated.

Chrissy

A Note From the Author

Greetings from Tasmania, Australia.

Thank you for reading my book. Could you please leave a brief online review, as this will help other readers find my work?

Her Perfect Smile is the first book in my *Billionaire's Jeopardy* series. The long-term plan is for Natasha and Greg to continue their adventures as secondary characters in the forthcoming volumes.

If you want to receive updates on my progress about other titles in this series, or other writing projects, please visit www.chrissygarwood.com and complete the form. Links to social media can also be accessed from my webpage.

Publishing a novel was a childhood ambition that lay dormant as I added mother, advocate for a child on the autism spectrum, mature age student, childcare educator, visual artist and chaplain to my life experiences.

The adventures my characters endure in *Her Perfect Smile* are fictional. Any resemblance to real people or actual events is unintentional. Within the yellowed pages of an unpublished 1989 manuscript, I found both the antidote for "writer's block" and enough inspiration for other novels in the series. My growing cast of fictional characters is impatient for me to give them their Happy Ever Afters.

I have learned more about myself and my ambitions while pursuing the writing dream. The confidence I am gaining as a storyteller has enriched my character. It makes me a humbler disciple of Jesus Christ, a stronger 21st-century woman, a more determined encourager, and a better friend.

Chrissy

Her Perfect Smile